Praise for

AS FAR AS YOU'LL TAKE ME

A Kids' Indie Next List Pick

"An honest, affecting novel about the lengths we must travel to find ourselves, and an ode to the people who sustain us along the way."
—**Andrew Eliopulos**, author of *The Fascinators*

"A heartfelt and unvarnished portrait of the growth queer people experience when they finally set themselves free."
—**Caleb Roehrig**, author of *Last Seen Leaving*

"Ardent, poignant and gripping, filled with lush descriptions and a witty narration, *As Far As You'll Take Me* is a moving tale of found family, letting go of the past, and forging a future determined by no one but yourself."
—**Sophie Gonzales**, author of *Only Mostly Devastated*

★ "Stamper does a beautiful job with his characters and their intricate relationships."
—*Booklist*, starred review

"The book's real strength is Marty's complexity: even when his anxiety flares up, he finds ways to maintain his mental health and cope with the things that threaten his dreams."
—*Publishers Weekly*

Praise for

THE GRAVITY OF US

"The first love, first launch, astronaut story I didn't know I needed." —**Becky Albertalli**, *New York Times* bestselling author of *Simon vs. the Homo Sapiens Agenda*

"A big-hearted, witty, and intensely relatable debut." —**Karen M. McManus**, *New York Times* bestselling author of *One of Us Is Lying* and *Two Can Keep a Secret*

"You will want to stand and cheer for Cal at every step of his heartstring-pulling story." —**Jeff Zentner**, Morris Award–winning author of *The Serpent King*

"Cal and Leon are fierce and sweet, and I never wanted their story to end." —**Shaun David Hutchinson**, author of *We Are the Ants* and *The Past and Other Things That Should Stay Buried*

"At once a tender love story and an honest exploration of anxiety, ambition, and family dynamics." —**Caleb Roehrig**, author of *Death Prefers Blondes*

"Equal parts thoughtful and heartfelt, this book never misses a beat." —**Julian Winters**, author of *Running with Lions*

"This funny, poignant novel will captivate space nerds and hopeless romantics alike."—**Chelsea Sedoti**, author of *The Hundred Lies of Lizzie Lovett* and *As You Wish*

★ "A sweet-spirited romance that will capture readers' hearts and imaginations."—***Booklist***, starred review

★ "Phil Stamper's *The Gravity of Us* is so interesting and well crafted that it's hard to believe it's his first novel."—***BookPage***, starred review

AS
FAR AS
YOU'LL
TAKE ME

Books by Phil Stamper

The Gravity of Us
As Far As You'll Take Me
Golden Boys

AS
FAR AS
YOU'LL
TAKE ME

PHIL STAMPER

BLOOMSBURY

NEW YORK LONDON OXFORD NEW DELHI SYDNEY

BLOOMSBURY YA
Bloomsbury Publishing Inc., part of Bloomsbury Publishing Plc
1385 Broadway, New York, NY 10018

BLOOMSBURY and the Diana logo
are trademarks of Bloomsbury Publishing Plc

First published in the United States of America in February 2021
by Bloomsbury Children's Books
Paperback published in March 2022

Bloomsbury books may be purchased for business or promotional use. For information on bulk
purchases please contact Macmillan Corporate and Premium Sales Department at
specialmarkets@macmillan.com

ISBN 978-1-5476-0864-5 (paperback)

The Library of Congress has cataloged the hardcover edition as follows:
Names: Stamper, Phil, author.
Title: As far as you'll take me / by Phil Stamper.
Other titles: As far as you will take me
Description: New York : Bloomsbury Children's Books, 2021.
Summary: Seventeen-year-old Marty Pierce leaves small-town Kentucky for London,
hoping to explore his sexuality and find work playing oboe, but homesickness,
anxiety, and his dwindling savings worsen even as his dreams are coming true.
Identifiers: LCCN 2020034586 (print) | LCCN 2020034587 (e-book)
ISBN 978-1-5476-0017-5 (hardcover) • ISBN 978-1-5476-0018-2 (e-book)
Subjects: CYAC: Coming of age—Fiction.| Musicians—Fiction.| Gays—Fiction.| Dating
(Social customs)—Fiction.| London (England)—Fiction.| England—Fiction.
Classification: LCC PZ7.1.S7316 As 2021 (print) | LCC PZ7.1.S7316 (e-book)|
DDC [Fic]—dc23
LC record available at https://lccn.loc.gov/2020034586
LC e-book record available at https://lccn.loc.gov/2020034587

Book design by Danielle Ceccolini
Typeset by Westchester Publishing Services
Printed and bound in the U.S.A.
2 4 6 8 10 9 7 5 3 1

To find out more about our authors and books visit www.bloomsbury.com
and sign up for our newsletters.

To my family.
The one I was born into,
and the one I found along the way.

ONE

AS IT TURNS OUT, I'm pretty good at lying.

On paper, there's nothing about me that says I'd be a great liar. I follow whatever obscure rules have been set by fake authority figures—*No running near the pool! Turn off your phone in the theater!* I won't even jaywalk. I was shoved into Christian youth groups for most of my upbringing, and, well, the Bible is pretty clear on what happens to liars.

But maybe that's why I'm so good at it. I'm incognito. Why *would* Marty possibly lie? The answer, of course, is simple:

I'm gay, and I'm suffocating.

I came to a realization about the former a long time ago, but the suffocating? That crept slowly into my chest, shortening my breaths until I realized I wasn't breathing at all.

"You're being melodramatic." Keeping one hand on the steering wheel, Megan flips her long hair out the car window so strands sway and tangle in the wind.

She has a habit of doing that. The hair flip *and* the dismissal. Like my worries don't matter. Like my *looming international trip* is nothing.

"My flight leaves in five hours. I don't have a return ticket. My parents don't *know* I don't have a return ticket." I grip the oh-shit handle harder. "I'm freaked."

"I can tell. You're panting harder than when we did that hot yoga class."

"God, don't remind me."

"You've got to believe me when I say this. You know how I hate giving compliments, but this is just fact. You are the most competent seventeen-year-old on the planet."

Her voice puts me at ease. It's a suspended chord—unsettling at first, both soft and harsh, followed by a clear resolution that feels like home. I lift my double chocolate Oreo milkshake out of the cup holder and wipe the French fry crumbs off the bottom of the cup, these now-ancient reminders of all the fast-food adventures we've gone through in this car. Megan in the driver's seat. Me, the passenger.

Always the passenger.

"I don't know how I could have prepared so much, yet still feel so unprepared," I say. "It defies logic."

I know it's partly because of Megan. We've got this yin-yang thing going on. She's so chill it's like she's constantly high on pot, and I'm about as high-strung as Hilary Hahn. (Because she's a violinist. And violins are high-pitched and have strings. High-strung? Okay, never mind.)

"You graduated early," she says. "You saved money working

at that shit diner all year. You performed in about every ensemble in the tristate area to beef up your resume. You figured out your dual citizenship and visa process in the middle of Brexit." She lowers her voice to a whisper, the wind in the car taking away the words as soon as they leave her mouth. "You've been trying to escape Avery for years. You're more than prepared for it, Marty."

Her words sting and soothe at the same time. Is she bitter that I'm abandoning her? My best of two friends—no offense to Skye. But a lot of history is there. It took me ten years to meet her, five years to stop hating her, and two years of hanging out near constantly to get where we're at now.

"I'm not escaping." Of course I'm not escaping.

"Finish your milkshake," she says. I do. "We've got two more ice cream stops before I roll you into the airport."

My gaze drifts out my window at the glory that is I-75 just before rush hour. The evidence of downtown Cincinnati evaporates from the exit signs, and we're left with the suburbs—Arlington Heights, Lockland, Evendale.

"Maybe we should abandon the milkshake plan. 275 will take us right there, and I'll have extra time."

She sighs. I knew she'd sigh. "And what, exactly, would you do with this extra time?"

"Read?"

"If by 'read' you mean get to the gate and stare at the screen, freaking about delays that aren't going to happen, then—"

Now *I* sigh. It's like a steam engine in here. "I get it. Carry on. What's next?"

"Young's Jersey Dairy. We can feed the goats there. This is going to be an *experience*."

I appreciate Megan's need to make even the most mundane drives to the airport into an adventure, but I can't let it go this time. In just a few hours I'll be up in the air. Away from Avery, Kentucky. Away from the shitheads at my school and the shittier shitheads who ate at the diner where I waited tables.

Away from my parents.

"Maybe I feel bad for lying to them," I say.

"The Bible-thumpers?"

"Yes, that's their official name." I roll my eyes. "Though I call them Mom and Dad."

Megan hasn't said two words to my parents since everything went down last year in London. Not like she was even there, but she got the full story. And, well, she is not one for nuance.

"You know how I feel about *them*." Her voice softens and I soak it up. "But I get that this is hard for you, Mart. Really I do. When do you think you'll tell them you're not coming back?"

The planner in me wins out this time, and a confidence rises along with my chest. "The summer program lasts three months, which means I have plenty of time to get a paying gig. Maybe that's what I'll do. Once one of these auditions works out, I can announce it. They'll be so happy their son got a spot in the London Philharmonic, they won't be mad that I'm—"

Megan butts in. "—never seeing them again?"

"Okay, *now* who's being melodramatic?"

Three months. That's plenty of time—and it's not like I'm super picky. It doesn't have to be the London Phil. It could be the Royal Opera House, or a regional theatre like the open-air one in Regent's Park, or . . . well, we'll see.

"It would have been a lot less complicated if I actually got into that summer program." I'm kind of rambling, but what else do you do when you're nervous? Make sense? Not a chance. "But I think it's a good thing. Because otherwise, I'd be wasting so much time in class and not out there booking gigs."

The program is at the Knightsbridge Academy of Music. According to what I told my parents, I auditioned last year and got accepted. I even have a letter to prove it.

But that's not the truth. Unbeknownst to my parents, I flopped at the audition after the whole London Pride melt-down. Hell, technically, that program started a couple of weeks ago. Thank god no one researches everything to the extent I do.

After everything happened last year, it didn't take me long to realize how much I actually *needed* this London thing to work out. How much I needed to get away from them. Get out of that tiny place. And all it would take was a forged letter, some time to ease my mom into the idea of going back to *that sinful place*, plus a little help from my cousin Shane.

Long story short, I was able to convince them to let me go this year. Fully on my own dime. I'm going to London, but I'm not attending the academy. I've got my own plan, and I'm not coming back.

Megan's right. I was trying to escape.

And I freaking did it.

* * *

Well, it was almost a clean escape.

Megan just drove off, her hair flying out the window (and she calls me melodramatic?), and I'm standing here just inside the Columbus airport, trying to mentally prepare myself for everything to come:

- Being lost in this behemoth of a building.
  - Maneuvering around this building while also being lost.
- Going through security.
  - Waiting in lines.
  - Emptying my pockets.
  - Taking out my toiletries and laptop.
  - Triple-checking that I've followed every rule.
  - Inevitably ending up leaving a full water bottle in my bag somewhere.
- Finding my gate and flying off to *an entirely new life in a new country*.

What I did *not* account for is that standing between me and security right now are my mom, my dad, and my grandma. For a moment, I'm stricken with the kind of fear that grips your lungs and sends shocks through your whole body, because the downside to lying is that at some point you'll probably get found out. And I was really hoping to not get found out until sometime after I touched down on UK soil. (Preferably not until I turn eighteen in a few months and there's even less they can do about it.)

But then I see Mom's holding one of those shiny Mylar balloons, helium shortage be damned, in the shape of a rectangle with the Union Jack on it—the flag of the United Kingdom.

"Mom?" I ask. She's scurrying toward me with an emotion that's half panic, half grief, and hands me the balloon before wrapping her arms around me. I drape an arm around her in response, still kind of dumbstruck.

"Nana wanted to say goodbye," Dad explains, "and we thought with all your planned milkshake detours we could beat you here."

Grandma insists on being called Nana, but she's never really struck me as the nana type. She's so fit she moves faster than I do half the time, which is not bad for someone who just turned seventy a few weeks ago.

Mom takes my rolling suitcase from me as I greet them. Mom's family is spread throughout Europe, but Dad's side never left Avery. Long as the census goes back, really.

The four of us exchange oddly formal pleasantries, like they didn't drive an hour and a half just to pop up and say one last goodbye, and I feel way too many emotions churning in my stomach along with the ice cream. It doesn't feel great.

"We really should let you go," Mom says, after a lull in the conversation. "Looks like everything's still on time. We'll follow your flight on that tracker. Once you get your SIM card set back up, just send us a text so we know you're okay."

"Three months," Dad says. "That's not so long."

I'm lying to you.

"I made sure Pastor Todd added you to the prayer chain at church," Mom says.

Even if I get a good gig, after finding a place to live and rehearsals and performances, there's no way I'll be able to come back.

"Not long at all," my grandma says. "Take lots of pictures for your nana, and send me a postcard if you have a chance."

I force a smile and walk toward airport security. I'm making my big escape, and everyone I love is watching me do it, completely unaware. My parents were shitty to me before, I know that, but is this any better?

What am I doing? What have I done?

They'll never forgive me for this.

TWO

THE EAGLE HAS LANDED.

I've just gotten off the plane, and I feel like I've been walking for a half mile just to get to customs. My eyelids are heavy.
Sticky, almost. It may feel like a dream world, but nothing's too
different yet.

I take a step into the customs area, and I let all the other
passengers rush around me and split into two lines. On the left,
Europeans. On the right, Americans. Well, that's what it looks
like, at least. I roll my shoulders. Stretch my arms.

Good morning, Heathrow Airport.

I reach into my shoulder bag to grab my passport, but stop
when I see a pale green envelope. *Marty Pierce* is written on the
front, in too-perfect cursive to be Megan's handwriting. She
and Skye gave it to me at my posh bon voyage party—or what
Megan and I dubbed the *My Mom Still Uses Pinterest* party—
and forbade me to open it until I landed in London.

Don't get me wrong; the party was definitely *cute*. The invites were red, white, and blue. Not our stars, but their stripes. Dozens of our church friends were there along with extended family I hadn't seen since Easter. Mom set up a fancy tea station that I didn't touch because tea is disgusting, but I *did* eat the pastries and biscuits. By "biscuits," I mean cookies. And though every detail was polished and fit perfectly with whatever aesthetic she'd found online, my mom bought one tacky thing, just because she knew I'd love it.

A large cake. Big Ben in the night sky, with four children flying around the side. Three in pajamas, and one in bright green tights. Admittedly, I had a weird obsession with Peter Pan as a kid. Like, I dressed up as him for every Halloween I can remember. We're not too different, he and I. I'm half a year from being an *adult*, but as I'm obviously gay and completely unable to grow a beard, I still identify with Mr. Pan.

Being a gay kid with sometimes shitty parents isn't easy. Their red voting record contradicts every "I love you" that comes out of their mouths. The money they spend at Chick-Fil-A used to go right to the organizations that want to make sure I never marry. To make sure I can never be truly happy. On the flip side, it felt like the cake was a peace offering, a subtle nod that "I know who you are."

This thought causes more thoughts about lying and how long it'll be until I see my parents, which . . . brings out all the tension in my body, then the guilt for feeling sorry for people who don't deserve it.

But I can't think about that. I won't. I'm always reading into the little things, but the big things never change.

Love is complicated.

I take in my surroundings. White walls, red rope to keep us lined up properly. (Properly! Sounding like a Brit already.) I'm technically in England, so I'm allowed to tear into Megan and Skye's letter. I pull out the card and examine the front. It's the kind of design you look at and know it costs more than a Hallmark card. The typeface you see boasting artisanal foods in your local overpriced organic market. Kombucha. Kimchi. It's Skye's style if I've ever seen it—he's careful and neat, while Megan's not above doodling over a used index card and handing it to you unceremoniously.

I open the card.

Marty,

As your best friends from the small, lowly state of Kentucky, we want to wish you, Mr. Britain, the best of luck in London.

However, this serves as a binding legal contract. You, the undersigned (we've forged your name, so don't worry about signing), commit to one (1) hour of FaceTime, every Friday night. We'll still need an excuse to miss all of those Avery High bonfires.

You're going to do great. And we're going to miss you, Mart.

Love,

M&S

P.S. It's Skye—Now that you're too far away to kill her, I need to confess. Megan told me. And I think you're awesome, dude.

Crap. Of course she told him.

My tidy, five-person out list has just become six. Mom, Dad, Shane, Aunt Leah, Megan, and now Skye? He's a friend, a good one, but how did that give Megan the right to out me like that?

I clench my hands, and the edge of the overly designed card crinkles within my fist.

A presence behind me clears her throat. She's dressed sharply in a uniform that notes her status as a customs officer. "Keep moving along."

"Right, sorry." I jam the card back into my bag and start riffling around for my passport. Instinctively, the officer ushers me toward the US passport holder line. The *queue*, that is, because every word apparently needs a different word in London.

I stop again, and the lady's stare ventures dangerously close to glare territory.

That's just *not* how you welcome someone to your country.

Finally, I spot the red passport and flash it at her. The passport that took ages to get, and is the only reason I'm even on this journey. I pray a silent thanks for my mom being born in Ireland. Her birthright citizenship meant I had this chance to come here. For school, for work, for anything.

I separate from the officer and join the (much shorter) queue to the electronic passport check. Where the other Americans with me on the flight get inundated with queuing, questions, and stamps, I simply walk through with a blank look at a camera and a scan of my passport.

As soon as I leave the area, I look up and see an ad showcasing a wildly British—albeit gaudy—vision. A pub dinner, a pint of beer, and the Union Jack in the background. "Welcome to London."

The words swirl around in my head. Welcome. To. London. Every step is a new revelation, a new reminder of this mess I've gotten myself into. Okay, maybe not a *mess*, but it's causing me some anxiety.

Some questions:

- What if I don't like living here? I have no backup plan.
- What if the charming accents lose their charm?
- How long is it going to take for my luggage to come out on that carousel?
- What if it doesn't? They've definitely lost it.

Cue the panting. Again.

Almost instantaneously, my fears about luggage negligence turn out to be for nothing. I grab my suitcase, which was maybe the fourth one to hit the carousel, and I'm on my way.

As I'm shuffled through the airport, I get bombarded by airport shopping. We go from point A to point B in a snake pattern through the shops, carefully placed so you're forced to see as much merchandise as possible. Toblerones out the ass. Do I look like I need a perfume sample? And why would I want a sample shot of honey bourbon at ten thirty in the morning? I can see the exit, but I can't get to it, and I don't need to make a list because that alone will make me lose my shit if people don't stop rushing by.

Imagine being in a corn maze back in the States. It's like that, but you're sneezing because of perfume, not hay. It's wild. But as I walk through the green passageway, declaring that I have nothing to declare to customs, my confused fury melts into confused . . .

Feelings. There are definitely feelings here.

Some guy's holding a sign that reads *Pierce*. My last name. There's a smiley face after it. It takes me a second to process this information because I'm a little too busy looking at his face, but by the time I do, he's running around the rope and stanchion (which I don't think you're allowed to do) and coming toward me.

"Marty!"

"You're not my cousin," I say. I've got to assume he knows this, but forming words is hard for . . . well, a few reasons right now. But he greets me with such instant familiarity that I ask, "Have we met?"

Which is the most ridiculous thing to say to this perfect creature. I'd have remembered us meeting. Trust me.

"Ha, no. We haven't met, and you're right—I'm not your cousin Shane. But I'm a friend of his!"

He's got a great face, a perfect-yet-too-flawed-to-be-on-the-cover-of-*GQ* face with a faded scar above his right eye, patchy stubble, and one dimple that just won't quit. Under the fluorescent lights, I see the slightest bit of pink brushing his otherwise light tan cheeks.

It's like he just looks at me and I know I'm having my sexual awakening. (Not really; that crown goes to Ryan Reynolds in *The Proposal*. I had an early start.) But I can actually see his pecs through his sweater, and that's a lot? I pull down my T-shirt. It's a little short, and I've got zero abs there. I consider grabbing my hoodie to further cover up my flabby stomach, but it's a little warm in here. And . . . I'm staring and not saying anything. Shit.

"Sorry. Um, zoning out. I didn't get an ounce of sleep on that red-eye."

I actually slept okay, but the spontaneous lie that leaves my mouth sounds better than *"A combination of jetlag and infatuation has made me fall madly, immediately in love with you, random dude, because you smiled at me once. Yes, we can all see the red flags from here."*

I don't even know his name.

"I'm Marty. Who are . . . and, um, sorry, why are you here?" I stretch out my hand to meet his. Mine's sweaty, which shouldn't be a surprise at this point, and his is dry and smooth.

"Right, a real introduction. Hi, Marty Pierce," he says by way of introduction, then points at the sign he's holding. "I'm Pierce, oddly enough. And a certain world-renowned stage production phoned Shane this morning about an audition. So he sent me instead."

Silence creeps between us as I process what he said. My cousin finally got an audition? A *real* audition? A pang of

jealousy hits me, and I curse myself for it. Shane's been balancing a near-full-time job at a local bookshop with applications
and rehearsals since he graduated in May.

But it's what we decided to do together. We even joked
about ending up in the same orchestra. The unease of doing
this alone hits me, which fits in well with the unease I have
about being so selfish about this.

"*Les Mis*," he continues. "If that wasn't clear."

I nod, remembering the extensive application process it
took to get him there. My chest starts to untangle when I think
about how excited he must have been to finally get a call. *The*
call.

"I hope that's okay?" Pierce strikes me as someone who
doesn't enjoy silence.

"Yeah, of course. That's amazing! I hope he gets it."

"He deserves it," Pierce says with a laugh. "Don't tell him I
said this, but I'm extremely jealous. I was in orchestra with him
in secondary, and now I go to Knightsbridge Academy of Music
just down the street from his place."

"Oh, you go to the academy?" Meeting another musician
calms me down a bit. It's like we've already got this shared
experience, even if we've never been in the same room. "What
do you play?"

"Trumpet." He looks away as he says it, then changes the
topic. "You ready to go? Shane planned on hiring a minicab,
but I was hoping we could take the tube? The subway, that
is. And I could show you the academy—for when you describe

the place to your parents. They still think you're attending, right?"

"Oh. We're going to take the train?"

- That wasn't in the plan.
- I'm carrying a lot of shit, and I'm going to get left behind.
- If I get lost, I will not be able to find my way without a working cell.
- I want to appear to be chill and breezy, so I can't *not* be okay with this.
- We didn't even take the tube the last time we were here. I knew I'd have to do it at some point, but not now. Not here.

I shrug, trying not to let the panic creep into my muscles. "Um, yeah. Smart! I guess a cab would be more expensive, anyway."

"Ah, plus! You'll get to take the Piccadilly line toward Cockfosters. Americans usually find that name hilarious."

He has to raise his voice at the end of that sentence because of my snickering. The sudden laughter kind of shakes me out of my spiral, just enough that I can get a grip on the situation.

I am doing this for me, I remind myself. I need to be uncomfortable. I need to try new things. And if I can just get past the burning feeling in my core, I might even enjoy this.

Maybe.

"Let me help you with your bags," Pierce says. The gesture,

while a little much, causes a smile to creep across my face. He leads the way, almost triumphantly, as he carries my bags. He *is* a trumpet, from the volume of his voice to how he commands attention in a space like this.

Suddenly, we're standing at a coffee bar, and the smell of freshly ground espresso hits my nose.

"Quick diversion. Want some tea?" Pierce asks, then narrows his gaze. "Or, let me guess, the American wants coffee? Hot chocolate? A mocha?" He pronounces it *mock-uh*, which brings another smile to my face, despite the fact that he's *mock*-ing me.

He makes a gagging sound, and I laugh, even though my mouth waters at the thought of chocolate in *any* form. "Just coffee is fine. With milk and sugar if you don't mind. Here, let me get this." I reach into my pocket and pull out a few bills. Dead American presidents look back at me. "And . . . I just realized this is basically Monopoly money here. Can I Venmo you? Or I can go to a currency exchange. Or—"

He places his free hand on my shoulder and looks me in the eyes.

"No worries. It's my treat." He laughs. "Well, technically, it's Shane's treat. He may have given us money for the cab."

He winks, and my cheeks heat up. There's something about his smile. The fact he's holding my bag. The way he can poke fun at me but not make my defenses tighten up. It makes all the lies that got me here feel worth it for the first time, and it reminds me of the unusual path my life is taking. I feel older than I was before. Which, okay, sure, technically is true—I understand how the passage of time works—but there's something tugging at the corners of my brain, at my emotions. It's something like infatuation, sure, but as I watch Pierce rock on the balls of his feet, bringing a whole new intensity to something as mundane as ordering coffee, it's also totally different. Something like home.

Pierce hands me a steaming Americano and guides us toward the tube. He flashes a soft smile at me, the kind of smile that's brimming with possibility. With hope of what's to come.

"Welcome home, Marty."

Now *that's* how you welcome someone to your country.

DIARY ENTRY 8

I'M GOING TO REWRITE this entire journal. It's a shitty piece of shitty homework for shitty teachers at this shitty school and shitty town full of shitty people. Am I missing anyone? Basically, it's all shit.

But, fictional reader, you'd know that if you read my other entries.

Shane is the only one here who gives me hope. Maybe Aunt Leah too. Now that we're leaving for Ireland to see my extended family—days earlier than expected—I think my aunt really understood me for once.

A few years ago, me and Shane decided we would both come out to our parents on the same day. There were tears all around, in both families. Shane's? Beautiful, artistic tears. Like when Jennifer Garner tells her son "You get to exhale now" in *Love, Simon*.

Mine took a different path. Different tears. Hotter, heavier ones, weighed down with the last strands of hope I had. And I've been grappling with this fire in my stomach ever since.

As no one will read this, I might as well give out some more details about the whole *coming out* extravaganza. Shit hit the fan, and I barely left my bedroom for days. I took my entire family's numbers out of my phone, Shane and Aunt Leah included. I deleted my social media accounts, fell off the grid completely. But . . . it turns out taking someone's number out doesn't really stop them from reaching out to you, and we live in 2020, where you're ALWAYS on the grid.

Shane didn't take the hint. And neither did his mom. They spent weeks clawing their way back into my life. They even got my mom to come back to Europe for the first time since she was a kid, *and* bring us all! She and Dad inched further and further outside their comfort zones. And . . . now it's all pretty much destroyed.

Again.

THREE

"HOW'D YOU MEET SHANE, again?" I ask Pierce as an escalator takes us deep into the underground.

He scoffs. "I'm honestly a bit offended he hasn't mentioned me. Truly, I've known him as long as you have. Though I guess we weren't close mates until a few years ago."

"My best friend and I are like that," I say. "We've known each other since we were, like, ten. But god, I hated her for ages."

"Nothing so dramatic for us. I . . ." He hesitates. "I came out a few years before Shane did, and I think he worried people would catch on if he hung out with the only other queer guy in school."

A chill runs through my body, just from the confirmation that Pierce likes dudes. Even with the eye contact and apparent interest, the connection we had, how was I supposed to know? It's like how Megan used to joke that she always "knew" I was gay. Mom and Dad, too, always "knew" I was gay. But, fuck, if they really knew I was gay, why'd they leave me in queer isola-tion for a full-ass decade?

We stand on the train platform, and though there are doz-ens of people brushing past me and Pierce, we're still able to lock eyes for one brief moment. One smirk, and he's driven some emotion straight into my heart. I don't know what this connection is, but it sure as hell isn't anything I'm used to. We step into the train car and take our seats.

Let me count the ways in which I am overwhelmed.

- I have just traveled—no, *relocated*—to a different country. Over an entire ocean.
- I am very aware of the amount of money in my bank account. I always knew it wasn't much, but for some rea-son, I didn't think about the conversion rate until I stopped to get some cash out of an ATM here, and let's just say the American dollar isn't doing so great.
- I am squeezed into a tiny-ass seat, rubbing upper arms with one of the most attractive men in the whole country. I'm exaggerating. Kind of.

I'm nearly silent, but Pierce talks and talks. I only get the gist of it, because instead of focusing on that dream-world accent—lazy A's shoot from his mouth in a reservedly bouncy cadence—I'm focusing on his lips. His thin beard. Or how I can see his sculpted arms even though he's just rolled up the sleeves of his sweater. Or how his arm hair is totally touching *my* arm hair.

"It's a shame you're not actually going to Knightsbridge. The summer program has been pretty interesting so far, but it's preparing me for officially starting uni there in September. I tried out for every trumpet solo, even though first-years rarely land one. And guess what? I didn't make it. They made me play third trumpet, which was just a huge step down. We're auditioning again next week, but I don't think I'll move up any. The lecturers here definitely have their favorites. But . . ."

I expect his words about the academy to hurt more. In any other version of last year's audition, I would have made it too, and I'd be right here bitching about solos or placements alongside him. But spending the last nine months revising my plan has actually done me some good.

I let him drone on about the school. It's time for me to focus. I look around the train car and try to get my bearings. I'm on the Piccadilly line, I know that. After studying the big train map, I can locate the line. The blue one. They all have names: the Northern line is black, the Central line is red, the Bakerloo line is brown. I've never seen a subway map with so many colors (colours?) before.

"I know Shane's really excited to introduce you to our friend group," Pierce cuts in. "You'll get on with the lot, I'm sure. Dani and Rio are probably our closest friends—they're both in the program too. Well, for now, at least. There's a lot of drama between Rio and another clarinet. I wouldn't be surprised if one of them dropped out. Of all the audition pieces in the world, they picked the same solo, and they both nailed it in totally different ways. Right now, they're sharing principal clarinet duties. Which . . . is not how that works. So there's been tension."

"Do people drop out a lot? The tuition is not cheap."

A more serious look comes over his face. "It happens. It's already happened, for a couple who just didn't like the program, or the people. I've heard of people dropping out for better reasons, though! Like they booked a great gig, or something."

"I can't imagine giving it all up," I say. "When I commit to something, I will complete it. To my own detriment, even."

He runs a hand through his hair. "I wish I could say the same thing. Maybe I'm not as disciplined as you."

"I wouldn't call it discipline."

He pauses, and looks at me. My cheeks feel hot, and I know I'm supposed to say something, but I wish he'd go back to his monologue. There's comfort in that. I did that enough with Megan. Always the passenger.

"So, you talk a lot." I wince. Why did I say that?

"I do, when I'm nervous." He doesn't stop looking at me. "And I get a little nervous meeting new people, don't you?"

"I think that's why I'm *not* talking."

He laughs, and I join in.

"Anyway," he starts, "I'm excited to hear you play. There aren't any oboes at Knightsbridge. And the ones in our school orchestra were all off-key and annoying—or maybe that's just how they're supposed to sound?"

I roll my eyes at the oboe slander, but he nudges me with his elbow. "It's a joke, Marty. I've been working up this oboe and trumpet duet for my end-of-term recital with my friend Dani, but she plays it on the flute, and it's not the same."

A chuckle leaves my lips. I can play both instruments—the flute was my first way back in middle school—and I know the differences well. They're two woodwind instruments, both in the key of C, but their similarities don't go far beyond their key signature.

"If you're half as good as Shane says you are, I might have to enlist your help."

"Sure," I say. It's hard to tell if it's genuine, or if it's just one of those polite offers. But I can picture it, briefly—me on stage at the academy. It'd be nothing like my botched audition.

A jolt in the train car brings me back to the present. I've been on subways before. The metro in DC is easy; there aren't nearly as many stops. Though there aren't nearly as many trains, so you end up waiting on the platform for two years just to get downtown. New York is fast, like this, but it's dark and dirty—you need to take an acid bath just to get the bacteria off you. I wouldn't say I love the tube, but it has its benefits. (But seriously, why don't people make more sexual jokes referring to tubes? It seems so obvious.)

"But anyway, I think you'll have a good time here."

"I . . . think I will too," I say. *If everyone's as welcoming as you.*

Though he probably knows little about me, he's already treating me like an old friend. And for once, I feel myself opening up to this unknown situation.

A brief silence settles between us. It could be awkward, but the train's wheels rattle and the car squeaks, and no one else in the train car is talking, either. I welcome the silence in the stress of the morning, but my leg bounces against his, restless.

Near the doors, a woman stands guard over her behemoth of a suitcase. I think I recognize her from the flight. As the train pulls up to the next stop—Baron's Court; possibly the fanciest named station, in my opinion—her suitcase rolls away, crashing into three or four people. The woman apologizes, giggles (meanwhile, I'm so embarrassed for her *I* could die), and a businessman in a well-tailored suit flashes a strained smile, but doesn't offer to guide the suitcase back to its owner. The moment she turns, the guy scowls and shakes out his newspaper.

"That's British generosity for you," Pierce says. "Note the fake smile, the passive-aggressive demeanor. It's an art form."

"Hopefully I'll have time to practice this art," I say. "Though my parents would probably say I have the passive-aggressive thing down. Megan would too. Okay, maybe I will fit in here."

"You're seriously going to love this country. You plan to travel any?"

I think back to the money in my bank account, and my palms start to sweat again. Or maybe they never stopped. "No way. I mean, *this* is travel enough. For me."

"Ha. You say that now. Don't you realize you're in Europe? You can fly anywhere for cheap."

A shallow breath. One country at a time.

"It's overwhelming," I say. "This is only my second time in Europe, and really we never did any traveling when I came last year, unless you count staying with my extended family outside of Dublin. I'm from Kentucky, so, it's all foreign to me."

"The place with the chicken, right?"

I cringe. A state with a two-hundred-year history rendered down to a piece of mediocre fried chicken.

"It's more than that," I say. I keep my eyes open, looking around the car. "I don't *hate* it there. It's the farmlands—cute houses, fields, open spaces, and bright stars the moment the sun goes down. I'm the only one who left. Of that side of my family, that is."

"So let's say your plan works out and you get to live here for a while. Do you think you'll ever go back?" Pierce's draped arm drifts closer. So close his fingers graze my shoulder, making me shudder.

"No." I wouldn't. "I'll figure something out. There's just nothing for me there. I'd like to tour in a symphony someday, but I don't know. There are plenty of gigs out there. I'll find something."

At that last bit, I turn to him. His face is inches from mine. The edges of his lips perk up, and I pull back on instinct. His eyes flicker to the train map, and my gaze follows. We're just three or four stops away. We're supposed to get off at Green Park; that's why I'm so surprised when Pierce jumps up at Gloucester Road.

"But this is *Glow-chester* Road?" I say.

"It's pronounced *Glah-ster*, but never mind that. You never got to see Big Ben, right? Without all the scaffolding?"

"Right."

"Let's get off here. I can show you Big Ben, the Abbey. 10 Downing. Let's be proper tourists. Then it's a straight shot to Sondheim Theatre, where we can go surprise Shane after his audition—what do you say?"

My face feels hot. Really hot. Like in eighth grade, when Megan and I split a bottle of NyQuil because we thought it'd get us drunk (but it really just made us sleep for fourteen hours). My anxiety levels are off the charts.

- This was not in the plan.
- I'm carrying a suitcase.
- There are going to be a *lot* of people up there.

My brain also chooses this time to remind me how long it's been since I've had a shower.

He smiles—not a beaming smile, but a smirk. The doors have opened. I grab my bag and suitcase, while Pierce reaches out to me. My shoes feel glued to the ground. There's something in his eyes—a sparkle? A twinkle? Reflection of the dingy train lighting? Okay, probably the latter, but fuck it. I'm going to see this city. I'll follow that smirk anywhere.

Diary Entry 1

THIS ASSIGNMENT FEELS A little juvenile. (Note to self: erase that later.) I've been sitting in our Airbnb for like twenty minutes staring at this blank page. In my creative writing class last year, Ms. Hardin always said how sometimes writing whatever you're thinking will jump-start your brain. Even if it's crap. This is crap, but I'm trying to jump-start my jet-lagged brain, and it's going to have to do. Okay. Back to London.

There's no place like this. I mean, I haven't seen that many places. Like, I went to New York on that school trip once, and when I was really young my parents made me board a bus with about forty other people from our megachurch to do that awful March for Life event in DC. I can't look back on that mess of flyers and hymns and virtue signaling and not do a full body cringe. We trashed the city. When no one was taking our flyers, we were told to let God take them, and threw them into the air. God, of course, took them nowhere, and they melted into the soggy streets of Chinatown.

Wow, maybe diaries *are* therapeutic. That felt good.

Anyway, I'm going to have to delete all this. I don't know if Mr. Wei is super Christian, but pissing off the righteous is not a good way to start my final school year.

So wait, London. We're here! I'm tired. And also, it's *PRIDE*. No one told me, not even Shane. We haven't seen anything—no parades or anything like that—but we toured the city today, and the amount of rainbow flags I saw blew my mind. I think we have one bar around town that has a printed rainbow flag in its window—it's not a gay bar, but it's at least queer-friendly. God, the people of Avery *hated* when that flag went up. Here it's like there are entire neighborhoods where I'd be welcome, whether I came in draped in rainbows, with painted nails, or holding hands with a guy.

It's like a shock to my system that I feel all over. I didn't know anything like this existed. I mean, I *knew*—we do have the internet in Avery—but I didn't know it'd feel like this.

Right, so, I need ten diary entries about my summer. We're here for a full week, so I want most of them to be about this trip to London. I'm auditioning for the Knightsbridge Academy of Music in a couple of days, and we get to spend the full week with my cousin Shane and Aunt Leah. We haven't seen much of the city, really. Just whatever we went by on the drive in, which was actually pretty great. Rolling hills, sheep everywhere, stone fences, and there's nothing stranger than riding in a car that's on the wrong side of the road.

I think even *that* was a little too much for my parents. They're not the big-city type, but I see how it's wearing on them. Mom hasn't been back to Europe since she was six years old, when her parents' divorce left her on a plane with her dad, off to a new life in America. Even during those six years, her parents rarely left her town, except when her dad would take her into Dublin, where she'd sit at a pub with a cheese toastie, coloring in a book while her dad drank a pint, and together they listened to whatever folk band was playing. It was a mini-tradition, worth the hour drive.

But it's been like forty years, and London isn't Dublin, so I guess she doesn't feel so comfortable here anymore.

FOUR

THE STEEL DOORS OPEN, and we're suddenly getting shoved across the platform. I mean this literally. It's supposedly a weekend, but über-professionals keep darting around the two of us to line up at the stairs. We aren't exactly walking at a leisurely pace, but one can only move so fast when they're tethered to a suitcase. As we approach the steps, Pierce darts ahead, through the crowd. I can't see where he's going, but I stick to the path—there's only one way out of here, but this seems like the worst possible place to get separated.

I wonder where Pierce went, but then I spot him. The back of his head, at least. He's carrying half a stroller up the stairs, while the frazzled mother takes the front end, stepping backward up the stairs. People shuffle around them, but they don't seem annoyed, like this is commonplace or something.

I'm a few steps behind them, but I feel Pierce's energy with every step—he's saying "no worries" over and over again. And when they reach the top, she thanks him for the millionth time before she disappears into the sea of gray.

He waits there for me, and we carry on.

"Well, that was trusting of her," I say.

"I wasn't going to drop her baby." He pushes my shoulder. "It happens a lot here. Fucking buggies *everywhere*."

". . . Buggies?" I try not to laugh.

"Um, prams? Pushchairs?"

"There can't be this many Britishisms for 'stroller.'" I roll my eyes. "I refuse to believe it."

We file through a dark, low tunnel. White tiles line the walls and arc across the ceiling, while dingy concrete lies under our feet. Against a small semicircle painted on the wall is an older man sitting on a stool with a harmonica in his hands. The eerie chords sing out. It's a bit painful to listen to. His ragged breathing sounds louder than the music, though I wouldn't exactly call this music.

I take a deep breath. He may be terrible at this, but he's got bigger balls than I'll ever have, performing down here. That's a place you'll never see me.

"Looks like Gloucester Road's got B-listers busking this morning."

"Busking?" I ask, though I know it's another word we don't use in America.

"God, don't you know proper English?" He chuckles—I notice the dimple again. "Street or tube musicians. Or really any kind of performer."

"Do you guys ever do that?"

"I have before, but I don't have a license or anything. Our friend Dani's quite into it. I think she likes it more than any of the performing she's forced to do for class."

We take a sharp left, and I see signs for the Circle and District lines, yellow and green, respectively. My palms are sweaty—actually, everything is a bit sweaty, and it's getting harder to catch my breath. The crowds are getting to me. So I try to relax, thaw my body. Deep breath in, deep breath out.

Either way, I know I can handle it. My chest rises with the realization. I walk onto another train and file to the back, where we'll have the most room. (Okay, I file to the back because that's what the signs say to do and I can't not follow the rules of posted signs.) Pierce reaches for the bar over my head, and I physically fight the urge to pull him into me.

A few stops later, I hear the train operator say one word I very much recognize: Westminster.

We're here.

Pierce takes the stairs two at a time—I take them *one* at a time, lugging my suitcase behind me and panting. Then I take out the shiny new Oyster card Pierce got me to exit the station. In my prep for this move, I learned that their train card is called "Oyster" because with their card, the world is your oyster. So adorable I could vomit.

We file through the turnstiles, and even with my bag, I slip through like a damned local. It warms my heart a bit—no one likes feeling like a newbie here. Exhibit A: the two old ladies struggling to enter their paper card into the turnstile.

Freaking tourists.

We walk through the gates, and I start to feel funny. Not sick, but a little overwhelmed with the moment. I've been here before, but even still, I find it hard to prepare myself to stand before things I've mostly seen on TV and in movies. I sense that it's close. Tourists are everywhere. Pushing into me, running by me.

My breaths are shallow and fast, and I know that's not good. I can't pull in the air I need. Pierce grabs my hand and guides me through the crowd.

I'm in a haze, but I follow him to a spot between two newsstands—neither seems to be selling news, just souvenirs. We get to the edge of the sidewalk, and for a moment no one's around us, just the metal backs of the carts and the black cabs and double-decker buses. It's surreal.

He's looking at me, and I him. And I can't help but think how cute he is. Instant infatuation. An instant connection. It's *never* like this—gripping me by the chest and wringing my heart out like a dish towel. And for a second, the briefest second, I pull closer to him.

I don't know what I'm doing, so I stop. He raises an eyebrow.

"Sorry," I say, then blame it on my weakness in the moment. "I get overwhelmed in crowds."

That eyebrow of his stays up, so I divert my gaze a few inches south of his eyes. To be honest, direct eye contact can be overwhelming too. But then I realize I'm looking at his lips, so I look down even farther—no, not *there*.

He takes my chin and lifts it slightly. I settle on looking

at the bridge of his nose. I want to be in this moment, but something's holding me back. I want to enjoy this closeness, the softness of his touch on my elbow.

But everyone's staring at us. Or at least, it feels like they are. Maybe they are, probably they aren't. But besides all that, we're *in the way*, and that alone makes my chest feel itchy. Not to mention, this closeness has revealed a gaping hole in my heart I never knew was there.

Once, I thought I had a crush on Skye. It was more that we hung out all the time, and he's the sweetest kid in the world. Cute face, piercing eyes. But that crush had a pretty normal trajectory. It started off slow, grew to an annoying but not life-threatening high, then passed around the time he started getting crushes on every girl he came into contact with.

I pull back, giving enough separation for three or four tourists to push through us. This opens the floodgates, and dozens more pour through the gap between us. I take in a sharp breath and pull my free arm across my chest—they're way too close. Everyone is. I take a few steps back, into the sharp elbow of a Super Important Businessperson.

I can't do this.

My free arm folds across my body as I stomp away. Not far, but away. Around the corner, under an awning, anywhere. In Avery, I always had a way out or a place to hide. I knew that little town like the back of my hand. But London's scary as hell. Construction lines the street like castle walls.

"Marty! Wait, I . . ."

It's hard to hear him with the chaos around me. Families

herd their children left and right of me. I arch my shoulders in
and close my eyes. Breathe in. Out.

In.

Out.

Pierce stands beside me. I feel him there. When I open my
eyes, I see his hand hovering above my shoulder. He's unsure
whether he should touch me or not. He decides not to, so I lean
against the stone wall and avoid his gaze.

"Are you . . . ?" He drifts off.

Okay? I hate that question. No, of course I'm not, and I
don't know why, so I can't really explain any of it.

Though "Are you okay?" is better than "What the fuck is
wrong with you?!" which was Megan's personal favorite attack
back in the days of me hiding in the corner of the gym during
mandatory pep rallies.

Pierce clears his throat. "Are you aware how much shite I'd be
in if I had to tell Shane I'd lost you on the streets of London?"

He hunches to meet my downward gaze. Smiles, so I know
he's joking.

"Sorry, mate. I didn't realize—I could have taken you to a
better spot. Is there anything I can do?"

"It's nothing. It happens sometimes; it's really nothing."

He leans against the wall next to me, then bumps my shoulder with his. "Whenever you're ready, mate. I know a quieter
place around the way."

We're close again. And this time I just sit with the knowledge that maybe there are people here who understand me . . .
or are at least willing to try to.

FIVE

THINGS ARE BETTER NOW. There's a lingering feeling—a catch in my breath, an ache in my core—but for a brief moment I can push it out of my mind.

We stand on the sidewalk across the street from the parliament building, and Pierce resumes a monologue about nothing in particular while I collect myself. I appreciate it. A hush has fallen over the city. (Proverbially, that is. In actuality, it's a madhouse.) The view's a lot to take in. Everything's so ornate. I scan the lower parliament building, all golds and tans. It is lined with an intricate, gold-plated facade that must've taken ages to design and build—and I know it well from doing Dad's old, super-cool-but-also-kind-of-dated 3D puzzles.

A black gate lines the area, protecting the important Brits who live—or work? probably work—there from the massive onslaught of tourists. But jutting out from behind the gate is one of the more impressive things I've ever seen in real life. Big Ben.

"Last time you were here," Pierce says, "you probably couldn't even see the clockface. Big Ben was almost fully covered by scaffolding. Did you even take pictures?"

"We stayed in the cab," I say, remembering the car ride. The five of us staring awkwardly at each other in one of those cabs where the seats face each other. "I'm kind of glad we did, because it's so much cooler this way."

What I don't say is, *"And they deserved the bad view."* If they're not going to appreciate the things that made London special to me, they don't get to appreciate anything about it. Now entering Pettytown, population: me.

This view? It feels like it's all mine.

Big Ben is essentially a clock attached to a mini-skyscraper. London's a low, sprawling city, so this is one of the taller buildings I've seen, in this area, at least. It stands out from the buildings, among the hundreds of commuters and tourists.

I read once that an establishing shot in a movie is the first thing you see in a new scene that tells you where you are. The montage of the Chrysler Building and Statue of Liberty for New York or the White House and Lincoln Memorial for DC. Looking up at my tall friend Ben here, I find the term resonates with me.

This feels like it could be—no, this *is*—my establishing shot. I'm not in Kentucky anymore. I'm a billion miles away, and I don't know whether to do a little dance or pull an armadillo, curl into a ball, and never get up.

"It's a wonder, innit?" Pierce says as he puts an arm around

me. The movement makes me feel like I'm about to spontaneously combust, but in a good way. "*Technically*, that's not Big
Ben."

I tilt my head up, side-eyeing him. He has no idea the research
I've done. How many online guides I've read, the Google
searches that led to twenty open tabs about things I didn't even
care about.

But I did this so I could be prepared. So I would never feel
like the tourist. So I would never be the butt of an Ignorant
American joke. I know the answer to the trick question behind
his words.

Yes, the tower is not *technically* Big Ben.

And that's when I realize I haven't responded. I'm develop-
ing a bad habit of not responding when I'm around him. It's
concerning, but I'm not exactly concerned.

The glint in his eyes borders on cockiness, and I realize
there's a sort of power in letting someone think they've pulled
one over on you. I let him have it.

"So why does everyone call it Big Ben?"

He lifts his arm the length of the building. "That's Eliza-
beth Tower, but *that* . . ." The bells toll as he points to his ear.
"The bell is called Big Ben. Quick, name the pitch."

"It's an E." I nudge him in the side and he hunches over,
laughing. "It's maybe a quarter tone sharp, but it's an E."

"I knew you'd be one of those perfect-pitch freaks."

He mocks me, and I let him, mostly because being able to
identify any note by ear is not something to be ashamed of.

When Megan mocks me, her words are sharp, cutting. There's something in his voice, his all-teeth smile, when I call the pitch that brings out the ache in my chest. A good ache.

He guides me down a path, still chuckling, and the earlier mocking settles in my brain, putting my mind back on Megan.

She's my best friend, sure. But in many ways she's still my biggest antagonist. It wasn't simple teasing; it was pushing. Calling me spineless when picking up the phone to order pizza would stress me out to the point where I'd have to use my inhaler to breathe.

It's hard to explain why I get like this. With the crowds, or picking up the phone. Or when I think somebody might be mad at me by the fact they didn't text me back but they clearly used their phone to comment on someone's Instagram post. And that stress triples if someone's left their read receipts on. But I've been friends with Megan for so long I kind of forgot what it was like to have someone look at you when you're panicking, smile, and try to make you feel comfortable.

And Pierce did that without knowing me.

Another wave of tourists pushes through us, and just before we get fully separated, I feel his hand slip into mine. He grabs my suitcase with his other hand.

Pierce's hand grips mine firmly, and he holds steady as he leads me across the street. Westminster Abbey grows larger in my field of vision, and we pause in the open space outside it.

I take a deep breath. One more—in and out. When I turn to him, he does the same. The closeness should overwhelm me, but I feel grounded, here in this magical country under the constant, stereotypical British cloud cover.

In movies or books (or literally all media out there), this moment is frozen in time. The rise in his chest. The warmth of my cheeks. His fingers laced through mine, lightly now, but enough to send sparks up my arm.

My mind can't stop, and there's so much going on, all the time, right now that I can't stop it. I want to enjoy this moment. I want to lean into him, smooth the expression on my face, but I feel myself receding. Pulling back, slipping out of his grip, flexing my muscles and withdrawing. The shortness of breath. My head feels fuzzy; my eyes lose focus. I can't keep up with it all—the people, my feelings, the buildings. The people.

His expression falters when I pull back. His mouth's slanted but soft, paired with the same poor-poor-baby eyes I get from my parents or Skye or basically everyone but Megan when I freak like this.

But suddenly, his eyes darken in the soft daylight. His brows furrow, giving him an angular, tense expression.

"It may not be my place, Marty. But—" He pauses. Considers. "But, I think you need to work through this."

The moment's over.

"Really? My best friend says that to me all the time. *Get over it!* Pierce. What if I can't get over it? It's not something I can just get over. It's who I am it's—"

"Wait, let me explain." He places a hand on my chest, and I suck in my stomach, trying in vain to harden my core. "I didn't say to get over it. I don't think you can. I know Americans are touchy with mental health, but let me say this. You could talk to someone, you could try one of those apps, or something. Just start there. This summer's going to be a big change for you. I don't want you to . . . Never mind. Maybe I'm out of bounds."

"Gotcha," I say.

"Does your best friend really say that?" His tone is almost pitying, and an icky feeling takes over.

I don't know how to describe our friendship to others, because the more honest I am, the worse it sounds. She does say that to me, all the time. But she also brings me out of my shell.

"Without her," I say, "I don't know if I'd have even left my room over the last year."

He laughs. "That's good. Doesn't mean she gets a pass if she's saying things like that. It's an anxiety thing, right? Does she know that it's more than you being bashful? Have you told her how it feels?"

There's a vulnerability in his voice, and it resonates with the same vulnerable chord thrumming in my own chest.

"I have told her," I say, tentatively. "It hasn't always gone well."

"Clearly." His cheeks puff out as he releases a long sigh. "Marty, mate, just know it's okay. We've all got weird friendships, and I'm not trying to step in, but whatever you feel is *valid*. Anxiety is a beast, especially for those of us silly enough to pursue a career where we have to put ourselves out there every single day."

"Good point. For the record, I *do* like being pushed out of my comfort zone. Sometimes. But I hate when I feel bad for feeling bad, you know? Like, I can't help it sometimes." I flash him a smile. "Thanks, Pierce."

I've just gotten here, but I'm filled with a warmth that I so rarely get to feel. Progress. Something real.

He pulls me in for a cautious hug, and for a moment I think my mind will go blank. I feel his stubble brush my cheek as he puts his arm around me. I grip his denim jacket, and breathe. And breathe.

I want this to be some sweet fairy-tale moment so badly, but I'm very aware we're in public.

Per usual, things change almost immediately in my brain. Back and forth. There are so many people around. Pierce holds me close, but I've lost the will to participate.

I pull away. "Sorry."

He just smiles. "Nothing to be sorry about, love."

I blush, hard. If that's even possible. My cheeks actually hurt from being so tense—and I play oboe. Strong cheeks are kind of my thing. He's so charming, and relentlessly British, and more importantly, he already seems to care about me as a friend. All I know is I am definitely not ready to deal with any of this. But for the first time, I really *want* to deal with this.

And that makes me feel like I could.

SIX

MY PRE-MEGAN DAYS WERE a blur. I'm not the protagonist of anyone's story, and I'd accepted that from an early age. But when we became best friends, I became something else. I was *something*, I guess. Something was better than nothing.

Unfortunately, I'm still one-hundred-percent dependent on her to sort out my life. Make my decisions, force me to take chances. By "taking chances" I don't mean, like, shoplifting—which she still does even though she has the money and isn't a twelve-year-old thrill seeker anymore—but forcing me to stand up to my parents and tell them I wanted to go live in London. Helping me craft the lie and practice it.

She didn't just help me find my voice; she also made me use it.

I keep feeling my jeans pocket, instinctively looking for and failing to find a phone on which I could text or call her. I'm alone here and I can't handle it. Maybe Pierce was right about learning to manage my issues. But I wouldn't even know where to start.

"So this is Sondheim Theatre," I say to Pierce. A billboard for *Les Misérables* wraps around the corner of the building, and the charming buildings that line the street curve around a roundabout just in front of me.

"Marty, mate!" a voice calls out behind me.

Shane walks down the street toward me. He looks like he's in costume, dressed up with a tie and button-down shirt. His French horn case is gripped tightly in one arm as he throws the other around me. I let go of my suitcase and wrap him up in a hug.

"You left me with a stranger!" I say, laughing.

Pierce pulls Shane into a one-armed hug. "I'm a much better host than Shane, here. We saw Big Ben, the Abbey, 10 Downing, and—"

"And *I* had to wheel a suitcase over a mile of cobblestones." Pierce rolls his eyes.

"So I see you've met, then," Shane says. His Irish accent seems to have gotten thicker, somehow. It reminds me how Mom's is mostly gone, how she claims she worked to get rid of it as soon as she got to America. "I was about to take the bus back. Have you gotten yourself a pass yet?"

We walk to the bus stop, which is just down the street. Pierce makes a point to take my suitcase again, after my cobblestone comment.

"Congrats on the audition," I say. "Tell us how it went!"

He shrugs. "I don't know. I never feel good about these things. They were auditioning for a few parts, and there were loads of musicians in there. Kind of freaked me out, remembering just how many people are looking for the same jobs we are."

It's like his anxiety creeps into my body. But then again, I'm out here to do the same thing. There are a billion oboists out there going for the same parts, and if I don't get something, *and soon*, I'm out.

"You'll get it," Pierce says.

Shane shakes his head. "I admire your . . . unflinching optimism."

A double-decker bus pulls up to the stop, and Pierce takes a step onto it. "Sod off. I'm feeling positive today. Meet you at the top?"

Shane lets an old couple onto the bus before him, and leans back to chat with me. "Marty, I'm so sorry I had to leave you. There was no way to call you, and I didn't think you'd be checking emails. I hope he wasn't too annoying."

"Seriously, it's fine. He was really sweet."

My cheeks glow warm, which Shane picks up on immediately.

"I know Americans lose all sense when it comes to British accents, but can you not crush on my friend? I know too much about that wanker to let anyone I love fall for him."

I sigh as we both scan our transit cards. "I'm very tired. He's very cute. He has a beard! How is that even possible? Help me, I'm but a weak mortal."

"Don't call that patchy mess a beard; his ego will never recover."

We take the stairs to the top, where Pierce has staked out a front row view from the upper deck of the bus. The street shines before me, and I feel immersed in this wonderful world. Without thinking, I take the seat next to Pierce as Shane takes the seat opposite me.

"Mom's a bit gutted she won't see much of you this summer."

Aunt Leah. I smile. "Will I see her before she leaves?"

"One night," Shane says. "Then she'll be out teaching that design course in Rome for the rest of the summer."

My chest rises, then falls. One summer. That's all I have to make it here. My aunt didn't escape my clumsy web of lies either—she thinks I'm here for the summer program at Knightsbridge. When she comes back, I'll need to have all my shit figured out before I've overstayed my welcome—a source of income, a place to live, a life that can't be swayed by my parents *or* by my family here. When she comes back, I'll be eighteen. I'll have a home established here.

And I'm not leaving.

As we hop off the bus, Shane and I say our goodbyes to Pierce.

"Well, this is where I leave you. You're in good hands with Shane, here—thanks for letting me crash the welcome party." He points to a series of stout, brick buildings. Uninviting, but unsurprising. "This is where I live. I'd invite you in, but I've got about four hours of practicing to do."

Shane waves goodbye, but Pierce faces me, waiting for a response, as he takes a couple of backward steps toward his building. I grunt a thank-you. But it's really all I can think of to say. Thank you for showing me around. Thank you for having the perfect balance of smells, citrusy and fresh. Thank you for not making me feel like even more of an idiot when I panicked.

Thank you for lacing your fingers through mine. For the fact I can still feel the heat creep up my wrist.

We part, finally, so I take a deep breath and walk in step with Shane, dragging my suitcase behind me. Everything's better here in ways I can't even quantify properly. Patches of blue start to peek out from behind the gray sky. The buildings around me are different, manageable. They're not ornate like Parliament or Westminster Abbey, but simple and classic. Large stone bricks give them a castle-like feel, and the meticulously manicured round or square bushes and lawns that sprawl out toward the sidewalk put me at ease.

"Things are certainly . . . different here," I say. "Maybe I'm delirious, but things just feel right. I think this was a good decision."

This happens sometimes, after I get out of a super anxious moment and I have the chance to breathe normally. I feel the sun on my skin and things feel lighter. Right. If only all the moments could be like this.

Hanging in the back of my mind is the awareness that I'm not a tourist here. I've committed to this new life, and the responsibilities are about to tumble over me. I should start looking for auditions soon.

But I spent so long trying to get here, why can't I just let myself enjoy this first moment? I swallow hard, pushing down the bile and unease. A minor success.

"Can you see this as your home?" Shane asks.

"I can. It's nothing like Avery, but that's not a bad thing. Everything is prim and proper here. It's picturesque."

"I suppose," he responds. "It's a bit harder to feel that magic when you've been here for almost eighteen years."

We walk in silence, and I recharge. As a certified introvert, I need people like Megan or Pierce to kick me out of my shell. But I also need alone time to re-collect.

I'm spent—a plane ride, a cute boy, and jet lag will do that to you. I meander along the path, enjoying the energy rushing through my veins and pushing through my drowsiness, until we come up to a building I recognize. A pang of something— regret, anger, disappointment, all of the above?—echoes through my body as I think back to last summer.

I tense my shoulders and push through the doors, and say hello to my new home.

Diary Entry 9

WE'RE LEAVING.

That's all I got from my parents. Shane and I were basically hiding in his room as my parents and Aunt Leah had this intense conversation out in her living room.

"I haven't seen you in, what, thirteen years?" Her voice carried. "And you're cutting your trip short because you felt a little uncomfortable?"

I stopped listening after that. I couldn't listen to them talk about it anymore.

It's not like Aunt Leah to raise her voice, but I can't help but be on her side. We have tickets to things; we had two days left at the Airbnb. But Mom just closed up.

It's kind of like what happens when I have one of my panic attacks. I close off, and I want to run away. But it was different with Mom. It's like she had all this armor up with none of the actual panic. None of the shortened breaths, the chest pain, the world-falling-in-on-you feeling. Which makes me think this is kind of fucked up. (Yeah, definitely not turning in this project.)

Before I left their apartment, Aunt Leah stopped me. She said something like, "Marty, we might not get another chance to talk alone for quite some time. At least face-to-face." She held eye contact with me, and her intensity was catching. "If you need *anything*, you let me know. Anything."

Living in London is out of the picture, I know that now. I find out about Knightsbridge soon, but that doesn't matter. Maybe I should just give up on music altogether and choose something safer.

It's clear my oboe and I are meant for a different path, and maybe that's okay. Maybe since everything else is fully not okay this seems less important, or maybe it's that it really is okay. I don't know the answer. I just know that I only have a handful of allies in this world, and only one of them is back in Kentucky.

Aunt Leah's offer, though, it's *some* kind of offer. An opportunity. I may have blown my chance with the academy, but maybe there's a way I can still come here. I've got an opportunity, and I sure as hell won't be wasting it.

I think . . . I can get out of there, for good.

SEVEN

IT'S AROUND MIDDAY WHEN we make it back to the apartment, and jet lag has fully set in. Aunt Leah's flat is charming and quaint—a little small, but the perfect size for her two-person family. It's on the high street, so there's no fancy brick entryway, or double-decker building with a garden out front. But once you walk up the flight of stairs and into the space, that's when the charm comes in.

It's an old building, but the inside's clearly been renovated recently. Exposed brick lines one wall; a floor-to-ceiling window reveals a glimmer of the park beyond. Soft light creeps through the space, and I notice it's started to mist again outside. The apartment itself is sandwiched between two restaurants, so echoes of pots and pans and the ranting of wait staff on their smoke break settle into the space.

"Mum's room is all yours. She's got all her stuff packed

for the summer, and she's going to spend the night on the couch."

"She doesn't have to do that," I say. "I can just move in there tomorrow."

"Oh, I know. She insists, though, and we both know how stubborn she is. So you might as well take it. Remember to switch on the outlets when you want to use them or charge your phone or whatever. You probably have time to nap if you're tired. I can wake you up once my mum's back."

"Thanks," I say, acknowledging the exhaustion that's creeping into my muscles. My chest vibrates with tension as I think back on my spontaneous adventure. "I had fun today. It was nice to meet Pierce."

"Looked like it." There's no malice in his voice, yet the words themselves reveal more than he means to. I wonder if he regrets sending Pierce to pick me up. "Be careful, okay?"

His warning sends waves of frustration through me. I've been stuck in that life back in Kentucky for so long. I've just gotten a taste of freedom, of being comfortable with myself, and for once I don't want to *be careful*.

I just want to *be*.

"I think I will take that nap." The weight of the day crashes into me. I don't have the energy to convince Shane I can handle this on my own, that I don't need his warnings or his protection. I can sense my body screaming for an escape, so I wheel my suitcase into Aunt Leah's room and promptly pass out on my bed, dreaming less of my supportive cousin who brought

me to a new home, and more of the beautiful Brit who welcomed me.

A couple of hours later, I wake to a mostly silent room. Sun
creeps in from the window, and my jeans and tee are crumpled
from the nap. I change into a different tee and a pair of khaki
shorts, and venture out of my room.

This will be my home for the next three months.

That's not enough time, I know that. But I have to make it
work. Anxiety rips at my throat, but I swallow firmly and steel
my core. Deep breath in, long breath out. And repeat.

I peek into Shane's room. He's got headphones on, his eyes
are closed, and he's fully into his foremost musical passion. One
that makes entire symphonies, but one that technically pro-
duces no sound: conducting.

He's conducting in four, but at times switches to two, then
builds to a passionate stop. He swivels away from his computer,
to the left, to focus on fictional violins. He swivels right, to cue
the oboes, or maybe flutes, and opens his eyes.

"Fuck," he shouts. "How long were you there?"

I try not to laugh at his panted breaths and panicked face.
I fail. "You'd think I just caught you jerking it."

He thaws a bit with a laugh. "That would have only been
mildly more embarrassing. I guess I'm not used to having
people around."

"Sorry, roomie. You're stuck with me. What were you conducting? Brahms? It felt like Brahms."

He shakes his head. "Care to try again?"

"Well, it was way too loose to be Bach. Beethoven?"

"Close. Rachmaninoff's Second Piano Concerto."

This makes sense, as he leads a double life as a pianist. And a triple life as a good horn player. Actually, he can kind of play everything. It makes me sick.

The looming conversation also makes me sick, but I have to do it. I can feel the layers building around him after catching him in such a weird, vulnerable moment. He's turned back to the computer, and the silence has filled the space.

"Sorry if I was short with you earlier. Are you annoyed with me about what happened with Pierce today?"

He sighs, and begins to speak. "I'm not annoyed with you. I'm a bit peeved at Pierce for making a move on you, but it's my own fault. We've been planning this, you and I, for a year. I should have asked for a different audition date, or something. But he told me he could do it, and you seem to really like him. I guess I'm just being . . ."

"Overprotective?" I ask. The Shane of my trip last year was so much less serious, more carefree. Until the end, at least. "Is this because of what happened last year? Like, that sucked, obviously, but I'm here now."

The silence between us expands, and I worry I've said too much. Guilt gnaws at me, and I get the very real urge to flee.

"You were so good at pushing us out. I thought you got grounded; then I was worried maybe something worse might have happened. It was just like what you did to me after your coming-out catastrophe. Mate, you panic when I don't respond to your email within a day, even when I'm, like, working. Could you imagine if I dropped off the face of the earth after our families got in a huge fight?"

A pause. I don't really know how to respond to that.

"Yeah, I would be majorly freaked," I say, taking a seat on his bed. My body faces the door, and I realize even now I'm looking for an escape. "I didn't want to make you worry. But it was *so* bad."

"I know, I know." He rolls his chair over to me and wraps me up in a hug. "It's just, you're basically the only family I have. At least, the only family I have born in this generation."

"I was all in my head, but you and Aunt Leah *were* there for me. I don't have much of an excuse, but I am glad you two clawed your way back into my life."

"We always will." He smirks. "But *truly*, it's fine. I'm being cautious for no reason. Pierce is just a bit of a heartbreaker. And you know I'll support you through anything, but I need you to physically stay here in order for me to do that. I'm not going to lose my cousin again."

"Until you become that famous horn player from the *Les Mis* orchestra and get too good for me," I say, deadpan.

"Precisely." He sticks out his chest and spins gracefully away on his rolling chair. "I'm already starting to forget who you are."

A key clicks into place in the front door, interrupting the moment. I stand and walk to the doorway, so I have a direct line of sight when Aunt Leah comes in. She sees me and drops her groceries on the table hastily in a near sprint to welcome me with open arms. Literally.

I'm about a foot taller than her, but I'm still squeezed into her embrace so tightly I'm not sure I could get out if I tried.

"How was the flight? How have you been? You're a secondary—I mean, high school graduate now. Your mum showed me all the pictures." There's a pause as the weight of their strained relationship barrels into the conversation. "Well, I saw it on your dad's Facebook."

"That counts," I say to lighten the mood. "Flight was as good as it could have been. I've been fine, doing better now that I'm here. Shane's friend Pierce picked me up and took me to see Parliament and Big Ben, and now I never have to be a tourist again."

"Pierce? Pierce Reid?" She looks to Shane, who's just met us in the kitchen. "Why weren't you there?"

He blushes. "About ten minutes after you left this morning, I got a call from, uh, the *Les Mis* orchestra casting director. She liked my portfolio, I suppose."

"Shane? Did you have an *audition*?"

Her hands come up to cover her gaped mouth. He offers a shy grin in response.

"So *that's* why you're wearing your nice M&S shirt. I thought you were just trying to make a good impression with Marty." She shakes her head. "But more important, oh my god! Congrats, honey. Well done."

She nearly barrels him over with a hug, but I see his awkward expression from here. We've both always had trouble celebrating our successes, so I should definitely find a way to drop this jealousy and be more supportive of him.

"Let's celebrate tonight," she says. "I'll pop by the shop and get some bubbly. Oh, that reminds me—I got you groceries that should last for a while. I was going to cook, but between your audition and Marty's big move, let's do a proper Sunday roast down at the Alexandria. What do you say?"

We agree to dinner, and Shane and I start packing away the mounds of groceries. I see a few American staples slipped into the mix—boxed mac and cheese, peanut butter—which makes me smile.

"I had to raid the tiny American section for those," she says with a laugh. "Want you to be as comfortable as possible. I'm really nervous about leaving you boys alone here all summer, but I'm so happy you're here to keep Shane in check."

She winks and Shane groans. I try not to let my anxiety show. Three months is not a long time.

"I'm just so glad Lizzie was okay with this. She still won't return my calls, but I'll do for a nice email every once in a while." I flinch at the mention of my mother. At the mention of the email *I* wrote from my mom's account, assuring Leah I'd be fine in London alone, all summer, with Shane. Somewhere, just outside my mind's reach, is the knowledge that this is all going to crash down on me. But . . .

Once everything's already crashed down on you before, how much worse could it get?

EIGHT

I HAVE NO IDEA what time it is. Strike that, I *know* it's ten in the morning. But my body has no idea whether the sun is rising or setting, and the cloudy sky doesn't help the confusion. Aunt Leah just left, and I've spent the last hour trying to get sorted, which is another British term I've decided to lift. "Sorted" sounds much more *proper* than "organized."

My phone's all set up, so naturally I'm already on an early-morning FaceTime call with Megan. She's talking about her upcoming breakfast plans with Skye. I don't bring up the fact that she outed me to him, and she doesn't either. She's got to know she made a mistake, but now that I think about it, she's never admitted to a mistake before. So I don't know what I'm expecting.

The whole time I half participate, focusing more on the new reeds I'm making for my oboe. Though I tell her briefly about Pierce. She goes on and on about how I should "kiss that bloke" and live my gay life to really stick it to my parents. But Shane comes in, and I don't feel like talking about him anymore. I end the call and continue the meticulous process of making my own reeds.

It takes forever, and makes me wish I'd taken up the clarinet or something a little less hands-on, but it grounds me. There's nothing that makes you feel more connected to your instrument than crafting the piece—shaving the thin pieces of wood, tying them together with string—that you use to actually make the music.

"You're really in the zone there," Shane says. He's warming up his own instrument. Actually, just the mouthpiece, running a high-pitched duck call up and down in pitch until he feels his lips are warmed up enough to try it for real. He puts the mouthpiece in his French horn. "Duet?"

"Oboe and French horn?" I laugh. "That sounds like a disaster waiting to happen."

"Fine, a solo it is."

He's not the best technician, and I don't think he'd ever claim to be, but you can tell he really *gets* music. He puts more feeling in what he performs than most, and it's necessary— having the ability to emote makes him the perfect fit for a subtle, harmony-driven instrument like the horn.

His phone lights up with a text.

"That's Pierce," he says. If he's feeling weird about Pierce after our conversation yesterday, he doesn't say it. "They're doing a jam session in the park after classes end. Want to join?

They're usually quite fun. Dani knows a marching band teacher from the States, and she gets sent all this commercial pop music. It's not super challenging, but after the days they have at the academy, it's nice to unwind."

"Oh, um, sure." I think back to something Megan told me before I got out of the car at the airport. *"Say yes to everything. Even if it makes you shit yourself. Be the Nike swoosh."*

I embody the Nike swoosh. I just do it.

I've been up since, like, four in the morning, thanks to jet lag and my crash nap yesterday, so while Shane goes to shower and get ready for the day, I pack my laptop and take a walk. A sourness gnaws at my gut, because I know I need to call my parents before they freak out, but I don't want to FaceTime them from Aunt Leah's place. They bolted out of here a year ago with no remorse, so they don't get to see it.

Any of it.

It's a Costa Coffee, a chain I've seen often enough around here, even though I've only been here one day. I order a hot chocolate and take a seat near the back. As I connect my laptop to Wi-Fi, I idly swipe through my phone and ignore the woodsy tea smell that invades the entire space.

It's around noon here, so seven at home, which means Mom's already left for work. I send a FaceTime request to Dad's phone.

Under the table, my legs shake, as I wait for the call to light up my laptop. Each time I force my legs to stop shaking, they start again. It's the only thing that eases the worry inside me, the panic pouring through my body. I try to sort out what's causing the anxiety:

- I'm not really missing them, but *shouldn't* I be missing them already?
- Is it that my shoddily made tower of lies could crumble at any second?
- Will just hearing his voice invoke some sort of trauma?

Either way, this is a shitty situation. Dad's face fills the screen, and his voice tumbles into the speaker.

"Hiya, Mart." He leans back and flips the camera to the side, then back, to try to get the view. He's never really gotten the hang of this. "You're not at your aunt's?"

"Decided to take a walk and went to a Costa Coffee. That one we went to last year a couple times."

"How was the flight? How's *London*? I think you're starting to pick up the accent already." His voice is almost perky, which brings my guard down a bit. It's always hard to remember that even if they were shitty to me about certain things, they do genuinely care about me as a human. Even if they don't act like it all the time.

Dad's on the porch with a glass of orange juice. I recognize my home—my *old* home—in the background. A bit of warmth fills my insides at the familiarity of it all.

"It's all okay." Vulnerability creeps into my voice. "Just, you know, different here. It's finally starting to hit me just how far away I am from Avery. I'm not homesick or anything, but, you know."

He nods. Takes his time in forming a response.

"Hold on."

He taps on his phone to check a message. Or at least, that's what I thought he was doing, but when he looks back at the camera, he says, "Okay, you're at that Costa Coffee, right? I've got their menu up. I want you to go and get yourself, let's see . . . a sausage roll, a Bakewell tart—remember when they had to make those on that British baking show?— and a mince pie."

"Mince pie, like, a meat pie? No thanks."

"I'm on the dietary page and it's marked vegan, so I'm pretty sure this is a fruit pie. Or it's one sick joke by the baristas. Go ahead, do it. Or get something different that looks good. I'll put some money in your account later; this is our treat."

I laugh. "Noted."

A couple of minutes later, I come back to my table in the back corner with the goods.

"Okay, now what?" I ask.

"Well, you eat them."

"Sure. A sausage roll, here goes," I say. I take a bite, and the flaky pastry crust and boiled, reduced, or otherwise tortured meat hits my tongue. I chew. Consider. "It's not bad. It's actually better than it has any right to be."

"Exactly. Next, what do we have?"

"I got the mince pie," I say. "And some kind of tart. I can't believe you're force-feeding me junk food."

"They call them sweets there," he says. "Get it right or you'll never fit in."

After tasting both, I look into the camera and arch an eye-brow. "Okay, they were both *proper delightful treats*. The point of this?"

"The point is that everything you just ate? You can't really get them in Kentucky. It doesn't exist, even at the fanciest of coffee shops."

"You mean Starbucks?"

"I mean Starbucks." He smirks. "These pastries are different, but it's okay. You're still here. Life still moves on."

Nike swoosh.

"Look, your mom didn't want you to go. You know I didn't want you to go. But we can't help but think this is good for you. There's so much to experience. It's a different world, maybe too different for us, but I think you might like it."

I look down.

"I guess I'm just scared," I say. And I already feel vulnerable for saying it, but I have to. "I don't know how to make this—um, this school stuff—work. It's like I have this idea of a perfect life all planned out, but I'm not sure how to get there."

He laughs. Pauses. Then his voice drops. "I'm still trying to figure that out myself."

We share an awkward glance—you never know when a parent's going to decide to be way too honest about their feelings—then I avoid his eye contact, even if it's digital.

"That reminds me," he says. I watch his smile fade. "You might have already found this, but Mom slipped your necklace in your bag while we were at the airport."

"Oh, she did?" I groan.

I have *not* found that, or I would have been dreading this call even more.

"It's part of the deal," he says. "We can't keep an eye on you over there, and we know Leah's not religious so I assume Shane isn't either. But you know how important it is to us. How it's always been to you. Wear the cross, find a good church nearby. Be the person God wants you to be."

There's so much he isn't saying. So much lies beneath the idea of who he thinks god wants me to be. But I'm seventeen, for the next three months, at least, and I know that I have to keep the charade going.

So I keep lying.

"I will. Tell her I said thanks." I sigh. "I'll find a church, don't worry. There's one just across from here."

"What kind of church?"

The kind with pentacles all over it.

"I don't know, Dad." I'm over it, and he can tell. "Can't really be picky here."

I'll never understand how we can be so open, and how they can be so kind, then close up so quickly. How their version of god can drive a stake through the heart of our relationship, and they don't even realize it's happening.

We mumble our goodbyes, but it's already too awkward. I try to hold on to the good parts of our conversation, and our relationship. But it's hard, sitting here godless and alone, looking at a blank screen.

NINE

"ARE YOU READY TO meet the crew?" Shane asks as we walk down the tree-lined path to Green Park. We're both carrying instrument cases—his is a bit large and awkward to fit the size and shape of his French horn, and mine's petite and contained. Though I'm also carrying a little cup of water with my new oboe reed resting in it, tip down in the water to soften it before playing.

"Ready as I'll ever be. Remind me of the names again?"

"Right. Rio, clarinet. She'll likely boss you around. Dani, flute, and her boyfriend, Ajay, who's a pianist but he's not much of a public performer. He just sits around with us." A beat, and then he says, "And Pierce, of course. That's more or less our group."

I say the names and instruments in my head like I'm practicing with flash cards.

"That's a small group, I can handle that."

"Actually, a lot of people join this thing. Like twenty, maybe more—that's just our crew. Pierce and Rio can be a little protective of our circle, but you've already passed Pierce's test, clearly."

The way he says it makes me think I've done something wrong again. But am I being too sensitive? Am I reading into things?

"When did you start getting close with Pierce?" I ask, hoping to gain more insight into their friendship.

"Around the time he made it into our school's top orchestra," he says. His voice drops a bit. "I'd been in it since year ten. I thought that'd be it for our friendship after graduation, but then he told me he got into the academy and that he still wanted to be friends. I started working with Dani at the bookshop nearby, and she and Pierce got close right away at Knightsbridge, so it just made sense for us all to be mates."

"Ah," I say. "You still seem super weird about him."

"Yeah. He cycled through friends a lot in school, so I've always assumed he'd get bored with me and move on. As soon as the solo competition between Rio and Sophie heated up, he brought Rio into our group and started to ignore the rest of us. But even if he gets distracted by shiny new friends, he always comes back to me, so perhaps he deserves more credit."

We're into the park now, and the hand that's holding my oboe case starts to sweat. I grip the case harder as I keep an eye out for this group of people.

"That's good to know, I guess. But he seemed to like me a lot? And I'm not going to that school, so maybe you're reading into it some?"

"Yeah, that's probably it. I don't want to let my weirdness with Pierce affect your feelings about him."

I laugh, despite the growing anxiety that comes when I know I'm about to meet new people. "Well, you're doing a bad job. So tell me something good about him."

"He's mad passionate. He's fun; he's got a wicked sense of humor." We must be getting close, since he slows down and turns to me. "A couple weeks ago, he convinced the people at the London Eye—that big Ferris wheel on the river—he was a social media influencer, and he got the whole group of us on a private ride."

Shane nudges my shoulder. "He can be very charming."

"That sounds more like the guy *I* met," I say as a smile lifts my face. "Thanks."

We approach the group. They're mostly hidden behind trees, so I hear them before I see them. Trumpets blaring scales, up and down and up until the players run out of breath. A trombone blurting out notes like it was trying to be the loudest. Clarinets trilling faster and faster, with the flutes lagging slightly behind them.

For one bright moment, the vise loosens its hold on my insides, and I feel myself becoming calmer and more ready than I was mere seconds ago. This is my element, my world.

I come into the clearing, where a clarinet player—maybe Rio, maybe Sophie—warms up with a low trill that builds into a powerful glissando. Her hands fly over the keys until she's able to push the pitch higher with just her lips. It leads into the iconic riff for *Rhapsody in Blue*, and it's a little show-offy, but I find myself drawn to her anyway. Her tight braids fall neatly down her back, but her dark skin glistens with sweat. She pauses to wipe her brow with her forearm.

Shane's ducked off to the side to set his instrument up and take a call from his mom, who I assume just arrived in Italy. I'm alone, but I've come so close that Sophie's looking at me now, so I force myself to keep moving.

"That was fantastic," I say, beaming a let's-be-friends smile. "I'm Marty. Shane's cousin. I don't know if you know him. I play the oboe. Just moved here."

"Sophie," she says. "Nice to meet you, Marty. And yeah, I may have been showing off. I'm in a bit of a standoff for principal chair with this other girl here. It's really annoying—I feel like I always have to prove myself, even when we're not in class."

"Rio?" I ask.

"Oh right, of course you know her. You're part of her crew or whatever."

She turns away from me slightly and starts adjusting the neck of her clarinet. I piece together my oboe—which isn't hard: there's the bell, two pieces of the main body, and the reed. And I watch her attitude fall.

"I just got here yesterday. I haven't met her. Only Pierce, and now you."

"Well, I'm glad you broke the clique to come say hi," she offers bluntly. "Sorry, I'm being a bit direct. I like your friends, but once Rio got caught up with your crew, I've felt this tension. Between all of them. Like Rio's talking shit and they all think I'm this monster."

"Huh," I say. Not adding a ton to the conversation, but noting how we all have our own insecurities here. "If it makes you feel better, no one's said anything bad about you to me. I got the impression that you and Rio were not the best of pals, but that you were a really good clarinetist. Which you've already shown."

I follow Sophie's gaze to find a girl who's fake punching Pierce across the lawn, her red hair bouncing with every punch. I feel her intense energy all the way from over here, but I still don't sense much bad blood. But Sophie looks at her almost forlornly, like she wants to be friends, like she wants to be part of the group.

I know that feeling. It was me and Megan against the world for so long, until Skye came along. But even so, we just collected him from another friend group that dropped him. I didn't have time to make friends—I barely had time to keep the ones I had—over the last year of practicing, studying, and performing, but I'd watch a group of seniors sneak out for lunch, or dress up with silver and blue face paint for our football games, and a part of me would want to be a part of that.

To be in a big friend group, to not feel so alone.

Shane waves me over, so in parting, I say, "Look. If I'm getting folded into this clique, I could try to bring you along too? Pierce and Rio seem super intense. I think I need someone else who's on my level."

She laughs. "Don't worry about it. That group is locked tight; go have fun with the golden ones. We'll chat at the pub later?"

"The what?"

Shane's come to collect me, so I never get clarification on "the pub later." It surfaces more than a few anxieties, namely the following:

- Will there be drinking at this pub? I am not old enough to drink, even here.
- I was going to FaceTime Megan tonight since she was half-asleep last time, but I guess that's not happening.
- What if I don't get along with these people, and I'm stuck with them all night? I didn't even bring my key, knowing I'd be with Shane.

Ugh.

"Marty, I need to introduce you to someone," Shane says, waving a quick but genuine hello to Sophie before guiding me away. "She pulled marching band music, so there's obviously no oboe part."

"Right, so I'm playing off the flute score?"

"You can do whatever you want, but that sounds easiest, yeah?"

Oboes, flutes, and violins are in the key of C. Which means if I was to play off clarinet—a B-flat instrument—sheet music, I'd have to make every note a full step higher in my head as I play. I've done it before, it's not impossible, but it's not super easy.

"Do they have a horn part?" I ask Shane, knowing that his instrument is all alone in the key of F.

"Dani didn't get the horn part, so I'm going off the alto sax one." Alto sax is in E-flat, so that's a full step down. He shrugs, with only a little bit of bravado. "It's not like these pieces are particularly hard. I'll be fine."

I'm introduced to Dani, who's a little frazzled making sure everyone has the right piece, but still exudes a ton of warmth. Her golden skin actively rejects the dim British atmosphere, and surrounding her face is long brown hair, which she has to tie up in a scrunchie to play her instrument.

"I hear you're from America," she says. "I try to keep up with politics there because of my friend who works over there, and it sounds like a new mess happens every day. Not sure you escaped to a better country, but I will say London and its people are beautiful."

She talks about London like it's a new home for her too, but I don't have time to clarify because we're suddenly starting. Though Dani got the music, Pierce and Rio take control of the group, telling us our set list. It's actually pretty epic. Lady Gaga, Kesha, Rihanna—all icons I grew up with.

There's a moment in every rehearsal, every performance, where the scattered warm-ups and distracted players all snap into focus, to tune their instruments and start playing as one.

Pierce steps up to play a tuning note for the group, then hesitates. Looks to me.

"Marty, care to do the honors? We don't often get an oboe in our group. Concert A, everyone?"

My cheeks flush at the offer, and I'm inclined to say no. But I know it's not just a kind gesture. In orchestra, everyone tunes their instruments to match the oboe, because the instrument tends to stay in tune despite any temperature or humidity changes.

I stand next to Pierce, and everyone slowly raises their instruments to their lips. I play a concert A. It's spot-on. Pierce joins me, slightly sharp before easing into perfect pitch. One by one, the rest of the instruments fill in, until Shane gestures for everyone to stop. We're all locked into the same pitch, we're an ensemble now, and that feeling warms my heart.

I return to my spot as Shane counts us off, and we launch into "Applause" by Lady Gaga. I fade into the background with staccato notes, and Dani and I echo the melody briefly, but we're just there to support the trumpets. Someone helps us keep beat with a snare drum practice pad.

Once we have all the notes under our fingers, we run through it again. We get *into* it, the call and response from sax to trumpet, from clarinets to me and Dani. I can't help it; a smile is plastered on my face, making it a little harder to play properly, but I don't care.

We end the song with a stinger—an accented note, where we all play as one. A major chord, a full resolution, and a powerful end. Of course, we're not all exactly on the beat, plus one of the trumpets tried to play the note an octave higher and fully missed. But a rush of joy surrounds me when we're done.

We have so many pieces left, but the energy is high. Is this what it's always like at the academy? Blowing off steam after a long day of classes and work? A pang of jealousy hits me, until I remind myself that I have my own plan.

"You know, Shane's got it all wrong," Pierce says. He seems to have materialized next to me as we prepare the sheet music for the next piece. "He loves the hell out of you, but he worries too much about you."

"Oh," I say. "He's . . . he's seen me go through a lot, I guess."

"He's protective of his friends. I suppose it makes sense he'd think you'd need help fitting in, taking chances, enjoying life here. But I don't know, Marty. I could hear you across the circle. I hear people perform constantly, and to see you sync in and play so freely, so fully into the music . . . I don't know."

He places a palm on my back as Shane counts us off. I launch into a trill alongside Dani. Before he brings the trumpet to his lips, I hear him say, "You're truly something, mate."

Our parts play off each other for a bit, before he wanders back to the trumpets. We lock eyes, for one last second, and then I'm pulled back into the music. A warmth comes over me, and it feels so good I want to cry.

I've been in dozens of ensembles, performed everywhere. But now I really feel like I'm part of a group.

TEN

I STAND OUTSIDE THE Southey. Where the Alexandria looked more modern, the Southey is an unforgivingly British pub, and that's the most accurate way of describing it. An aged brick building, stately and reticent with its dark shutters and planter boxes along the awning. A glance at the petunias inside the planters gets me caught up in an all-teeth smile, because the same purple flowers hang in pots outside my Kentucky house.

I grab Sophie's arm, and wait for the other musicians to pass by. The others are nice and seem more welcoming than she lets on, but there's something super down-to-earth about her personality that makes me trust her. Maybe even reminds me of Megan—an altogether kinder version of Megan, at least.

After the jam session, she introduced me to the rest of the woodwinds—except Rio—she told me where everyone was from, what they did, and I found it easier to chat with them because of it. They're one big family, and I'm starting to feel like I fit in, even if I don't go to school with them.

"Are you sure I'll be able to get into the pub? I'm . . ." I lower my voice. "Seventeen."

"You're a hard case." Sophie cackles, in a way that doesn't make me angry. "Americans, I swear. Keep in mind the drinking age is eighteen here, and it's not like we're going to a club."

She pulls—literally, she's got my arm—me into the pub. The moment we push through the old wooden door, I feel oddly at ease. Hardwood floors that must date back a century creak under each step, but the word "cozy" doesn't begin to describe it. Light music pumps through the main room. It's getting late, but a few old men still sit at the bar, reading the paper or staring at the glowing TV screens.

"We usually take up the back room," Sophie says. "I got this round."

"But I can't—"

"Trust me. No one's going to give a second glance at a bloke who looks your age. Not here."

I pass portraits and old paintings as I walk the dim hall to the quote, unquote *back room*. It's all so comforting, the charming antiquey feel, the stately old architecture. When I press into the back room, things are decidedly rowdier. This is what I imagine college bars to be. People yelling over the music, standing in big clusters. Giant beers in hand. I wonder if any of these are Americans, taking in their newfound ability to drink legally. I want to fit in, but even for me this isn't legal. I'm still too young.

I sigh, but I catch Pierce's eye from across the pub and all the air in the room shoots back into me. He arches his eyebrows, flexes a quick smile, then goes back to his friends. His friends and my cousin.

But I notice Shane's not really talking with anyone. He just sips his pint (he's not legal either!) and listens to Pierce dominate every conversation. I wonder what it'd be like to be Pierce. To always have every eye on you. Does his throat ever get sore just from talking?

"You didn't get far." Sophie nudges me in the shoulder and offers me a pint. "I got you cider—that okay?"

I start to pull some pounds out of my pocket, and she forces the cider into my free hand. "You're good, mate. You can get me back later."

I stare into the golden liquid filling the glass to the brim. This is a big moment in my life. Drinking alcohol. Years of volunteering with the substance abuse groups in high school, coming down to this. It feels a little hypocritical.

To be fair, I never felt strongly either way. Skye used to hang out at parties and get drunk, but one too many hangovers led to one too many botched tests, which led to summer school. And that's when he decided to hang out with us. His B-group.

"You all right? You don't have to drink; I just assumed since everyone else here seems to."

"No, no, I'm fine. I'll at least try it."

I take a gulp of the cider, and it tastes like I thought it would—tart, sweet, and perfectly cold. I read that Brits drink some beer at room temp, which sounds even worse than cold beer, so I'm glad this one's refreshing.

"One of the saxes has a table at the back—want to find them?"

I look up to Sophie and shake my head. "You said Pierce and Rio are super cliquey, right?"

"Yeah."

I take a breath, and pretend Megan's just given me her trademark pep talk. This time, I pull Sophie along. "Let's put an end to that."

My cheeks are on fire; my ears must be bright red. Thank god it's dark in here. They stand at the table, with just enough room for two at the end.

It's uncomfortable, at first. You could cut the confusion, the tension, with a knife. But though there are a million tiny things that make me uncomfortable and panicked and stressed, I won't let this be one of them.

"Hiya, Marty! And Sophie," Pierce says, and gives a quick smile. His eyes dart back and forth between us. "Marty, you've met everyone already, haven't you?"

They still haven't offered us a seat, but I take one anyway, and make room for Sophie. Dani and Shane are at the table too, so I give them a quick nod.

Shane jumps in. "Marty, this is Ajay." He gestures to a guy with deep tan skin who's got his arm around Dani. His smile is as immaculate as his undercut. We shake hands.

"And Rio."

She's a bit too far away for physical contact, so I send a curt wave her way. She nods, not exactly smiling. She's glowing, though—her red hair seems to reflect the dingy yellow light. It falls past her shoulders and complements her ivory skin, light clothes, and green eye shadow. I can see Sophie tense up beside me.

"Welcome to the UK, mate," Ajay says.

"You should hear him play," Dani responds, then looks to me. "You're such a strong sight reader. So confident too—I'd love to hear you play a solo sometime; it's a shame you're not in the academy."

"Confident?" I say, blushing. "I . . . well, I think that's a first."

"Don't be humble." She smirks. "You know you've got talent."

Her accent is complex, with the lilt of Arabic. Her hair is thick and wavy, and her clothing is on point, and I can't believe this girl is so put together, yet so close to my age.

"I don't know about talent, but you've definitely got skills," Rio adds. "That one run during 'Shut Up and Drive' was hell— that arranger must hate woodwinds—and you nailed it."

All eyes are on me. Rio has an incredulous look, while Dani's pointing at me.

"I told you!" Dani says. "I tapped out about three notes in."

I respond with a glance at my cider, then say, "It's nothing, really. There was this arpeggio drill I used to do that was similar."

Rio laughs. "I bet. Tell me again why you're not in the academy?"

My cheeks flush with heat. "Decided to take a different path. That's all."

The conversation they ease into is stilted, brief, as if they don't really know what to talk about when they're not discussing class. Ajay's explaining how he fell in love with Scandinavian rap, which is a thing I wasn't aware even existed until now. But otherwise, it's clear that even if they're a bit cliquey, this friendship *is* relatively new and malleable.

I still feel a little out of place here—especially when I catch Pierce whispering to Rio, then meeting my gaze—but I feel a calmness come over me too. The table is a mix of so many races, cultures, and sexualities, and it feels like the most normal group in the world.

Some people back home would hate this, or at the very least be uncomfortable. They'd try to cover it up with strained smiles but inevitably say something off, a comment that points out our differences, regardless of the many similarities that bring us together.

They'd want us to feel like we'll never truly belong. But here . . . it's clear that everyone belongs.

"Marty, Sophie," Pierce says. "Help us settle this debate. From your perspectives as foreigners—"

"Oh, I never asked," I cut in, looking at Sophie. "Where are you from?"

"I'm a Kiwi, y'idiot."

I stare blankly at her.

"New Zealand. Christ, Marty."

My cheeks burn as the others laugh, but she gives me a

smile and an elbow nudge to make sure I know she's just joking.

"We're planning out our weekend trips," Pierce continues. "Before the end of the summer, we want to go to three different places—we decided on Brussels, Belgium, and Cardiff, Wales. For the third, I want to go to Florence, Dani wants to go to Copenhagen, and Ajay says anywhere but Scandinavia because he's going to Denmark for a convention later this year."

Dani shakes her head. "If we go to Italy, my mother will demand I come back to Malta and visit. I've visited three times a year since I moved in with my aunt, and that's plenty."

"Keep complaining about the pound," Ajay says, "but I dropped so much more money than I planned to on that convention because of the exchange rate in Denmark. The krone is obscene."

I turn and see Sophie, clutching her beer, looking altogether uncomfortable. I wonder what it is about this group that intimidates her. Everything stresses me out, but that doesn't mean I don't have a right to be here for the length of a conversation.

And when I pan from Sophie to Shane, I see the similarity in their expressions, and I wonder what I'm missing. Then Shane swaps seats with Ajay to sit next to me, and whispers in my ear.

"Sorry, should've warned you. They talk about travel *a lot*. They've already taken a couple weekend trips. But with my bookstore shifts, I can never go on these things."

I look back to him and nod, thinking about the low funds in

my bank account. I'm not traveling either. I don't mind them talking about it, but I guess this *is* my big travel. Shane's lived here forever and he doesn't even get to leave.

"Marty, what do you think?" Pierce asks. "Where would you go?"

"When I was younger, I used to be obsessed with the idea of international travel." I clear my throat. "That probably sounds dumb here, where international travel is a thirty-minute flight away, but it's a little different in Kentucky. My mom lived in Ireland as a kid, but we only traveled internationally once and my parents couldn't even handle that."

Where am I going with this? I take another sip of my drink.

"Anyway, I used to go to garage sales, yard sales, whatever you call them—I don't even know if you have them here. And I'd get any travel books I could find. I'd practice drawing flags of countries I'd never even heard of, like Lesotho or Luxembourg."

Looking around, I see a few smiles and heads bobbing. They're actually listening to me. Sophie looks to have relaxed too.

"But my all-time favorite guidebook was this one for the Tuscany region of Italy. I couldn't believe there was that much to see in one area—Il Duomo in Florence, Piazza del Campo in Siena, the Leaning Tower of Pisa. Well, that last one seems a little anticlimactic, but still. You've got to go with Italy."

Pierce pounds the table with his fist. "Yes! I knew you'd side with me." He gives me a wink, like I constructed the whole story to help him out. I roll my eyes.

"My sister went to school in Florence," Sophie says. "I never got to visit her there, but her pictures were amazing. I mean, it's worth going so you could say you've seen Michelangelo's David, to be honest."

"It's settled." Pierce laughs. "Then we can go to Malta and visit Dani's mom."

"Yeah, right. Malta's overpopulated as it is; it doesn't need you fools on it."

A laugh escapes my mouth, just before I get an elbow in the side from Sophie.

"Can we go join the others now?"

I survey the table and wonder if I've made enough of an impression. Something propels me to want to be around them. To want them to like me. I see the benefit in quitting while I'm ahead, though, so I leave the table with one last wink at Pierce.

Except it comes out as more of a pained blink, which kills my insides. I've never been good at being smooth. So much for quitting while I'm ahead.

"There, you've had your fun fraternizing with the cool kids," Sophie says in my ear, sloshing a bit of her beer on me.

The picture forms in my mind. Walking along the crowded Ponte Vecchio, too enamored with the old jewelry shops and art galleries to be anxious. Well, not actually, but a guy can dream.

In this fantasy, I walk under archways, on a path made of dusty cobblestones. Coming to an opening, I look out, downstream, on the Arno. The wind hits my cheeks and tells me I'm finally here, taking the lead on my own life.

I snap back to reality, and sigh. "I want to go with them. To Italy."

I don't hear her overly dramatic sigh as much as I feel the air shifting around us. Her eyes fall; her shoulders fall too. She looks like these people have personally hurt her, but that can't be the case.

"Why them?" she asks. "With the exception of maybe your cousin, they're exclusive and a bit snotty."

I pause, fully aware I'm about to out myself to one more person. And I feel comfortable doing it, but something about it always feels weird. The confession bubbles up in my chest, and I feel hyperaware. Does she already know? Could she?

For a second, despite her worried face, I smile. I want to trust more people with this. I take a breath.

Then, "I may have a crush on Pierce."

We stop.

"Oh, love. Come, sit down."

We take seats at the booth where a few musicians sit. Eight empty pint glasses crowd the table, along with various plates of fries and a bag of chips. Er, a bag of crisps. A plate of chips. Whatever they're called.

"Look." The crowd around us starts getting louder, so Sophie raises her voice. "You're cute and funny and a little neurotic—I get that. But Pierce isn't . . . and I know I've only known him for a month or so, but . . . he goes through guys pretty quickly."

My insides freeze. "Define 'quickly.'"

I glance back to the entrance. As I scan the crowd, I can't

even see the door anymore. Students stand in large groups all around, laughing, swaying. I turn to Sophie and focus on breathing.

"He dated this flautist, who was one of my first friends in the program," she explains, "but Pierce bailed the moment things got too serious. A week later, he was making out with some pianist in that booth over there. Long story short, my friend doesn't go to the academy anymore."

"Oh." I absorb the message, and embarrassment creeps through my body. I remember how sad Pierce looked when I asked him why someone would drop out of the academy. "But I'm—I'm not like that. I can play it casual."

I look down at the table and tighten my core. Back home, this feeling of anxiety in big crowds would pummel me at pep rallies or county fairs, sports events or even graduation, when the chaos around me became too much. I get the urge to run, to hide, like always. But there's no avoiding this.

Play it casual? I chide myself. I am the least casual person on this planet.

The temperature spikes. I coach myself through shallow breaths. Breathe in. Breathe out. Repeat sign. *D.S. al Coda* until my lungs cooperate.

"Hey, Marty. Look, I'm sorry—are you okay?"

I'm exaggerating. I'm making a scene. But I can't help it; anxiety's fingernails scrape at my chest. I open my mouth, but the words don't come out. My brain's a combination lock, and I need a different code to get out each word. God, I need some air.

"It's nothing. Really. But I mean, we held hands? I know it sounds immature, but we did and it felt like something more than just being buddies, you know? I'd never done that with anyone before where it *could* mean anything."

"Ah, sorry, mate," Sophie says. "I didn't know there was something already brewing there."

"He took me to Big Ben and said nice things and was being really cute, and I believed him." I wonder if this is why Shane continues to be weird about him. He has to know the story of this boy who was so heartbroken he dropped out of the program.

I suck in my stomach to protect myself from embarrassment. The temperature's skyrocketed, the noise in the pub is unrelenting, and I don't know which is affecting me more. To Sophie, it must seem like I'm being overly dramatic about a boy I like. But how do I explain that it's like the wind's been knocked out of me?

I know the air's all around me, but I can't find it.

"I'm sorry," I say. "I feel like an idiot. I have to go."

I take a few steps toward the front, but all paths are blocked. People are everywhere, just like around Westminster, only I'm inside and trapped. Breathing turns to panting, and the burn sets into my lungs.

I squeeze through two people, step around a third, and trip over someone's bag. But I see the door, and if I can hold it together for a few more seconds, I'll be okay, so I take a step and I take a breath and I tell myself it'll all be okay, and—

I stumble out of the pub and into the night. My lungs fill with much-needed air. I'm alone, and I'm on my own.

And it's already so, so hard.

I've been sitting on a bench outside the pub for about ten minutes now. I'm a little calmer, and I can breathe, and I take the time to process what Sophie said while I wait for Shane to come out of the pub. They've only been in this program for a few weeks, and Pierce's already dated someone, dumped them, and made out with somebody new?

I mean, wanting to have fun and not be tied down is not a bad thing. But with how things went down with the flutist, it seems like they were not on the same page about what their relationship actually was. And whose fault was that?

I don't have enough information to freak out. And it's not like we really even did anything. My feelings for him aren't that strong.

"Marty," a voice says in front of me. "Hoped I'd find you out here."

Pierce's eyes glow in the pub's soft outdoor lighting. Passersby keep up their chatter, but it all gets muted when my gaze meets his.

He holds my oboe case out to me, his expression unreadable. "You left this inside. Shane said he'd take it back, but I figured I could catch you."

There's room on the bench next to me, and he takes a seat. He goes to put his arm around me, but stops halfway, resting on his elbow and draping his hand next to my arm.

"Need to chat?" he offers, and I shrug.

I don't know what he wants from me, from whatever's going on between us. And it's becoming clear that all warning signs are saying that he doesn't enter any relationship if he doesn't want something out of it.

"Not really."

"Understood. Is it okay that I'm here? Or should I leave?"

I pause, considering the question. If you remove everything I've heard about Pierce from others, all I'm left with is a slightly obnoxious but super passionate guy. A guy I like, who's maybe even the first guy who likes me back. A guy who knows how to respect the boundaries that matter, while pushing me out of the ones that hold me back.

"You should come with us sometime, on one of the trips. Shane never goes, and I'm not sure why. He blames work and money—which are valid, don't get me wrong—but even during short, cheap trips where he has enough time to request off in advance, he gets weird. He was like this in secondary too."

I grunt an approval so he knows I'll consider it, and then we're silent for a bit longer. He builds the courage to move his arm again, this time draping it over my shoulder. I welcome the touch and unconsciously lean into him.

"Why did you agree to come pick me up from the airport?"

"Because Shane needed help." He says it plainly. Despite myself, I smile. Even if he does go through guys quickly, he's still clearly a good guy on some level. "Well, I suppose there's more. Shane talked about you coming a lot. And I thought you were cute. And I knew you were a good oboist—I even saw the navy scholarship finalist performance you gave. I wanted to get to know you."

"Get to know me as an oboist, or as . . . something else?"

"Both. Is that so bad?" he says. I turn my head and our eyes meet. "I like getting to know you better."

I don't have Megan here to vet all of my choices. I don't have hours of solitude to overthink things. I have this moment, and I have a decision to make. I like him, and he seems to like me. But is that enough?

Leaning in, slow enough that he can stop me if I'm reading all the wrong signals, I plant a soft kiss on his lips. He puckers as I do, offering the slightest bit of suction between our lips. My chest floats as I give in to one more kiss, one more pull— this one firmer than the last. More confident. Real.

We release, and I feel like I'm panting. It couldn't have been thirty seconds, but my entire body is charged with electricity. It's like I'm a whole new person, and I find myself getting addicted to the feeling. Sure, kissing Pierce might be a risk.

If you ask me, a good kiss is worth the risk.

DIARY ENTRY 2

IT WAS MISTY AND gross all day. Mom didn't feel like walking all around the city, so Aunt Leah suggested we take a tour of the city on a double-decker bus. I thought this sounded pretty awesome, but the concept of public transportation makes my parents uncomfortable. Look, I *get* anxiety—like, right now, I can feel an ache thrumming through me. Why? I don't know. Because I'm separated from Megan? Because I'm in a new environment? Because I'm so far from home? Who knows, but it's always there.

But even though I'm uncomfortable with new experiences, I still want to *have them.* Sometimes. And really, if I could make it all the way here, through airports and cabs and so many people . . . what's one more semi-traumatizing experience?

So anyway, that idea was swatted down pretty quickly. Finally, my aunt got them to agree to taking a cab tour. We drove *near* a lot of things. We drove over the bridge that goes to Parliament and Big Ben, and I almost missed Westminster Abbey completely. We drove by Harrods, that fancy store everyone talks about, and even went by some of the theatres.

Shane was pointing things out to me as quickly as he could, but eventually the joy of being *near* things fizzled out, and I just tried to enjoy the lackluster ride through this magical city.

It was kind of a flop, but I did learn one thing. I refuse to just be *near* things anymore, even if it kills me.

ELEVEN

A FEW DAYS LATER, I'm walking through Hyde Park, because I've gotten used to exploring the city by myself. Shane and I eat dinner together, and sometimes we'll watch old episodes of *Drag Race*, but we don't spend all that much time with each other. What Pierce said about Shane is true—he's focused fully on practicing and working.

I haven't seen Pierce since our kiss, but the pangs of this crush aren't dying off. Each time I think back to our tour of the city, I feel this rush that starts in my gut and spreads out, filling my chest with electricity. He sends me texts within seconds, rarely ever leaving me on read. Though I take Sophie's warning to heart, I don't want that rush to go away.

"Marty!" Sophie beams. "You ready?"

"Ready for what?" I clutch at the oboe case in my hand. When I complained to her about the applications and not getting anywhere, she reminded me that it's not even been a full week and I need to chill, then offered to help me with my auditions.

I never asked what she meant by "help."

"There's a busking platform in the tube station here that has great lighting."

"Okay?"

"And I'm going to get a video of you performing at it."

"No."

"*Yes.*"

My brain screams a red alert. I have a few audition pieces that I can whip out at any point, but that's for a real audition. Not for an impromptu show while people are running to catch their train. I feel my heartbeat punch through my body.

"I can't do this."

"You can," Sophie says. "Most of us at Knightsbridge have done it. It gets easier after the first time."

"There's going to be another time?!"

Sophie laughs. She explains the full plan: I need a video portfolio that includes more than just my stuffy award performances. A social media presence that shows my personality, she explains, and then she goes into detail about all the benefits of being active and building a following. And it sounds like a whole lot of things I'd rather not do.

But in the end, I want a job. Even if that means performing a solo in front of hundreds of people. And don't get me wrong— I like performances. I like playing my oboe for people.

Except, I like playing for people who (1) have volunteered to hear one of the shrillest instruments on this planet and (2) are sitting down and paying attention. In the tube, people are neither.

"I wish Megan were here," I say, mostly to myself.

Sophie veers off the sidewalk, taking us through the grass. "Who?"

"My best friend. From home, that is. She's really good at pushing me out of my shell."

"Want to give her a ring?" she asks. "I'm sure you could use a positive pep talk right about now."

I laugh at the idea. It's almost a scoff.

"It wouldn't be positive," I say. "She can be pretty aggressive about it, actually."

Sophie stops to lean against a tree, and I feel an enormous relief knowing this pit stop could delay us for a few more minutes. I take in a breath.

She puts out her fists in a fighting pose. "What, need me to give you a couple punches? Whip you into shape?"

I roll my eyes.

She gives me a smile. "Just trying to be a supportive friend here."

"Well, she's never hit me," I say. "But she's . . . I guess she's been pretty rough, verbally."

She stares into the trees for a bit, and I feel a calmness surround her. I can already tell Sophie's a lively person, excitable at times and cautious at others, but she seems to know how to choose her words. I envy that in her, right now.

"But when it comes to my anxiety, it's like I can't do *anything*." I start to sweat, and I realize it's a cold one—my body starts to shiver in the eighty-degree heat. "I don't want to be like this, you know?"

Before we go into the station, she pulls me to the side and looks right at me. "Oh, Marty. Don't say that. And don't beat yourself up about it. So you need a push sometimes? Tell you what: I'll push you out of your comfort zone, but I won't be a bully about it. How's that?"

I don't know if Megan's a bully, or if she's necessary in my life, or what. But I've never been this transparent about it.

"Thanks," I say. "I still don't think I can do this."

She laughs. "We'll see about that."

I clutch my oboe case and take the stairs one at a time. Drawing it out as much as I can. Sophie grabs my arm and pulls me through the station.

And I hear something. Music, the sweet pluckings of a classical guitar. It almost makes sense in this setting, tinny chords splayed out by fast-moving fingers.

I turn the corner, half expecting to see some Spanish guitar master slash bullfighter, cape and all, even though I know that's a horrible generalization of an entire culture. Damn, my American is showing.

But when I turn, I see . . . well, a cute guy. His eyes are pressed closed as he sways to the music. He's in all grays— light jeans and a V-neck sweater—and he flips his head back like he's got this massive head of hair, but his buzz cut isn't budging.

I've apparently stopped, because now Sophie's in my face.

"This one's reserved for Knightsbridge students, and I

grabbed the spot just a bit ago, so I'm not sure what he's doing here. Let me go talk to him."

"No! Well, maybe after this song."

She rolls her eyes and walks over to him, and I launch out after her to join her.

I take a deep breath, and try not to let him affect me because I have been a swooning mess since I got here. I hate confrontation, and I just want this over with.

"Hey, didn't see your name on the schedule," Sophie says.

He looks up, and his fingers stop picking at the strings. His eyebrow curls, so I hold up my oboe. I fill the silence. "Yeah, um, I'm supposed to play here, now, I think. Did we double-book? Is this not how it works? Should I come another time?"

He smirks, and his eyes light up. I can't help but smile at him.

"Play with me," he says. His voice is unusually deep, unmistakably not British.

"Excuse me?"

"You heard me." He points to my case. "That a clarinet?"

"Oboe. Look, I'm not even playing a full set. I just need video evidence of me playing here for, like, a few minutes; then you can start playing again. And"—I point to his empty guitar case—"if anyone throws in some money for me, which they won't, it's all yours."

His fingers run over the strings, and the chords melt deep into my core. The tune is playful, mocking. It matches his all-teeth side smile. I wish I'd shut up and let Sophie deal with this, and I wish she'd come save me. But she's now just hanging back with a sly smile like she's enjoying this.

"Also, I can't play with you. We don't know the same pieces. I don't think there are oboe and classical guitar duets. I'm likely to piss enough people off with this squeaky thing on my own."

"What pieces do you know? I can figure it out and pluck along. People will think we planned it."

"The Bach Partita for Oboe in G minor was my audition piece."

His eyes light up. "I thought I remembered you. You auditioned for Knightsbridge last year, right?"

I sigh. "Let's not talk about that."

For once, he's the one who looks uncomfortable. "Right, sorry."

I've started putting my oboe together, more out of necessity than anything. Double reed instruments—where you basically make the noise by tying two special reeds together—are peculiar in every way. On the walk here from Hyde Park I had my reed resting tip-down in a cup of water. I took it out and let it rest a few minutes back in its case. If you don't do this right, you can't play well.

If I wait any longer, I'm going to have to repeat the entire process, and I already threw out my cup of water. So, I don't really have a choice.

I nod as I push in the reed and feel the familiar squeak of the cork padding as it slides in. I stand and bring it to my lips, take a deep breath from my diaphragm, and release it into the oboe. I run through quick scales, arpeggios, and do the quickest warm-up I can think of.

He side-eyes me, stops playing altogether. "Did you just run through the world's fastest version of 'Gabriel's Oboe'?"

"You know it?"

"There are people who don't? It's, like, the best film score of all time."

My features lighten, and I show some teeth too. (Then quickly cover them, because his are ten times whiter than mine, I'm sure.)

"Play it with me," he says. "I can figure out the background, just play the first note."

I sidle up next to him and look out in front of me. Stark white subway tiles creep along the wall, stopping to highlight the Marble Arch station sign under the tube's classic branding—red circle, blue rectangle. I take note of the advertisements along the wall too. Two book ads stare at me, asking what I would do if my family was in danger, or what if my wife's secret could ruin my entire life.

It's all a bit melodramatic.

I play the first note of the piece and wonder if we're any different from the ads. Trying to stand out when everyone wants you to fade away. Grabbing people's attention, then making them roll their eyes.

And suddenly I'm playing. It all kind of disappears. Not my worries, of course—I'm still very much aware people can see me and are probably judging me. But it softens, at least. My emotion for the piece fills in, and the support of the classical guitar moves me. Chills creep up my back as he nails the chord progressions by ear.

I sway back and forth as I play, and I wonder how we look together. Do people think we planned this? The petite guy with the big guitar and the tall guy with the teensy oboe. But then I hear something oddly validating.

A woman unzips her bag, and the abrupt sound makes me open my eyes and throw her my gaze. She pulls out a couple of pounds from her change purse and tosses them in his case.

Ennio Morricone is a master, and "Gabriel's Oboe" is his masterpiece. The most compelling contemporary melody over a light harpsichord. It's the piece that made me pick up the oboe for the first time. Mom is a film score buff, and she'd play this over and over. I'd go back to her old CDs, ignore all the gospel ones, find *The Mission* soundtrack, and put the piece on repeat. And that was where it all started for me.

And then we finish, somewhat abruptly, because I could have kept repeating it ad nauseam and this guy was willing to let me.

"You're amazing," I say. "How'd you play that by ear?"

"I've listened to the piece a lot."

"Me too."

His gaze falls to the guitar box. "We got, like, ten pounds for a two-minute song. That's a record for me, and it's off-peak hours."

He reaches in and hands me a five. The queen stares at me. "I can't accept this; you really helped me with—"

"Take it," he says, with such authority that I do. "I'm not

exactly an oboe expert, but I have played my share of duets, and you're quite the musician."

His eyes burn into me, so I divert my attention and focus on a freckle on his chin.

"Are you okay? You seem embarrassed."

Naturally, this makes me feel . . . doubly embarrassed.

"Well, anyway. You're a confident player, and a very supportive duet partner. So thanks. That was fun."

"Did you seriously just have a film score jam session?" Sophie busts in, showing us her phone. "This is amazing. But I'd expect nothing less from the prodigy golden child who graduated from the academy at sixteen."

"Always nice to, uh, meet a fan." He laughs, almost mocking himself. "I'm Sang. Sophie, right? I work part-time in the office, so I can usually put a face to a name."

"And I'm Marty. But wait, let's back up," I say. He's so young. "You graduated from the academy?"

"Last year. Now I just play gigs around the city for not great money." He rolls his eyes. "Living the dream, eh?"

But what he doesn't realize is that *literally is my dream.*

"So, Marty. You want to take over my spot here?" he asks.

My heartbeat speeds up, and I know I'm not ready to play here alone. And now that I know this is his livelihood, to some extent, I don't want to kick him out of here.

"No, I think we're okay. That video's enough, right?"

"It's a start," Sophie replies, with a slightly disappointed tone.

I ignore it and start packing my oboe away. We say our goodbyes and make our way to the exit. The soft plucking of Sang's guitar follows us as we go, and a part of me feels empowered. If he can make a life here piecing together various gigs and side jobs, so can I. So can Shane.

This plan we've worked up might feel far-fetched at times, but for once, it actually feels doable.

TWELVE

SOPHIE AND I SPLIT up so she can finish classes for the day—Music History and Music Theory, respectively—and agreed to meet up afterward for a late lunch at Pret a Manger, the go-to lunch spot for all of the academy.

My heart beats fast, almost humming, as I sit down with my prepared sandwich and chips—okay, crisps, whatever. The way Sang played was nothing short of magical, prodigious. I can't help but wonder if there are other duets I could be doing, even if just to mix up my portfolio. And to have some fun.

It's probable that Sang and I couldn't even if we wanted to. Unless he's knowledgeable about obscure classical oboe solos, I don't have much else we could play together. And considering I have no way to contact him, I can either hang around Marble Arch or the Knightsbridge office and cross my fingers, or I could move on.

But I want to know how he makes a career out of this—even part-time. I wonder who he's auditioned for, or why he's still busking for money if he has real gigs.

Sophie takes a seat across from me, and I feel a presence to my left. I look up.

Pierce.

He has a tray of food and an awkward smile on his face—like he's uncomfortable or something, which is impossible because he doesn't strike me as a guy who gets uncomfortable.

And he's pulling a chair over to this two-top table. Oh god, are we the type of friends who share meals together now?

"I hope you don't mind," he says.

I sit up straight and shake my head. "No, of course. I'll make room."

He takes a seat, and we rearrange our trays and food so there's enough room on this table for all of us. While he's unwrapping his tuna melt, I take a second to really look at him. We haven't spoken much since the kiss, except the occasional text and promise to meet up.

Are we becoming friends?

Are we more?

He's wearing a bright patterned shirt buttoned all the way to the top. He trimmed his beard down to stubble. Like a magnet, I feel myself pulled into him.

I grip the table to make it stop, but it doesn't stop.

There's too much to concentrate on.

- First, there's the feelings.
- Second, there's the "don't worry, guys, I'm cool" attitude I'm trying to display.
- Third, there's the fact that I have no idea how he feels about me, but I know he's not exactly the most trustworthy person in the room, plus—

"You okay?" Sophie asks.

"Oh, yeah. Just distracted. Still thinking about today."

"Sophie showed me your video in Music History," Pierce says. "That was amazing. I can't believe you just met Sang and you could play together like that."

I *blush*. The kind of blushing that makes your cheek muscles cramp. I couldn't doubt the connection between me and Sang. I couldn't doubt the connection between me and Pierce.

Sophie gives me a wink when she sees my face. That's an unexpected connection too.

This didn't happen in Kentucky.

Megan and I only had each other for so long. She ripped me out of my shell when my anxiety made me retract, and I gave her perspective when she couldn't see it. If I was an INFP, idealistic and introspective—which I am, I looked it up—Megan was an ESTJ, pragmatic with an intense sense of right and wrong.

We've had so much fun together.

I keep waiting to miss Megan. To feel the ache of our separation—she was my crutch, my bandage holding me together. And now that I'm free from her, I'm making my own friends and people are connecting with me not because of

Megan's self-deprecating humor, but because of me. My humor. *My* words.

Sophie kicks me under the table. "You are hard-core zoning out right now, Mart."

"Sorry," I say. "Didn't sleep well last night. Is it possible to still be jet-lagged one week later?"

Pierce's bare knees are touching mine. Deep breaths. I eat a crisp. Normal, normal. I am so acting normal right now.

"Sang was the golden child of his year, but even so, there was so much emotion in your playing," Pierce goes on. "People were literally throwing money at you. It was brilliant."

"I have to agree," Sophie says. "This is what I was telling him stands out—on YouTube, on portfolios, whatever. A classical guitar slash oboe duet on the London Underground? Fucking smashed it."

I smile, and the tension in me releases slightly.

We eat in silence for a bit, listening to the ambiance of the restaurant around us. I try one of Sophie's crisps, because it's a sweet chili flavor I've never seen in the States. Pierce's attention drops toward his own food, and it takes me a second to understand what he's doing. He inspects the nutrition information of his tuna melt with a disapproving glare.

"There's so much fat in this," he says distractedly as he takes a bite. "It's basically all mayo. No wonder I can never eat the whole thing. Oh well, can't be too choosy."

It's a quick observation, one that he seems to make without much thought. Sophie and I meet eyes, and neither of us seems to know how to respond in any meaningful way. I self-consciously shield the remnants of my own, fully eaten, tuna melt from his view.

"Anyway, I have a proposition," Pierce announces. "Completely unrelated to this conversation."

We both turn to him, and Sophie's eyebrow is cocked.

"Dani's got a car. We're going to Cardiff with Ajay, and we got an Airbnb in the Welsh countryside for cheap, but it'd be even cheaper if we got some more people." He pauses. "Would you two like to come with us?"

Sophie's eyes widen, and I remember how she's not used to being part of this group.

"Is Rio going?" she asks, curious if the cliquey woodwind she seems to dislike was asked first.

"She didn't seem interested when we were talking about it. She's into more *European* trips."

"And Wales isn't European?" I ask.

"She's from Belfast. Northern Ireland. Totally unenthused by anything in the UK." He turns to me. "And Shane has to work, so he's out. Shocker."

"I'll go . . . if Marty will." Sophie looks to me expectantly. "Otherwise I'd feel like I'm crashing your party."

"Yeah, I'll go too." I say the words before I think of them.

It's not Italy, but it's *something*. A weekend with Pierce in Wales. I nearly shudder at the thought. He looks at me and seems so genuine. I subconsciously pull an arm over my stomach, and wonder why he's so into extended eye contact.

Sophie excuses herself to go to the toilets. As soon as she's out of earshot, Pierce leans in.

"I have a second proposition, actually."

My cheeks must be bright red with how hot they feel. Is it possible he's going to ask me on a date? There's such sincerity in his eyes right now that I'm unable to reconcile that with the monster from Sophie's story.

But then he's reaching in his bag, and as he's pulling out sheet music, it clicks before he says anything.

"Will you play in my end-of-term recital?" He's almost pleading. "I adore this piece, and it's not working with Dani. Dr. Baverstock said I could get outside help. I want to spend more time with you, and this seems like a great reason to do so."

He sighs. "I knew I wanted to ask you after hearing you play in the park, but after seeing that performance, I couldn't wait. What do you say?"

"We'd be practicing this the whole summer?" I ask. "We don't even know if we're compatible together."

"Oh, and the best part! These end-of-term recitals have a really intimidating guest list. Scouts from the Philharmonic, big production companies. It could help you out too."

Megan's advice about taking chances rings in my head. I'm not naive—well, maybe I am, but I know he's not exactly doing this to become buddies. So maybe he's using me, a little bit. Then why can't I use him right back?

Why would I *ever* turn down a chance to impress someone from the London Phil?

"Okay," I say with a smile. "Yeah, I'll do it."

The rest of lunch is uneventful by comparison. We talk more about Sang and how brilliant he is. I nod along, still feeling the rush of excitement about our upcoming trip. The many different ways I see my life playing out spin inside my head. And for the first time in a long, long time, I'd be happy with every one.

When I get back to the apartment, Shane's in the living room. He throws up a welcoming wave, so I take a seat at the dining table across from him. He's nursing a warm tea, and the bitter aroma fills the air.

I open up Sophie's video on my laptop, not realizing the volume is up as high as possible. My performance pierces through the air, and Shane jumps. I rush to adjust the volume.

"Sorry," I say, cringing in my chair.

His laugh replaces the awkward silence. "Is that you? I mean, I'm assuming it is because you play that piece constantly. Where are you in that?"

"Marble Arch, the tube station."

He gives me a confused look, which fades into a smile. "Never thought I'd see that."

"I know it hasn't been long, but I haven't gotten any bites on jobs. I don't know how else to stand out. I keep seeing these applications that ask for portfolios, and Sophie thought this would help. I'm starting a YouTube channel."

"You don't even have Facebook."

"I used to!" I sigh. "But you're right, I have no idea what I'm doing."

"Here," he says as he gets up and sits next to me, "let's work on your social presence. I do this stuff for the bookshop, when they let me."

In thirty minutes, I have a website. It's a pretty weak one: my bio, links to my YouTube (which is still empty), and my headshots. Which are starting to look weird to me. Why am I holding my oboe so close to my face? Why is my grin so creepy? Is this why I'm not getting auditions?

I play the full video for Shane.

"This is . . . epic. Of course your first time busking you'd be thrown into an impromptu duet with Sang."

"You know him?"

"We all do. At least, we know *of* him. He was in the summer program last year, and got to tour with *Jersey Boys* recently. All of the Knightsbridge people see him as a god or something."

My phone starts buzzing on the table—it's Megan.

"Go ahead," Shane says. "I've got your video uploading now."

I walk into my bedroom and answer the call.

"Hey, loser." Megan chuckles. "I thought you'd suddenly become too good for us."

"Hey." I hear my echo. I'm on Bluetooth. "Isn't it, like, nine in the morning over there? What are you doing in your car?"

"Skye and I are making the most out of our summer. First stop, Waffle House."

"I think I already miss our breakfast runs. Get your hash browns double covered for me." In Waffle House slang, that means two slices of American cheese.

"What's happening over there? Kiss any charming British boys yet?"

I pause, searching for a response. Too long a pause.

"Wait, I was joking." Megan gasps. "You *didn't*!"

I'm two parts embarrassed, one part flustered. "Just one . . . time."

"Good going, Mart!" Skye shouts from the passenger seat.

I cringe. Here's the thing. I've been open about my sexuality in London. I feel comfortable telling these people I've just met, and it's not been a big deal.

But it was a big deal back home. Not because Skye or Megan are gay-haters (they're not), but being raised in a conservative shithole of a town means you're around a lot of closed-minded people. People leave divorce court and get in line to picket a gay wedding for destroying the values of marriage.

And beyond that, this was *my* secret to tell. I've held it for a decade, and she robbed me of a chance to tell Skye in a way that felt right for our friendship.

"You guys, this is weird. I don't know what to say."

"Come on," Skye responds. "You can trust us. And apparently you've been open about it in London."

"Tell us about the kiss, you whore."

"Harsh, Meggy."

A pause. She hates being called Meggy more than anything. I let it sink in.

"It was good." There are more words for this, but I don't know how to say them. I feel weird saying them. "It felt real, I guess. It was that cute guy who picked me up at the airport for

Shane. He kind of held my hand when he was showing me around the town. And I kept feeling this connection whenever we made eye contact, like there was something more there. But it was still so unexpected."

"So are you going to date?" Megan says, some seriousness to her voice. "Or is this just a . . . thing?"

"Oh, it's a whole thing. And I don't know. He doesn't have the best reputation here, but he's been super nice to me. I think I want to find out for myself, though, and not just take other people's word for it." I sigh. "I mean, that's what I'd like someone to do if they heard stuff about me. Is that silly?"

"I get why you'd want to be careful," Skye says. "But, like, this is a really big deal. I feel like you should be celebrating it. You're happy about it, right?"

"Yeah. I'm very happy about it, actually." The realization hits me, and a warmth floods my body. "It's all happened so fast, and I think he's a bit of a risk. But I actually *want* to take that risk. And I never want to take risks."

"Huh. I don't even know how to handle you crushing on someone." Megan shuts off the car. "Look, we just got to Waffle House, but we'll catch up, and you can show us all your hickeys on Friday."

"Friday?"

"Yeah, you committed to our weekly FaceTime."

I laugh. "Riiiiight. I think my signature was forged, but I guess I'll oblige. Call me whenever. I'll be around."

"Lurrrrrves you," Megan says. Skye cracks up in the passenger seat.

"Yeah. 'Bye, weirdo. You too, Skye."

My breath catches as I hang up the phone, and I blow air out and tighten up my face so I don't tear up.

I think of all the experiences I haven't told them about, and I try to sort through what I will and won't say. But I don't even know how to tell these stories to Megan, mostly because before this week, all my stories involved her.

Diary Entry 3

I'VE BEEN ON BRITISH soil for about three days . . . so I had to have my catch-up call with Megan. You'll have her in class next year, Mr. Wei. You'll have many arguments with her, and you'll lose more than half of them. Also, fair warning, Megan's already started researching every education law to see if she can get out of doing this project over the summer while you're not *technically* her teacher. You probably know this by now, but no teacher makes it through the school year unscathed. I'll try to be extra calm this year to make up for it.

We have a balancing effect on people. Which is why I needed this phone call.

"Got any glitter on you?" she asked me immediately upon answering the phone. "Here's what you should do."

She went on to tell me, in detail, how I should sneak out to the London Pride parade, decked out in glitter and rainbows, and, while that sounds nice, the issue with family trips is that while on them, you can never actually *escape your family*. Even if Shane and I could get out of here, I'd never be brave enough to do something like that.

I tried to get an update on her own family trip, but shockingly, I didn't get much. I know it's been hard since it became just her and her mom, staying on the same beach they all went to year after year when she was growing up.

I know this, even though she's never said it. It's hard to have a real conversation with her sometimes. Can you really be so close to someone, know everything about them, and still . . . not *know* them?

She's my very, *very* best friend. But just between you and me, Mr. Wei, I don't think she knows me either. And that makes me feel lonely.

THIRTEEN

THE CORK PART OF my reed makes a squeaking sound as I ease it into my oboe. I close my eyes as I do it, inching it closer and closer to the base until it's in the right spot. Too far in and the tone will be sharp, too far out and it'll be flat. Of course, I won't fully know if it's the *right* spot until I play, but after you do it fifty thousand times, you have a pretty good idea of where it should go.

It's a ritual.

My breathing's slowed a bit, and I can feel the tension easing throughout my body. I'm shut in this soundproof box, and I couldn't be more thankful that the practice rooms on the Knightsbridge campus look, sound, and feel the same as the ones back home. This even smells the same—kind of sterile, lightly perfumed by the wood oboe in my hands and the reed near my face.

I place the reed between my lips, and force air through it.

A warm sound fills the space, and my fingers pad the keys without my mind expressly giving the order. I'm transported back to my hometown bedroom, practicing runs until my cheeks go numb. I slow down, though, and pull air into my diaphragm.

Though I mock it from time to time, I really do love this instrument. There's nothing like it. Clarinets don't have the character; flutes can't pierce through you in the same way.

As I practice, my mind keeps nudging me back to the cross necklace that's stuffed into my bag, for some reason. For so long, music was how I escaped religion, escaped feelings of inadequacy and shame, and just got to be myself.

But my oboe playing isn't too different from a religion of my own: the steady rituals, the inpouring of emotion, the full belief in something more than you. In that way, it's almost filled that god-shaped void in my heart. I was *always* there for my religion, but my religion was *never* there for me.

And I guess I'm still not over it.

But I manage to feel full and find peace here, in these moments, connecting with music. Finding god in my own rituals.

I think back to my duet with Sang, or the jam session in the park. A smile tugs at my lips, breaking my embouchure and pulling my tone sharp. That's a kind of organized religion too.

A knock at the door shakes my already broken focus, and I jump when I look through the soundproof window.

Dr. Baverstock walks in, and my mind goes flying.

- I'm not supposed to be here.
- He witnessed the absolute flop of an audition I had last year.

By the caution in his expression, he one-hundred-percent recognizes me.

"Mr. Pierce, isn't it?" he says, before I can spiral anymore.

"Ah, yep. You can just call me Marty. Hi, Dr. Baverstock." I pop the cork out of my oboe and reach for my case. "Sorry, I know I'm not supposed to be here."

"No, it's quite all right. A bit slow today, wouldn't you say? Sorry to interrupt, but I was taking the short distance between the orchestra space and my office when I heard a most unusual sound."

I don't respond, but he smiles. "You see, I don't have any oboes in my orchestra. It is *my* principal instrument, so I'm naturally very picky when it comes to the instrument. And we had one promising young lad audition with this piece just last year. Came all the way from America to do it."

My cheeks must be glowing red. I wish I could just melt into the padded walls. But he gives me a genuine smile, and his support is what's keeping me together right now. Just barely.

"Marty, I don't know what exactly was going on last year, but I do know that if you had played that piece how you just did, I would have happily accepted you into the program."

Embarrassment creeps over me. I'm overwhelmed with the feeling of failure that followed me all the way back to the States. I wallowed in that feeling for so long, until Shane helped pull me out. Until I made a new plan.

"Thanks," I say. "But . . . I didn't. So."

"So you figured something else out?"

I pause, and let my gaze drift. "Yeah, I think so."

"Good." He gestures toward me. "What you have here is special, the hold you have over music and how it connects perfectly with your emotions. I can teach technique all day, but I can't teach people that."

I nod. "That means a lot, coming from you."

"And for technique," he says as he flips my sheet music back a page, "get this run under your fingers with a metronome first. When you drop and build after the sforzando, you start to lose it by the end. It's almost there."

I grab a pencil out of my bag and make some light notes on my music.

"Thanks," I say. "Are you sure it's okay I'm in here?"

"I hear you've been recruited for Mr. Reid's end-of-term recital," he says. "Since you're helping Knightsbridge, for what I assume is no pay, the least I can do is give you access to the practice rooms whenever you want."

He winks and then steps out of the room. The heavy door closes with a *hiss*. And I'm alone. I can't help but flash back to the audition I ruined. How everything fell apart. How *I* fell apart.

The pieces of my oboe are spread around me. And I know the only thing that'll put *me* back together is to start the ritual all over again.

FOURTEEN

THERE ARE MOMENTS, LIKE this, when the landscape flies by my window and it feels a little like home. Straight roads, livestock farms, and not much else.

But then I remember we're driving on the left side of the road. And I'm on the right side of the car, but the driver is in the seat in front of me. And all of the farms have sheep. Miles and miles of sheep. And every few minutes, we course through a roundabout, which is like an intersection that never stops moving in a circle, and by some magic you learn which lane you're supposed to be in when you exit.

"I can't believe how calm Baverstock was today in recitals," Ajay says.

Each Friday, all of the school comes together for an hour of short recitals, where a few people perform one piece each. They're technically open to the public, so Shane and I were able to sneak in and watch.

Rio and Sophie both performed solos—possibly to prove a point—and it was clear to see why the conductor, Dr. Baverstock, can't decide on a first chair. They're both extremely talented in different, but equally captivating, ways.

"What did he say—he's 'never been so impressed by a crop of summer musicians.'" Pierce dons a posh accent while quoting him.

Dani shakes her head. "I'm tired of talking about those recitals. Sorry, Soph—you were epic. But I don't want to talk about school anymore."

"No offense taken," she replies. "I'm just glad I got through it."

"What *I* want to talk about," Dani continues, "is how you and Marty just happened to run into Sang, and then he gets to go and play a duet with him."

"The video's really good, mate," Ajay says. Pierce grunts in agreement.

"You're welcome," Sophie says. "If anyone else wants to commission me for an iPhone recording, I'll send over my prices."

Pierce nudges me. "Your portfolio is going to be looking great."

"I don't know if it'll make much difference. I played one song. From a movie. That I've been playing since eighth grade. I'm nothing like Sang—he just figured it out and played it alongside me, acting like we've practiced this our whole lives."

Pierce releases a dry laugh. "Hey, sometimes it's okay to ride on someone's coattails, if it gets you where you want to go."

A chuckle escapes me, and my gaze falls to my hands in my lap. I try to ignore Pierce's hands, when I notice they're fairly close to mine. Yes, hand-holding was all the rage at age twelve, but I kind of missed out on that, and the one time we've done it was *not* enough to satiate this need.

Pierce puts a hand on my leg, near my knee. But I'm wearing shorts, so his hand is definitely touching my leg hair, and that's a gross thing to think about, but it's definitely sending chills up my leg and into my *special regions*, but I can't show how this is affecting me, so I turn to him and smile like I'm the most normal kid in Normalville, meanwhile I'm shaking on the inside, and shit I forgot to breathe and . . .

His body slides down a bit in his seat. He's smaller than me in every way, so when he slouches and leans into me, he's able to rest his head softly on the side of my arm.

I glance over his head to see Sophie's eyes widen. She looks to me and nods in approval.

This is real.

No amount of googling can prepare you for this moment. When you inch your way toward a relationship, testing boundaries and learning limits. He made the first move, putting his hand on my leg. He made the second move, resting against me.

If I don't do something fast, he'll pull away. He'll think I'm rejecting him.

I take a deep breath and coach myself through this. My lungs are about to burst with excitement, but I have to keep my cool.

I slowly lift my arm and lean back against the window. This prompts him to pull into me, resting his head on my chest.

(Side note: I am definitely getting excited in ways that are one-hundred-percent not okay in a car full of people.)

I place my arm around him and pray I don't look as awkward as I feel. He's warm on my chest—it's warm in here—but I could let him stay forever. The fresh, fruity smell of his shampoo hits my nose.

We stay like that for a minute before I can breathe again. I see him rise and fall on my chest as I take in air, but he doesn't seem to mind.

He made two moves. I made one.

Time to even the score.

His hands are pressed together and rest somewhere in the void between my leg and his lap. I bring my hand around and place it over his. God, his hands are warm and mine feel like they've just come in from a blizzard.

This moment is sweet and it's never going to last.

Sophie's stopped watching, but I wonder what she's thinking. I can't get her warning out of my head. She thinks he's just going to make me fall for him, then kick me to the curb.

But right now that idea lies beyond the constrains of my comprehension.

Before I know it, he's asleep.

Before I know it, I'm falling asleep too.

Some minutes, or hours or days, later, he sits up and jolts me out of my nap.

"Now I see why you demanded the middle seat," Ajay says, chiding him.

"Oh, sod off. I know how to pick who's most comfortable."

We all chuckle at the line, but my laugh is hollow. I *know* I'm the most comfortable. I'm the only guy here with extra padding on his chest, and everywhere else for that matter.

I pull my arm around my gut again, and suck it in. My mind flashes back to Pierce's spontaneous chatter about tuna melts and mayo and fat content and the disgust that was on his face when he said he could never eat the whole sandwich. The same whole sandwich that was residing in my own stomach.

I remind myself that he didn't mean anything by that, just like he doesn't mean anything by this. This is just another overreaction by yours truly. Self-sabotage. My body tenses, and I curse each shallow breath for making my stomach stick out more than the last. Megan would call it shutting down, but I don't care.

I lean against the window again and pretend to fall back asleep.

FIFTEEN

WHILE I REST MY head against the window, I plan my next move.

There are two ways he could have meant it. In one, cuddling, in general, is comfortable. He made the "most comfortable" remark flippantly, and it meant nothing. In the other, he meant I was the most comfortable, which means he meant I was overweight, which means he meant I was nothing more than a pillow to him.

I open my eyes.

Option two is ridiculous.

But why can't I let go of the fear that it's true? Or that he misspoke. Freudian slip. Which is also probably not what happened. So I take a deep breath and shake off my angst. But it won't let go. I feel like a wounded bird trying to conceal myself from prey, but the predator isn't in the car. It's in me.

When will I ever be free from my own brain?

Somewhere in the middle of my spiral, I realize the car's slowing to a crawl. Sophie's peering out the window, and I look around the car for any clue about what's going on.

Ajay groans. "Why must you insist on taking this road? It's so far out of the way."

"Because it's nice for the Stonehenge virgins," Dani says, "and it only adds twenty minutes to the drive."

Pierce palms my knee. I turn to him, slightly confused.

"If you have a camera, you might want to whip it out now." Pierce points out my window. "Stonehenge is coming up, in all its underwhelming glory."

"Like, right here?" I ask. "On the side of the road, a couple hours outside of London?"

He rolls his eyes. "Yeah, marks of the oldest civilization ever, treated as normal as seeing, I don't know, one of your red barns in America."

"I appreciate the American analogy," I deadpan.

The car inches over the hill, and rising up in the distance is Stonehenge. It's literally a bunch of rocks sitting on the side of the road. I know how old they are—over five thousand years— and it's massively impressive and confusing.

"Here it is," Pierce says with a laugh. "A very old pile of rocks."

But when he looks at me, a genuine smile is there. He even leans back to give me a better view. The car inches forward through near-standstill traffic as I survey the megalith, and again, it hits me just how far away I am from my hometown.

"Ah, fine. It's not all rubbish," he says, looking back to the site.

His resigned awe brings a smirk to my face. If nothing else, it's taken me out of my earlier spiral enough for me to enjoy the moment. I shake off some of my worry and grip Pierce's hand. We stare at the pile of rocks like it is the most wondrous thing in the world.

We get to the cottage just after nine, but the skies have already faded into a stunning Welsh night. I pause a moment to take it in—the smell of grass and trees is the same in Kentucky. The forest spirals around us, and if I didn't know better, I'd say I was home. It brings me back—the cool night air under a starry sky. Sure, the constellations are different here (I looked it up), but the feeling's still the same. It's been a week, but I'm starting to get restless. Eleven weeks left to find *something*. It's not nearly enough time.

I'm invited in by the smell of tea. Pierce has already fired up the electric kettle and has made himself a cup. A platter of chocolate-covered biscuits sits on an ornate, antique dining table.

"Dani and Ajay claimed one of the rooms upstairs," Sophie says. "Pierce took the other. We can share the pullout down here, or . . ."

She glances in the direction of Pierce.

"Anyone want a cuppa?" he asks. "Earl Grey, chamomile—Twinings brand. It's the good stuff."

Sophie looks at me. Pierce looks at me.

"No. Yes." My gaze darts between the two. "I mean. No tea, thanks. Yes, Sophie, the pullout."

I set down my bag and run up the stairs to the bathroom to re-collect. That, and to relieve myself after a four-hour drive. Before I step downstairs, I take a peek into the two rooms up here. Ajay sits on his bed, and looks up at me.

"It's kind of weird to stay in someone's place, isn't it?" I ask.

"Not usually. Flat sharing is great, and cheap, and you're not stuck in hostels." Ajay points up. "But occasionally you'll have a two-meter-long picture of the host's grandchild hanging above your bed."

I laugh and continue walking through the hallway. Pictures of a family line the wall, and it makes me feel a little weird. The second bedroom up here is much smaller—just a double-size bed fits with a small dresser and not much else. Pierce has been in this room for less than a minute, and the whole place smells like him. It's impressive. I turn to see a travel-size bottle of cologne on the dresser. When I bring it to my nose, it starts to make sense—he must've given himself a spritz before he came back downstairs.

And then his hand is on my shoulder.

He pulls back, gently, and I turn to him. He has a mug of tea in his hand, and he raises it to me.

"Have you actually had tea before? I mean, real, properly steeped tea with milk and sugar?"

"My mom usually microwaves her water and dunks the tea bag in." I smile. "Is that not how you do it?"

He throws his head back, sloshing some of the tea on the floor. "Your mum is evil. Americans are the worst."

"I'm joking. My mom may be a coffee convert, but she *is*

Irish after all." I roll my eyes. "I did a ton of research on how to fit in here, and I came across this three-thousand-word rant by some Brit about how Americans ruin tea. I thought I'd test the waters. Turns out all British people are just as intense."

He brings the tea to my lips. The tan liquid rises toward me, and I think this is an intimate moment where I should be sensual and turned on, but I'm really just worried about him burning my face with this hot water.

But he's careful about it. He presses the rim of the mug to my lips, and he tips it toward me, slightly, until the liquid meets my mouth. I take in a sip. He pulls away.

It's warm, comforting. A hint of that bitter, earthy tea flavor cuts through, but it's softened with a brush of sweetness. It's something I could get used to.

He sets the mug down on the dresser and puts his arms around my neck. He looks up at me, and we stand there like we're about to get taken out of a high school dance for pressing our bodies too closely together. And I kind of want to sway back and forth, to dance with him. To redo my one prom night and take him. He'd look damn good in a tux.

My breaths get heavy, and he puts his head on my chest.

"I know how to pick who's most comfortable."

It echoes through my mind, and I can't get it out. I can't let this moment pass, but I can't put my guard down. I can't let him hurt me when I'm hurting myself enough as it is.

I gently push him off me, and he looks into my eyes. And I get lost in his, which is a supremely cliché thing to say, but have you ever actually looked at someone's eyes? I refuse to believe anyone else has eyes like his, shades of brown and green and a million new colors in between.

I'm falling deep, and he's not stopping me. I don't have anyone to tell me what to do. Do I kiss him? Do I stay with him? How do I stop myself from getting hurt? Why is there not a guidebook, an easy resource I can google to tell me how to rationalize what I'm feeling? Help me help me he's too cute and too nice and his lips are too soft and I can't I can't but maybe I can.

I bring my lips to his, and I fall.

He closes the door. He presses into me with such force that I step backward. I take small steps back, knowing what lies behind me. But I don't want to stop. I pull his face closer, and he wraps his arms around my waist. Then I fall, this time literally, onto the bed.

I lean back, elbows propping me up on the bed. He stares at me in consideration. Is he trying to read me? The messages my face might send could range from "I very much like you as a friend" to "Take me now." Though I don't exactly know what the latter would mean in this context.

"What's going on in that head of yours?"

"Excuse me?" I ask.

"Tell me. You look freaked, but excited."

"Pierce, I—I don't know. I can't explain a feeling I've never felt." One I never thought I'd feel. "Aren't the others waiting for us?"

He shakes his head and sits down next to me. "Don't think about them. Think about you. Me and you. What do you want?"

It doesn't take a Google search to figure out what he means. He's talking about how far I want to go. How many bases. How far we'll take this tonight. If we'll ever leave this bedroom. He wants to share this with me, and that's the most mind-blowing thing I've ever experienced, but it feels wrong.

I need to decipher whether it feels wrong because it is wrong, or because it's how I've been raised. Or if I've seen one too many movies where person A gets screwed over by person B because B was fucking around but A loved B and B didn't really care about anyone but B.

"Honestly, I don't know."

"Yes, you've said that."

I smile. "Can we make out for a couple more minutes? Then go downstairs before people start talking?"

"They're already talking."

He leans into me, kisses the side of my nose, which causes chills to explode down my back. Apparently that's where all my nerve endings have been hiding.

I bring him into me. His lips meet mine. His tongue pushes in, and I let it happen. I taste him, and the taste is so uniquely . . . Pierce. Tea and sugar. Spearmint lip balm. I breathe him in when he exhales. I can't remember ever feeling this close to another human before.

We lie back on the bed, lips still locked on to each other, but now I pull him as close to me as possible. A million firsts already, but I want him to be my first everything. I want to be with him, from grabbing lunch between classes to flying to America to meet my parents.

And that's what stops me.

I want something real. And he might want something real too. But we're not going to figure that out by mashing faces.

I'm panting. He is too.

My face still stings from his rough beard.

"Let's go downstairs, now." I give him a last kiss. "Or I'll never leave this bed."

His lips perk up into a smile, and it makes me want to start the whole make-out session all over again, but I can't. My chest aches to have him close to me. But I can't I can't I can't I won't. I am stronger than this.

Sixteen

THERE IS NOTHING, IN all of life's existence, more putrid than instant coffee.

But it's all I can find here. So I choke down a sip, because it's *early*. Wales seems brighter than England, but I could be making that up. Sophie's still on the pullout—that girl can snore—and everyone else is asleep upstairs.

So I'm stuck in the kitchen with my toxic sludge.

My ears perk up as I hear someone come down the stairs, and my heart aches, since I have a one-in-three chance that it's Pierce.

But it's not. It's Dani. Her hair's a massive, stringy mess, and she's thrown on the same clothes from last night.

"Morning, love. You all right?"

I nod to the living room, where Sophie's snoring echoes throughout the house.

"Not great," I whisper.

As I take another sip and fight the urge to gag, she reaches into the purse she discarded on the kitchen table the previous night. She pulls out a set of keys.

"Can't believe you're drinking that. I'm going to the café we saw on the way in—you want to come?"

I smack my tongue against my mouth, begging the taste to get better. Then I slam down my cup.

"Yes. God, yes."

We leave the cottage and jump in the car. The passenger seat is a whole new world. We're wildly close to the left curb, and everything feels off. But it also feels exciting, somehow. Different.

"Ready for the most fire opinion of film composers you've ever heard?" Dani asks.

I laugh. "Go for it."

"Ennio Morricone's a hack."

"Excuse me?" I fake a gasp. "You saying you didn't like my piece?"

"Look, I think your performance with Sang was beyond epic. But I'm a film score aficionado, and his are not the best."

"Right." I roll my eyes. "Let me guess, you're a Hans Zimmer fan."

"Ouch. That physically hurt me." She gives me a light punch from the driver's seat. "Love, I know everyone's here to perform, go on to orchestras and symphonies and tour the world, but I want to be a film composer. Like Carter Burwell—emotional and simple."

Her hands fly as she talks, her passion bringing a brightness to her face.

"Sure. I really wanted the *Twilight* score to be better, though," I admit.

"Those are fighting words. But come on! *Carol*?"

"I actually don't know that one. I guess I'm not much of a buff—my mom used to listen to them a lot, so I know a lot of the older ones."

"Well, you'll know mine. Guarantee it."

"I support that," I say with a smile. "But you have to give oboes the best parts. And hire me to play them, because otherwise I'll be broke forever."

We pull into the parking lot of the café. Once we get inside, I take in the sharp, rich smell of coffee. It's all from an espresso machine, which isn't my scene, but it'll have to do.

"Do you have any recordings of your stuff?" I ask.

"I'm working on a piece for piano and flute at the moment. It's utter crap."

I grab our drinks and lead us out the door.

"You should play one for your weekly performance. Baverstock would go nuts over that, wouldn't he?"

"I may've hyped my skills a bit too much—pretend I never told you. I want to play in the London Symphony Orchestra! And other totally cliché things!"

I shake my head, and smile all the way back to the cottage.

"So what's our plan?" I ask as Dani parks in a garage in the middle of the city.

We step out of the car, and I see Pierce and Ajay smile at each other.

"Plan?" Pierce asks. "We'll walk around, maybe get lunch, definitely find a place to drink."

"Oh." I like having a plan. I feel anxious energy flood my body, and I feel flustered. It's not that I care what we do, but I hate not knowing, and not having a goal. We could go back to the cottage in an hour or fifteen for all I know.

I don't play things by ear.

"Could we do *some* touristy stuff?" Sophie asks. "We can drink shit beer anywhere. Cardiff Castle is only in Cardiff."

Ajay laughs. "Fine. Tourism, then we drink."

As we step out from the garage, it's clear this is a different place than London. Gone are the flags of England, the red cross on a white rectangle, and up are the official flags of Wales:

A fucking dragon.

This place reeks of coolness. People our age litter the streets, half speaking English, a quarter speaking straight-up gibberish (okay, Welsh), and the last quarter speaking languages from all over the world.

"There's no shortage of pubs here," Dani says. "Pubs and fourteenth-century churches. There's something odd about that."

"In my hometown, there are seventeen churches and nine bars." I shrug. "Only a couple thousand people live in this town."

"Huh," Sophie says. "I guess this is a universal thing."

We walk down the street together, a few paces behind the rest. What she said that first night about Pierce's ex burns deep in my core, warning me of the heartbreak that might come if I keep doing . . . whatever it is I'm doing with him.

He's directly in front of me, and I take a second to survey a different view. How can someone's jeans fit that well? Were they sewn on him?

And yes, technically, this mental conversation makes me a perv, but that is something I can deal with.

Dani's leading our group, but it's clear she has no idea what she's doing. We end up on a pedestrian path in the town square. We meander through stores, until we come across a pasty shop. It's a lovely concept—any ingredients you'd ever want, stuffed into crisp puff pastry.

I see Pierce's hesitation from here.

I'm hungry, but I'm not. The thought of eating anything like this (all fat, all butter) makes me feel gross. Well, it *sounds* great, actually. But Pierce's insistence on reading the nutrition information on everything he eats is really starting to rub off on me. The sugar content of the chocolate-covered biscuits we all shared last night, for example.

I realize I've started glancing at that info myself this week, and it's kind of hard to get it out of my head. The sodium content in those Kraft Mac & Cheese boxes Aunt Leah got us, the calories in a single bag of crisps.

I couldn't stop thinking about it, so I did the math last night—okay, I borrowed Dani's phone because there's no Wi-Fi here and I have no data, and a website did the math for me.

I put in my height and weight, and the site calculated my BMI, which is a number that supposedly corresponds to how much body fat you have.

The science behind it is questionable, but guaranteed to make you feel bad about yourself. Normal weight is eighteen and a half to twenty-five. Obesity is thirty. My number is twenty-seven.

Each pasty in the cart might as well be in the shape of the number twenty-seven, because it's all I see.

Everything affects me more here, and I don't know if it's because I'm away from home, or if it's because I've been left to my own devices for the first time ever. I miss when things were simple, cut-and-dried. When I had time and space to recover, or to hide. When I had Megan to make my decisions for me. To tell me when to push against myself. Everything here triggers the panic in my chest, the tension in every muscle.

I know I should eat something. But I can't bring myself to order it.

"You know, my stomach is a little upset," I say. "I might sit this meal out."

Sophie gives me a quick stare. "You skint? Broke, I mean. I can get you something."

"Oh, yes, totally, but it's not that." I smile so she knows it's not. "I'm good. Seriously."

The others don't seem particularly concerned, except Pierce, who briefly puts his palm on my back before reluctantly ordering a sausage roll.

I drink the water I ordered and zone out, looking through the windows and out into the plaza. As the others finish their lunch, I notice the red, green, and white dragon flag that flies outside a souvenir shop, simply called Shop Wales.

I excuse myself to take a look, and walking through the doors, I'm comforted by the rows of shot glasses, postcards, and flags. Mugs with pictures of the British royal family on them. Soccer jerseys out the ass.

I figure I should grab some souvenirs from each place I visit. Some I can send to my parents or Nana, but some for me too. I will save one from each place to remind me of the trip.

Since I'm trying to keep to a budget, I focus on the cheap postcard section. It's dull, to say the least. Historic pictures of the town, a million pictures of the castle we've yet to see. Nothing here strikes my fancy, as the Brits say—even though I've never actually heard them say it. Until I find the tackiest one in the whole shop.

What is love? the postcard asks, followed by an image of a Welsh sheep and *Baby don't herd me.* Tacky postcard and a tacky pun that quotes a tacky '90s song.

Perfect.

Sophie comes in as I'm paying, and giggles out loud at the postcard.

"Real mature," she says. "Sending that one to your mum?"

"Absolutely not. She hates puns." I chuckle. "It seems like that group does a lot of traveling. If we keep going on trips, I'd like to have a postcard from each one."

"Good idea." She grabs one of her own from the counter.

She's looking down at the postcard, but I feel the tension in her stance. I place an arm on her shoulder, and bend to look at her face.

"Sorry," she says. "Lost in thought. Those guys are . . . nice. Nicer than I expected."

"Of course they are. What do you mean?"

She shakes her head. "I don't know, they never seemed that way. I've been burned before with friendships. I tend to be the one you're friends with until someone better comes along."

She's not making eye contact, but I still look into her face. Megan and I have always been each other's number one. We have our issues, but I can't imagine not having that one person. That real best friend.

The Welshman at the register smiles at us as he completes the transaction.

"*Diolch.*" Sophie smiles as she speaks.

I stare at her, and the cashier chuckles. "Thanks to you too. Glad you like the joke—'What Is Love' is a funny song on its own." He leans across the counter and drops his voice to a whisper. "Did you know Cardiff is the *city* of love?"

"*Is* it, now?" Sophie draws out her sentence, while my cheeks burn red.

"No, not really. But I tell all the couples that—it sounds rather nice, don't you think?"

"The city of love," she echoes. She turns, her braids fanning out around her, and walks out the door. "Well, for one of us, it is."

Her words sit with me for the walk to Cardiff Castle. And it's a long walk. It should have been a fifteen-minute journey, but I guess signs are hard to read and no one bothered to look it up.

I grit my teeth as we walk through the gates to Cardiff Castle.

I can go with the flow. I'm the flowiest goer there ever was.

We've just walked onto the castle grounds, and it hits me so hard—America is freaking young. An expansive lawn is spread out before me, with trees and grass and only a couple dozen tourists littered throughout. We're flanked by the walls that divide the castle grounds from the city of Cardiff. In here, it's different. It's peaceful and stately. The smell of freshly cut grass hits my nose.

Dani and Ajay take pictures of each other in a touristy re-creation of medieval stocks. She hangs her head low while putting her hands through the holes. They're a cute couple. The type you'd love to go on a double-date with. They complement each other, and neither one seems to take anything too seriously. They walk away together, hand in hand.

Sophie has run off too, possibly to learn more random Welsh phrases.

That leaves me and Pierce, alone in the fake city of love.

"The castle was built in the 1000s," I explain. "Like, one thousand AD. It's crazy, isn't it? Over seven hundred years older than America." Pierce eyes me. "What? I—"

"Googled it?" He snickers at me. "What don't you google?"

"I like to be prepared. To know what I'm getting into, you know?"

"That's why you knew the castle cost seven pounds, and how many kilometers we'd be driving, right? If you didn't admit you googled everything, people might think you're a genuine know-it-all."

"Hey!" I snap.

We cross over the moat and start to scale the ancient stone staircase to get to the keep of the castle. He shrugs as he places a warm, guiding hand on my back. "I'm teasing you, love. Tell me more about these rocks."

I hesitate before I continue speaking. "It actually dates back to first century AD. This spot, at least. It was a defensive fort for the Romans, left mostly abandoned until the eleventh century. There are conflicting theories about who built it up first, but the castle was built in the late eleventh century and continued throughout most of the millennium."

Silence.

"Are you even listening to me?"

Through the castle walls and into the keep lies a simple but stunning yard. The top of the castle is behind, and I try to imagine the activities that went on here. It's a small space, but it's hallowed ground. Stonehenge was impressive in a "hey, those rocks have been sitting there for millennia" kind of way. This is different. Rich with heritage.

A stronghold.

Pierce is already up the stairs to the top of the keep, and I follow behind him, inching past a group of younger schoolkids coming down the staircase.

It's dark in here. We're alone.

There's a stone window that's no wider than the size of an

index card and the length of my forearm. Pierce presses his face into the opening. I lean over him and look out the top half of the window, and see the city of Cardiff unfold beyond the castle walls. Another ancient tower stands on the grounds, with the rugby stadium behind it. A weird pairing of modern design with medieval architecture.

"I've never seen something like this," I admit. "There's so much here. There's too much here. I'll never be able to see it all."

"Not with that attitude we won't."

We. Are we a we? I like that.

My stomach growls, but he ignores it. I ignore it. He puts his arms around my waist and smiles at me.

"We'll get you to Italy. Don't worry."

I pull him into me and hold him close. I kiss his forehead. He places his head on my chest, which swells with excitement and energy and . . .

Hope.

Opening up to Pierce reveals a soreness, a vulnerability I never knew I could have. But I cling on to this boy. I'll cling on to my new friends, and my new life. It's only been one week, but I'm starting to feel like this could be home.

Cardiff really must be the city of love.

SEVENTEEN

THE CITY CENTER OF Cardiff isn't too dissimilar from some of the more modern streets of London. Wide pedestrian walkways are flanked by stunning new buildings, public art intertwines with restaurants' outdoor seating, behemoth trees poke out from the concrete to provide shade for the many public benches. People converse in a myriad of languages, and tourists dart about in every direction—it's crowded, but not so crowded I get that pang in my chest that tells me to go hide in a bathroom.

It's nice.

And apparently, it's a perfect spot for a street performance.

"So . . . you do this everywhere?" I ask as Pierce sits next to me on a bench that overlooks the towering Cardiff Central Library.

Dani puts her flute together, while Ajay paces around her,

trying to figure out the best lighting for the video he's about to shoot.

"She does," Pierce says with a laugh. "She has no shame, it's astounding. Not that she should, mind you. She's really good."

"Oh, yeah. I shared sheet music with her in the park; she's great. It's kind of weird, though, right? I don't mind performing, really. I can shut everyone else out and feel the music. But that duet with Sang in the tube was a whole different experience. I felt so exposed."

Pierce settles in next to me. There's definitely enough room for the two of us on this bench, but he's pressing into me just slightly, his shoulder resting into my arm. My stomach growls, and I wrap an arm around my gut to try to suppress the sound.

"Let's go, Dani!" Pierce shouts. "We need that beer money!"

He laughs, and I silently roll my eyes. But he gets things started by tossing a five-pound bill in her upturned flute case. Dani gives a nod of approval, then starts.

The piece is melodic and slow. Our marching band medley was full of songs that were snappy, loud, and fun, but what pours out from her instrument is a complete one-eighty. Soft, sad, at times barely audible over the din of the crowd, but when she builds—and wow, does it build—it causes people to quite literally stop in their tracks.

"Wish you'd brought your oboe?" Pierce asks.

I shrug in response.

A group forms near her, not a super obvious semicircle, but mini-crowds dotted across the walkway. A woman nearby hands something to her toddler, who toddles toward the upturned flute case in front of her. He throws a couple of coins in, then returns to his mom, who stays for the full performance.

Others follow suit, mostly as they pass by, but I find it hard to focus on them. I close my eyes as the clinking of small change adds an off-beat rhythm to her piece, accenting the swell and fall of her phrasing.

"Okay, this is kinda cool," I admit. "No one seems annoyed at all. If anything, they're delighted to have some music interrupt their day. It's wild."

"They're annoyed sometimes," Pierce says. "Especially when I bring my trumpet out, as that's a bit *louder*. But yeah, you'd be surprised how many people stop to take it in."

"It's cool that we have that power. To pop out of nowhere and make a group of people bond over music."

"So you wish you'd brought your oboe."

I laugh, as a wave of anxiety sweeps over my body. There's no way I could do that again. Or could I?

"Almost," I finally reply.

We're back at the cottage, which is still as adorable as humanly possible. Their goal was to get pissed tonight—"pissed" meaning "drunk"—so they each bought a handful of the big 440-milliliter cans of cheap beer, financed by Dani's spontaneous busking. Sophie and I got a cider each, because drinking underage gives me more anxiety than it supposedly relieves. Why she's nursing her drink is anyone's guess, but with the way she casually watches the conversations, she *still* doesn't trust this group.

"Come outside with me," Sophie says.

My eyebrows arch, as I find the proposition a little weird. But I go along with it, and no one seems to notice or care. When we get outside, she walks a few steps into the gravel, and I watch as she takes a deep breath. I do the same, subconsciously. The air's nice here. Woodsy. Green.

"Should have brought a jacket out with me. Assume you don't smoke?" She pulls out a large yellow pouch, a pack of gum, and some erasers.

I shake my head, and when I come closer, I see the pouch is tobacco, the pack of gum is actually a pack of filters, and the erasers are in fact filters. She's assembling her own cigarettes.

"I didn't realize you could make cigarettes." Could I be any more naive? "How does that affect your clarinet playing?"

"Everyone's a casual smoker in London. Well, not you. Guess that group isn't either."

I shrug. "I'll keep you company anyway."

"Good. Can I talk to you about something that you won't like?"

I turn to her. She looks at the moon.

"I guess I'll just tell you," she says. "I almost told you last night, after you left his room."

"This is about Pierce."

"It is." She sucks in smoke and blows it out quickly. "I'm starting to like Pierce too. And I feel bad for what I said at the pub, just unloading all that on you with no context. But . . . I think you need the full story."

"Okay," I say, drawing out the word.

"See, the flautist I told you about? Pierce's ex?" She looks to me for recognition, but my face is frozen solid. "Right. You know. I thought he and I were going to be best friends. We clicked so well, and so did he and Pierce."

I turn from her, because whatever she's about to say, I don't want her to see my reaction to her words. She continues.

"When things ended, Colin was devastated. Pierce didn't even break up with him—just kept putting off his calls, texts. Pierce was on to someone else so fast, and revealed that information to Colin forty minutes before his Friday recital. To paraphrase Taylor Swift here, he gave it all to Pierce, who changed his mind. He was a mess. He cried on my shoulder until the stage manager pried us apart."

There it is. The pain that creeps back in my chest, leaving a burning residue as it slithers down my insides. We're not even a thing, and it's complicated. Aren't things ever just okay? Can't people fall out, but not fall apart?

"The performance went as well as you'd expect," she says. "His playing *sounded* like he'd gone through a breakup minutes ago. Weak, sad, dead inside. After the recital, I couldn't find him. He disappeared, then went to the main office the next day and dropped out of the academy."

Deep breaths. I clench my fists, and fight the urge to hide from my anxiety. Seems like I never have that option here. I let Megan take control of my life back home, but here I'm on my own.

I have to face things head-on, again and again, even though it's too exhausting. *I'm* too exhausting. The others might not think my reactions make sense, but they don't see everything compounding through the day.

- The stress of a car ride
- The pangs of early love
- The constant worry about how my every movement and every word are being taken

But I breathe. Because that's the only thing that grounds me.

"I think . . . this could be different, and I hope it is. I just don't want to see a friend go through this again."

"Sophie," I say. "I'm not Colin. I'm not going to just disappear."

She drops her cigarette on the gravel, and I clutch the cider I've barely touched. I've never felt so young. The can crinkles under my grip.

"Then what should I do? How do I stop it?" I turn, take a sip. "I've never felt this way. I see him and I think my heart stops. I can't breathe. And I can't hear everything you're saying and not think that this is different. Even if it's not, how can I not think that?"

"Marty . . ."

"Sometimes, when my anxiety gets too bad, I make a list of the things I worry about on my phone. Bullet points— sometimes three of them, sometimes twenty. But no matter how I try to break down that list, I can't get rid of them. It's what I do, it's how I function, but worrying about it doesn't help me make the right decisions, and it sure as hell doesn't prepare me for what could happen. I know the stakes are high here. To fall for someone in your only friend group? To be on trips with a boy when I should really be practicing and applying for jobs 24-7? I can't stay here if I don't get a job. I'm running out of time, and I'm clearly getting distracted. But it's also the first time I've ever been able to *do* something like this."

Her arms are around me, and she's squeezing tight.

I start to breathe again.

"You're going to be okay," she says. "But you strike me as a guy who likes to be prepared for all outcomes, right?"

I nod.

"With Pierce, this is a potential outcome. Prepare yourself for it. And don't fucking run off on me like Colin, because I'm really tired of making new friends."

I crack a smile, even if I'm a bit peeved at her for repeatedly warning me about Pierce. We're a lot alike—calm but worried, perky but snarky—but she seems like she's put together. She was instantly inviting, yes, but it's more than that. It's early in our friendship, but I can already tell. We just work.

"Soph," I say. "I'm your friend. And not temporarily, until someone better comes along."

The front door creaks, and Pierce takes a step into the night sky. He's changed into a graphic tee and mesh shorts. He looks at me, and I feel it again. Dry mouth, caught breath. I'm in deep.

"Yeah, yeah. We'll see about that," Sophie says with a chuckle.

She pats Pierce on the shoulder as she goes inside. It's just us.

He comes to me. Kisses me on the neck and looks up at me. I bring my mouth down to his, and we share a light kiss.

"Stay with me tonight," he says. "In my room."

Sophie's words run through my head, over and over, crowding my happy thoughts but leaving room for the doubtful ones to punch through. I want to say no. I want to say yes.

I don't know.

I want him to be my boyfriend. I want him to fall in love with me. There are too many factors outside my control, and usually that makes me panic. I'm kind of stressed, but I wouldn't call it panicking. Not yet, at least.

Maybe that's why I say, "Okay."

I exchange a long glance with Sophie before Pierce and I go upstairs. There's so much I didn't consider before the door shut. Like how I'd feel when he rips off his shirt and throws it on the antique chair in this room. He turns to me. He's got a slender frame, with a built chest and a faint six-pack. God, those arms.

This is the time when I should say words. I should try to act cool. But I can't do these things. I gawk at his body, which slowly comes closer to me. His chest hair is sparse, but present, and it trails down, lightly gathering at his stomach before it disappears beneath his shorts.

I've thought about this moment for a long time.

He puts an arm around me, and the lingering smell of deodorant and his musk hit me, and I know it's a feeling, a setting, I'll never forget. I turn off the light. We kiss, push and pull into each other in the fragile light of stars. He lifts my shirt over my head, and I freeze. He looks into my eyes, and I press my lips to his, while keeping my gut away from his body.

He sits on the bed.

I slowly remove my shoes and socks. "I left my paja—um, shorts downstairs."

"That's okay." He slips his off, revealing tight black boxer briefs.

I pull down my jeans, take my time folding them, and walk to the bed. We get under the covers. I'm on my back. He's on his side, looking up at me, holding on to me. We kiss again, and I wrap my arm around his back. Our breathing intensifies, and he pulls off me to pant. His hot breath on my neck sends chills.

His hands start at my collarbone and slide lower. His fingers graze my stomach, and I flinch. He pauses. He slides lower and I almost moan. I suck in a breath—if he goes any lower, we'll have gone too far. I'll be Colin, who had his first everything with Pierce before he moved on to another.

I don't want him to stop, but I do.

But I don't.

He looks at me, his fingers tiptoeing back up my chest.

"You're panicking."

"I'm panicking."

"Right." His smile pierces through the night. "Should we go back to making out, then?"

Eighteen

THE RIDE BACK IS uneventful. Shane's working when I get back, so it's just me in the apartment. The highest highs of my weekend away with Pierce make these lows feel even lower. I open my laptop to check for new jobs, knowing I need to treat it like I did all my homework back at Avery High.

I'm an overachiever by nature. Not in that intensely smart, know-it-all kind of way, but the fear of failure drives me harder than anything. Back in high school, the few times we'd blow off homework to stay out through curfew, I'd always get up at 5:00 a.m. to finish it. Skye would turn papers in a few days late, taking the lower grade. And Megan would calculate her overall grade and convince herself she didn't even need to do the work.

These little peculiarities in my friend group run through my mind. My email loads, and a dozen emails light up the screen.

They're mostly from Megan.

"Fuck," I say out loud, to no one. "Fuck fuck fuck."

I connect to Wi-Fi and make a call. It's still early Sunday morning in Kentucky, but she'll pick up. Two rings. Three.

She picks up.

But she doesn't say anything.

"Megan? Megan, I'm so sorry."

"Did you just get back from the hospital?" she asks. "Did London's power go out?"

"No. I'm sorry I missed our FaceTime; it totally slipped my mind. I went to Cardiff—in Wales, you know?—with that guy I was telling you about and a couple friends here."

Again, she's silent.

And then she's not. "This was intensely hurtful. You are thousands of miles away from me and you go completely MIA, I can't find any social media updates *because you have no social media*, and I can't even leave you a voice mail."

I rest my face in my hand.

"You've always had this fucking problem, Mart. You check out and you're oblivious to everyone around you."

"That's not—" I start.

"Not true? Sure. Did you talk to your parents about this Wales trip? It's Sunday, so you know they're going to want a full report on your 'new church' or whatever—what was the sermon? Tell us about your new pastor. I shouldn't have to remind you to do that, but I know you, and I know *them*." She pauses. Her breathing comes in shallow puffs, but it feels heavy coming through the phone.

Fuck.

"I know, I know," I say. "I'm sorry. Tell Skye I'm sorry too."

"I'm not your housekeeper. Clean this up with him yourself."

It's hard to handle. I did this. I know I did. I want to shut down. I am shutting down. Like I always could do back home. Like I can never afford to do here.

"I, um . . . I have to practice."

"My family is going to the Outer Banks next week, so you're off the hook," she says. "Might want to put the following Friday on your calendar now if you want to salvage this at all."

She hangs up. I hang up too. I ignore the emails on my computer since none of them are about auditions. I grab my oboe and storm out of the apartment, ignoring the pain in my gut that's half from skipping a couple of meals and half from the abject horror that just happened. I know I have to make it up to her, to them, but I don't know how.

But she was wrong about me being oblivious. For the first time, I feel present. I'm falling for someone, and I am incredibly aware of the points of pain all across my body: chest, shoulders, neck. Tension holds me together like a suspension bridge, and I beg for that normalcy, that complacency, that's followed me along my entire life. It's like I've been thrown behind the steering wheel of a semi and I'm doing my best not to overturn and cause a sixty-car pileup.

I check out the practice rooms at Knightsbridge, but all ten of them are full. I make a mental note that midday Sunday is not a great time to get a room. I could practice at the apartment, but I don't even want to be there, with my computer and all my emails mocking me.

My stomach growls. I need to eat something. But every single time I think about getting food, the thought of Pierce's hands grazing my stomach hits me. I feel stuck. I feel trapped. I can't practice, and I can't eat.

I wander down the tree-lined, stone-paved street until I come to Regent's Park. It's not too far. A girl jogs past me on the right; two dogs play off leash to my left. Everyone seems more content than me, or more driven or something. I can't place it. Is adulthood learning how to fake it? Maybe. Probably.

Local parks in my part of Kentucky are sparse, often flat. They usually have one track that wraps the perimeter. They might have tennis courts or swing sets, but that's about as exotic as it gets. London parks are massive, sprawling. You could go on a run here every day and never take the same path.

I don't mind getting lost in here. Turn after turn, I pass some amazing sights—a charming open-air theatre, a mini-rose garden—and now I find myself immersed in a statuesque path. Meaning a path with a lot of statues everywhere.

It's modern art. It's where I'd take my parents if they ever visited again. Something stately to show Mom how cultured this move was. She's always been the type to push for better grades, and urge me to practice daily. I wouldn't be here if it weren't for her, but I wonder if I'd be someone different if I took after my dad. Funny, loud, someone who really owns the room. I'd be more like Megan, like Pierce.

I have no idea how I'm going to answer all the church questions I know are coming, but I pull out my phone anyway to see if I can find Wi-Fi and give Mom a call, when . . .

When the music hits my ears. I stop. Delicate fingerpicking classical guitar realness coming from the next bush over. Music that takes such concentration, even to listen to, that I find it distracting. Even healing.

I turn the corner to see Sang sitting cross-legged on the grass with his eyes closed. His short dark hair peeks out of a worn-backward ball cap. He's got a huge smile on his face.

My feet take me to him as he plays a perky song. I'm sure I've heard it before, some classic Spanish guitar ballad. His fingers fly over the strings, faster than what I heard back at Marble Arch. Faster than I ever thought possible.

I sit next to him, a safe distance away.

His music's making me sway back and forth. We're all alone here, between two rows of bushes. The music drifts away with a decrescendo. I want to play with him again, I realize. I let the final notes sing out into the sky, and then I clear my throat.

He opens his eyes. "Marty!"

"Sang," I say, with a smile so big it makes my face hurt. "What are the chances?"

He laughs. "Probably pretty good. I work at the academy, remember? The glamorous life of sorting and copying choir and orchestra music."

"I like that piece you just played. What others do you know?" I ask. "We should do a duet again sometime. The video

I put up has gotten a little bit of attention, a few dozen views and, like, two comments."

"Oh, I can share it. I don't have a ton of subscribers, but that was fun. Know any pop songs?" he asks. "Those are always big hits on the tube—on YouTube too. I do some arrangements of everything—from Rihanna to Spice Girls. They *really* love Spice Girls here. Still."

I laugh out loud as I put my oboe together. "My mom dressed up as one of them in college with her roommates or something."

"Which one?"

"No clue. I can never remember their names."

He just smiles and shakes his head.

We spend the next hour on his phone, finding chords and sheet music for whatever songs we can think of. I play a passionate Adele song, while he makes a Rihanna track fit underneath it. His grasp on music is unlike anything I've heard—beyond mine, for sure.

The ache in my shoulders has gone. I breathe easier, though I'm a bit out of breath from the whole oboeing thing. Music is calming. Friends are calming.

"All right, my fingers are aching. I think I'm done for today. Want to grab dinner? I can give you some pointers for your portfolio and applications and all that—not that I'm a big success, but I've gotten a few paid gigs."

I grab my stomach. The pangs are there, but they've receded. I could go the rest of the night without food, probably.

But I like having him as a friend, and I want to hang out with him more. And I definitely need all the help I can get.

I swallow the guilt as it rises up from my stomach, and I agree.

"Can I invite my cousin?" I ask. "He's doing the same thing and could use some advice."

NINETEEN

"GIVE ME THE SECRETS," I say, passing Sang the ketchup for his chips. "Everyone talks about you like you're some god."

"It's true," Shane says as he unpins his work badge from his polo. "It's actually a bit mad."

A smile comes over Sang's reddened face. "There's no way to answer this without sounding like a git, but I'll try. It helps if you're a prodigy."

"Oh, you're one of *those* musicians." I shake my head. "Socially stunted, cocky, performance-ready at any moment?" Laughing, I roll my eyes so he knows I'm joking.

"Suzuki method from day one," he says, talking about the music lesson regime that churns out prodigies by starting them out early and using proven methods to teach. "Which is why I got into the academy so young."

"Thought Suzuki was only for piano and violin. At least you're a virtuoso at something unusual. Well, outside of Spain."

I poke at my salad. As it happens, pub salads are as appetizing as they sound, in that they're not. But the menu listed the calories next to each item, so I forced myself to order one of the low-cal options. This option is apparently also low-*taste*, so I take a sip of my water instead and let my stomach grumble.

I can't even remember making the decision to diet, or to try to lose weight, but it feels like this insecurity has had a hold on me for so long. And maybe this is something I can control. Something I can fix. Sure, Pierce hasn't called me out for my weight or put pressure on me to eat healthier, but he must think it. It's in the subtext of every meal we share and every pointed comment he makes about his own diet.

"Yeah, but that bit me in the ass," Sang explains. "I'm a glorified intern for the academy and busk on the tube for a few quid, since there aren't enough classical guitar gigs out there." He shakes his head. "That's enough complaining for one day. So what kind of gigs are you looking for?"

I laugh. "The type that pay money, preferably."

"Cheers to that," Shane says between bites of his burger.

"Shane, I kind of know your story, but Marty, I've got to ask . . . why here?"

I sigh, not sure how to condense so many emotions, so many hopes and dreams, into a short answer. "I wanted to get away from Kentucky. America, really."

"Marty's on the run," Shane says, laughing.

"Nothing so dramatic. I realized one day how much that town held me back. Or I felt like I needed to hold myself back.

My best friends are great, but I was always in their shadow. I was in everyone's shadow."

"That's a lot to run from. And you're not in the shadow here?"

I shrug. "Maybe. It doesn't feel like it. I'm making my own decisions, making friends—the people here are great. And I love being in a more, um, queer-friendly environment."

We all clink our glasses, actually cheers-ing at that.

"I feel the same way," Sang says.

I take a bite of tomato, and feel remorse take over my body. I hadn't planned to eat dinner. It wasn't in my plan, and if I want to lose weight to prepare for my next shirts-off experience with Pierce, I have to keep it up.

"So what brought you here?" Shane asks.

"Well, I'm from Calgary." He turns to me specifically. "Canada, that is."

I roll my eyes. "I know where Calgary is."

"Well, you might be the first American ever to know that." He smiles.

"I . . . google things, a lot. I like maps." My face burns with embarrassment. "Let's not get into it."

He throws his hands up, dropping a chip on the table from a foot in the air. My embarrassment fades as we all start to laugh. His smile cuts into me, and I chalk it up to good friendship. I never made friends this easily in high school, but here I am: Pierce, Sophie, Dani, now Sang.

There's a part of me that knows Sang is hella cute. I'm not blind to that fact. It's like our cheeks are attached—he can't smile without my face mimicking it. He's bursting with energy, and everything about his hair and personality is so effortless. But I may have a hormone issue happening, and I will *not* be the guy who falls in love with every boy he meets.

"You're funny," Shane says. It's almost a whisper. He bites his lip and stares into his glass of water.

It's a good thing I'm focusing on one boy at a time too. Because otherwise, I might have some competition. I kick Shane under the table, and watch his cheeks redden.

"Anyway, my parents found this school," Sang explains. "It seemed like a fun experience. Came here and loved it so much I couldn't go back." He looks down now. "And I'll stay here if I can find a job to prolong my visa."

"Is that hard to do?"

"I've tried to get jobs. But not all of them count toward extending visas here, like that *Jersey Boys* stint was just to cover a maternity leave. I need a full-time, long-term opportunity to come up, fast."

He grips his napkin harder, and he still won't make eye contact.

"I'm glad we're all in this together." Shane gingerly places a hand over Sang's. "Everyone at Knightsbridge is so starry-eyed and gets feedback from professors. They perform in all these cool venues. But they're just delaying the inevitable. We're good enough to get these gigs, I know it. Especially you guys."

"I've been searching for a little bit longer, so maybe I'm jaded." Sang offers a sad smirk to Shane, who in turn looks defiant.

"Some days," Sang continues, "it's like the universe is giving me a sign. Telling me to move home, hang up my guitar, and give up this whole thing."

Shane clears his throat and hesitantly grips Sang's hand with his own. "Forgive me for being dramatic here, but some days the universe is just wrong."

Sang lifts his gaze, but I see the exhaustion taking its toll. Sang's the experienced one of our group, but he's only eighteen.

"Is there anything I can do?" Shane asks.

"This helps." He offers each of us a smile. "I didn't come out of the academy with many friends. And you'll find out the longer you get into this mess—London on your own is not easy. It's expensive, and I have two roommates, and we live out in fucking Tooting."

I chuckle. "Where is that?"

"South," Shane answers, while Sang says, "Nowhere charming."

I look up at my phone. Sighing, I grab my bag. "I hate to say this, but I have to call my parents before they have a full-on meltdown. Texting isn't cutting it. Did you want to walk back, Shane?"

He looks from me to Sang, who's got his eyes locked on Shane. I feel my cheeks burn from the secondhand romantic tension.

"I think I'll stay for a cup of tea."

Sang's smile shows all his teeth. "Yeah, me too."

Back at the apartment, I call my mom. She picks up the phone on the first ring.

"Hi, hello?"

"Hi, Mom."

"Oh, there you are. I've missed you. We haven't gone this long without speaking since . . ."

Since I came out? I finish in my mind.

"Well, it's been ages," Mom says, deciding to not go there.

We talk about everything, and I line up my list of lies:

- Aunt Leah's doing great. She's not at all bitter that you unfriended her from Facebook last year and won't take her calls, yet trust her with your only child.

- The school is great. The professors are really helpful, and I've learned so much from my classes already. I can tell this program's going to be great.

But then she brings up the one topic I want to talk about least—even less than talking about boys: church.

"Did you get my necklace?"

"I have. Been wearing it every day," I lie. "Thanks for dropping it in there."

"Good, great. You would have loved the sermon today; it was on putting God's will first. Really training your mind to know and choose the Lord's way, so that when you are faced with tough choices and temptations, you'll be better able to make the right decision."

I pause, not really sure if this is her recapping her day or if she's trying to tell me something. Living as an out gay kid in a Christian household is actually not just cliché passive aggression and Bible verses thrown out everywhere. But for me, it's the knowledge that the one thing that brings ultimate security and peace to your family is the same thing that threatens your emotional well-being (and in some cases, your life).

"So did you take a look at that church? The one across from that coffee shop? Dad was telling me about it, but I wasn't able to learn much from the internet about the pastor or their sermons."

Slowly but painfully, it sinks in that this is all my mom wants to talk about with me. I haven't talked to her in a whole week, and in that time I've had my first alcoholic drink, my first kiss, I'm falling for someone so completely, and I have no guide for it. I want to talk about my friends. About how Dani had the audacity to call Morricone a hack. I'm living my life alone in a new, beautiful city filled with the most amazing people.

And all we can talk about is some sermon about learning how to put god's will first?

I know what I'm supposed to say, what Megan trained me to do. I'm supposed to pick a new sermon, summarize it blandly but enough that it appeases my parents, and throw in some specific but minor details about the church—the creaky pews, the out-of-tune piano, the lack of air-conditioning, anything.

I can't cut out all my lies—they're the only thing keeping me sane and safe. But I can't do this either.

"I didn't go to church," I say. "And I'm sorry, but I haven't been wearing the cross either."

There's a silence on her end.

"I'm not sure what god's will says about this, but I'm not going to look for a church here. I am just starting to feel comfortable in this brand-new city—which you haven't even asked me about, by the way—and I'm not going to throw some biblical trauma into the mix."

"Well," Mom says. "I don't even know how to respond to this. I just wanted to have a nice catch-up, but I don't know what else I expected. One week with her and you're already like this, I swear."

Aunt Leah isn't even here! I scream in my mind. But I don't let it slip, because that would not work out well for me. I still don't know if they could make me come back—I guess legally they could—but as long as they think I'm technically safe here and that I'm busy with school (and that I only have eleven more weeks left here), they won't do anything.

At least, I hope they won't.

"Don't do that, Mom." It's not a demand, but I'm not pleading either. "Aunt Leah's letting me stay here for free, she stocked the pantry with American snacks for me, Shane's going out of his way to make sure I'm happy and making friends. They're *good*."

She sighs. "Be careful, Marty. I can't watch over you from here."

I don't say it, but I think it: *That's kind of the point.*

DIARY ENTRY 7

IF I HAD TO give a few adjectives that describe my cousin Shane, I'd probably pick words like "chill" or "sweet" or maybe "easily distracted." But the Shane sitting on the floor next to me is none of those things. He's *pissed*. Angry, explosive, likely to spontaneously combust if someone doesn't throw some cold water on him.

Everything feels a little hopeless right now—okay, a lot hopeless.

I can't pull Shane into this. I can't pull Aunt Leah into this. These are *my* parents and this is *my* mess. At least, that's what I tried to tell him, but he's not having it.

"They're wrong, Marty." He's said this like eight times. "With so many things in this world, there's this gray area. I try to take other people's perspectives, I try to understand all sides of the story, but this is so obviously wrong."

He said something like that, at least. To be fair, he talked really fast and I'm so busy trying to forget everything that happened that even my memory from the last few minutes is getting fuzzy.

That might be one downside to this project. To the entire concept of journaling. I can read this diary months from now, and I will know what happened, how it all fell apart, and remember exactly how I felt. How do I feel? Awful.

My parents are making me feel awful for existing. My church tells me my very existence is wrong.

When will this pain stop? When can I stop pretending and just . . . be the person I want to be?

There's a rage building inside me too, and I don't think it's going away this time.

TWENTY

"NO." *NO.* "ABSOLUTELY NOT."

There are a million people here. And they're all annoying. We're at King's Cross Station, which is about a tenth as fancy as it sounds, and eight times more stressful than any station I've seen so far. I'm dodging people who dart left and right. It's like everyone's missed their train. It's like no one knows where their fucking rolling suitcase is supposed to go. It's been two weeks since I moved to London, and I still can't deal with crowds. I'm beginning to wonder if I'll ever get used to this.

The station's clean. At least I can focus on that happy fact. Stark white everything, clean floors, walls. When I look to the roof, I see crisscrossing white beams line the vaulted ceiling, letting soft light through their cracks. It's open and bright here. These are positives.

But then there's the chest pain. We're here to film one of Sophie's sessions for a class, but she's somehow convinced me to add another video to my collection and to film it. But at least mine is being filmed at Marble Arch, as that was the only reserved Knightsbridge spot Sophie could sneak me on at the last second.

She turns to me, takes a breath, releases it, and looks in my eyes.

"This is hell, I get it." She hands me her phone, which is a million times nicer than mine. "But you owe me for filming your portfolio videos, and this is my turf."

"You *chose* this venue?"

"Hey." She shrugs, pops a clarinet reed in her mouth. "Business travelers are loose with their change. Also, hello, the lighting."

We slip past the staircase, where a lone upright piano stands. Its pale wood is cracked, and I imagine the tuning can't be great, but the fact they have a piano amid the chaos is nothing short of amazing.

"Okay, I need five minutes of good footage." She smiles. "Think you can handle it?"

I pat her right cheek and wink. "Can you? Five minutes is a long time."

"Just remember, you and your dumb kazoo are next."

She takes a breath and sits on the piano bench, facing out toward me, toward the thousands of others. She pauses longer than I expect her to. She zones out a bit, her eyes focused well past me.

"Soph?" I ask. "You ready?"

She nods. "Ready."

I start the camera. Point it at her.

"Aria for Clarinet and Piano," she says. "Sans piano, that is. Eugene Bozza."

With half a breath, she's off. It's a slow piece, but the emotion is there. It's one you might be able to learn the fingerings for in high school, but you'd never be able to pull off the emotion, the clear tone. Between passages, her breaths are hushed. She builds, a crescendo over eight, ten measures. Even more.

And it falls.

A smile is on my face. I feel it tug at my cheeks before I register how happy it makes me. To hear music. Yes, I'm still very aware of the people around me, but being anxious and happy is marginally better than just being anxious.

"That was great," I say, once she finishes the piece.

She laughs. "It's no prodigious oboe and guitar duet, but it'll do."

"Please. He's the prodigy. I'm here because I was the only one who could handle the oboe headaches."

"Those aren't real, are they?"

"Yeah, they are. You're blowing out a lot of air, but the oboe reed only allows a teeny bit through, so the rest goes into your brain." I roll my eyes. "Or your sinuses. I'm not a doctor. It's probably not healthy, but it got me here."

She takes her phone back, then picks up my oboe case. "Here." She puts it to my chest. "You should play here."

"No way." The hell is she getting at? "Let's go to Marble Arch."

"Marty, that isn't any different. Except it's brighter here. People still ignore you."

I take a seat on the bench. "You don't understand. There are certain quirks I have. I'll try to explain it in a normal way. If you're okay with me being honest."

"Obviously. Go on?"

"These crowds here are more erratic. You don't know where they're going, they don't either, so it's a lot of crisscrossing and bumping into people. That's bad." I sigh, realizing how crazy I must sound. "In Marble Arch, people only go two directions. It's crowded, but there's a flow. It's not chaotic like here, or like Big Ben."

"You think it would mess up your playing?" she asks.

I nod. "There are some stressors I don't want to deal with. The worst part is that this wasn't part of my plan. When things get changed last second, it stresses me out."

It's the type of speech I'd prepared to tell Megan a hundred times, but could never get out the words. "We planned to go to Marble Arch after this. It's not like it's a safer, calmer experience there, but it's expected."

She nods. Her face is half-confused, half-processing. After I stand, I shift my weight from leg to leg. It's a bit awkward.

"Two things," she says. "One, you're in for a rough ride. You know that, right? You can't ever have a plan with this career in this city, oh god, especially if you start dating a guy like Pierce. And two, thankfully you have a friend like me who's willing to walk all over town to make you chill out. Let's go to Marble Arch."

But when we get there, twenty minutes and two trains later, there's an empty feeling in my chest. And again my mind compares my best friends, old and new. Megan would've shoved me out of my comfort zone. Yeah, maybe I'd have been fine with it, but I'd have been upset too. I would have spent the next week recovering, hiding in my room after school, reading something or playing video games. Which is why Sophie's response was what I needed.

So why, as I soak my reed and pace around the busking area, do I feel like I missed out on a new experience? One that could have been good?

I assemble my oboe and roll through my warm-ups, scales, and arpeggios from B3 to F6 and back. And I feel comfortable and safe.

Safe?

Since when does feeling uncomfortable mean feeling in danger? That's how I've always approached everything—big crowds, new experiences, making new friends. Sharp fear, pinching my shoulders tight and pushing me back. Holding me back.

"Are you ready?" Sophie asks, raising the camera. "I'll start filming whenever. And you're doing your old audition piece, right?"

But I don't need Megan to push me outside my boundaries.

I need to do that myself. I need to be my own advocate. To say okay and keep moving forward and panic later.

"Nope," I say. "I've been working on something new. I have it mostly memorized, I think."

She hits record, and I start to play. Bach's Oboe Concerto in D minor, the second movement. The melody flows through my fingers, and I purse my lips together, feeling the oboe reverberating throughout the space. I make a few mistakes, and I miss a whole measure, but I play it through.

My arm tingles; my fingers feel heavy. I've never performed a piece like that, underprepared and on the spot. It's like I've chugged a gallon of coffee; my body is vibrating with energy.

But a good energy.

"Damn, you are good with a melody. Do you want to try again to pick up the notes you missed?"

I shrug. "No, I want that moment played. It was a nice moment."

With Shane occupied in the main room, flinging his arms around erratically, conducting . . . something, I take a late afternoon shower. As soon as I get out and dry off, I weigh myself.

I can't see a difference, or much of one, when I look in the mirror, and it's a bit demoralizing. But I've lost weight, and I think that's the most important. I'm down from a hundred kilograms to ninety-three, and it's only been a couple of weeks. So, no, I can't see much of a difference, but the scale in our bathroom tells me I'm on my way.

My BMI's gone down too. Every time there's a change on the scale, I look it up. I weigh myself after I go to the restroom every morning, before I shower. Then again later on in the day to make sure the food I've eaten hasn't increased it too much.

When I put some product in my hair, I hear the front door open. Suddenly, Pierce's voice booms through the apartment, and my body freezes. I'm behind a closed door, but I still cover my stomach.

Wrapped in a towel, I duck into my room, not acknowledging the new visitor. I throw on my clothes in a panic, and check two, three more times that I look presentable. Then there's a knock on my door. And he's in my room.

Looking at my bed.

"Hiya, Mart."

"What are you doing here?" is my hello.

He rolls his eyes. "I was in the neighborhood."

"We live in the same neighborhood."

"Have you ever seen a sitcom? That's how friendship works—dropping in unannounced."

"Great," I say. "I love spontaneity."

I make eye contact with Shane, down the hall. He studies me wearily, which he's been doing a lot more lately. And if there's anything that makes me worse at dealing with people, it's dealing with those who can't deal with me.

"Anyway," I say. The eternal let's-pretend-this-never-happened transition. "Thanks for stopping by. This is my room. That's my bed."

I wince. There's nothing else to show Pierce about this box of a room, but is pointing to the bed presumptive? Especially after the last time we were in a bed together?

I wonder if my mind will ever stop running.

I decide it probably won't.

"I see that." He plops down on the bed. "I figured you'd be the type of bloke who makes his bed every morning. Not one who leaves it so messy." He shakes his head, because he knows I'm exactly that kind of guy and he's trying to get under my skin.

It's working.

"Normally, yes. But I slept in today."

I've been sleeping in a lot, actually. And I was hoping to get in a nap before dinner. It's an unfortunate side effect of skipping meals, but sleeping also helps me pass time and keeps the hunger pangs at bay.

"No plans for tonight?"

I shake my head, since naps probably don't count as plans.

"Want to *make* plans for tonight?"

My normal response for this would be a quick no. This is my default answer for any time someone talks about making plans, especially without notice.

My conversation with Sophie flashes back in my mind.

"Is that a no?"

"It's not a no," I say quickly. "Why, what did you have in mind?"

He smiles, the same one that melts me every time. And I want to say yes, whatever it is, just to be with him. But that's probably not a healthy outlook either, so I take slow breaths and put on the persona of a calm, reasonable person.

It's not working.

I take a seat next to him on the bed. My bed. I pull up my feet and sit cross-legged. He turns to look at me, and I feel elated and embarrassed. I feel light-headed too, but that's unrelated.

"You're not even listening to me, are you?"

I snap out of it. He laughs.

"You were zoning out, staring at that wall. Is that some sort of defense mechanism for when I invite you to do fun things? You seem very fun averse."

"Hey!" I shout. "I very much like fun."

He leans back on the bed, his core flexing with each deep chuckle. He's usually a button-up guy, all plaids and checkered shirts, but on this warm day he wears a thin T-shirt. It rises up as he leans back, and I see his abs peek through, his stomach hair. And I'd be lying if I said I didn't feel *all* of the feelings right now.

"I asked if you knew where Brighton is?"

"I . . ." Haven't looked it up, oddly enough. "No, I don't."

He smirks. "It's a two-hour drive away, the beach. It's been so warm, thought you might be keen to go down there a bit, so I borrowed Dani's car. Want to come?"

"Oh," I say, trying to remember all my responsibilities. "Who all's going?"

"Just me and you, I was hoping. I got a mate from school who lives down there, said we can crash at his place."

I feel my cheeks get warm. "Um, when?"

"Now-ish. I'd like to get on the road before traffic gets too bad."

They're on fire now. "Oh, wow. I guess so."

Then I remember what day it is. Friday. My rescheduled

FaceTime date with Megan and Skye. I can't bail on them again—they'd never forgive me.

"Wait, no. I totally forgot." And now I realize I really do want to go. "I have a FaceTime date with my high school friends tonight."

"Oh," he says. "Like, late tonight? I'm sure you can use my friend's Wi-Fi. You usually do it on your phone, right?"

My spirits lift. "That's right. I can do that! If you don't think he'd mind. It wouldn't be long, but I can't skip this one—I totally forgot about the last one because we went to Cardiff, and my friends were so upset. I couldn't do that to them again."

He puts a hand on my leg, and I guess he feels my panic. He winks. "Totally fine. We'll call them tonight."

"We?" I ask. "Are we a *we*?"

His response is simple, sweet. He plants a kiss on my lips, and I melt away.

We're a we.

TWENTY-ONE

HE GIVES ME JUST enough time to change and pack a bag. I could've pushed for more, but I couldn't even think beyond the pounding in my chest, the endorphins pouring into my brain like some antidepressant medication commercial. I decide, then and there:

I want to be with him. All weekend, all month, all year. I don't care.

As I'm heading out the door, Shane stops me.

"Here," he says, handing me a granola bar. "Um, in case you get hungry on the drive?"

His words linger, and I fight the growing embarrassment. I'm starving, maybe even literally, but I still flip the bar over to read the—

"Don't." Shane's features are tight, and he's biting his lip. "Don't read. Just eat. Please."

I walk out of the apartment while unwrapping the granola

bar. For a moment, I really do consider eating it. But then I see the chocolate. And the bar feels so heavy in my hands. So I drop it in the trash can before meeting Pierce at the corner.

It's different, this trip. My mind's in a haze as Pierce talks and talks, about the summer program, about our looming duet, which we still haven't gotten together to practice yet. I get in the passenger's seat of Dani's car, and we're on the road in minutes. Driving through the streets of London.

"We made it on the road in good time." Pierce is energy. After weeks of seeing other sides of him, some sweet, some subdued, he's back to how he was when we first met. He's let his beard grow a bit, the brownish-blond patches more apparent in the low light. "I'm going to take the long way out of here," he says.

"Oh, okay."

I'm oddly content with this human.

There are better ways to say that, I'm sure, but it's how I feel. I'm used to this kind of partnership, riding shotgun and feeling that connection with someone—a friendship based on the same destination. Even when you don't know where you're going, like when Megan and I would try to get ourselves lost in the winding roads of the Ohio Valley.

His hand's on the shifter. Mine's on my lap. I want this to feel like more than friendship. And I know it does for me, and I hope it does for him. And I feel ridiculous, because we're not twelve and at the movies. But it's not like I ever got to *be* twelve and on a date at the movies. So, yeah, I want to hold his hand.

I reach out. Hesitate.

His hand turns over and meets mine. His fingers lace between mine, and I feel so whole and comfortable. And his hands are big. I haven't done this much hot and heavy hand-holding since middle school.

He pulls my hand to his lips. Gives it a light kiss. He tilts his head and that smirk is out again, on a mission to melt my heart. He lets go, and I miss it immediately. My chest rises and falls, catching both ways.

"I've got to shift with that hand, love. Try again once we're on the motorway?"

I chuckle. "Noted."

We bolt down streets, stopping harshly at each light. He keeps checking the map on his phone, and I keep looking out the window. It looks like we're taking a detour out of the city, but I don't mind.

"You haven't seen much else in the city, yeah?"

"Haven't had time. Went to King's Cross and St. Pancras for Sophie's busking, walked around Soho a few times."

"Her performance was top-notch this week," he says. "And it seems like she and Rio have been getting on a bit more lately. I think they both figured out they are epic musicians and infighting isn't going to do anything. Did you have any drama like that in secondary?"

"No," I say flatly. "I just got all the solos."

He busts out with laughter. "I see. Any bad blood there?"

"Sure, some. There's always competition, I guess. But I graduated early, so our feuds ended pretty quickly."

"So why did you leave early? I know you wanted this

experience, and you wanted to get away from fried chicken land, et cetera, but why graduate early? Did you not get on with your mates?"

"When did you accept you were gay?"

"Ah, the age-old question," he says. "Are you asking me because we're going to Brighton, which you'll see is the LGBT capital of the UK?"

"No, not when did you realize you were gay, which every straight girl on television asks, or when did you come out, which everyone else asks, but when did you accept it?"

He shakes his head, slowly. "A few years ago, I suppose. It was in school. I broke up with my girlfriend and told her why. Hell, I think Shane and I were the only ones from our school who were public about it—and Shane only at the very end. It's a shame we weren't closer."

"He's a really good guy," I say.

"So what about you? When did you accept it?"

"I was six, Pierce. I would think about guys a lot. Like, I would think about kissing some of the boys in my class and it felt so wrong. But I accepted, eventually, that it wasn't how everyone secretly felt—it was me and I was gay. Even in middle school, when I tried holding hands and liking girls, I knew."

I clear my throat. "See, I love Kentucky. It's home. I feel more comfortable on the back roads there than I'll ever feel here. At least, I think that's true. I had my safe spaces, I knew how to survive, but it can't be my home anymore. When I was a kid, there was a gay hate crime on the news, just a couple counties over. My parents were generally appalled in an all-violence-is-bad sort of way, but they never acknowledged that it was a hate crime, which I thought was fucked up. But some of the kids at my middle school agreed with the attack and made jokes about it. Even after Kentucky was forced to allow gay marriage, that terrible homophobe county clerk, whose name I would never give the notoriety of saying aloud, refused to issue marriage licenses to same-sex couples. We went to this megachurch every Sunday that always had these sermons that were nothing but veiled homophobia. That's my home, Pierce."

"Love—"

"Fuck, I got out of high school in three years, but I wish it'd been two. I feel so accepted here. To be in a city with a real pride parade, and gay bars—have you seen all the pride flags in Soho? It's incredible."

He slows to a stop. We're stuck in traffic as a dump truck blocks all lanes. I see hands fly up in car windows in front of me. He places his hand on my leg, which ignites, sending waves of passion up my body.

I brush my fingers across his hands, taking in their heat. He leans in, halfway. I turn and look into his eyes, deep and light and perfect. Everything about him is perfect, even if it's not—like how his hair's grown out a bit, and it's a bit fuzzy on the sides, and how his beard looks patchy when grown out this much. And none of these are negatives.

I'm drawn to him, magnetically. His breath hits my face. The sides of our noses touch. The secret to time manipulation is somewhere in his hooked nose, chin dimple, and that accent.

I'm suspended in time and space while reality bends to bring us closer together.

His hand slides farther up my leg, and I shiver at the touch. His lips are so close to mine, but neither of us goes in for the kill. I know what it'd do. I couldn't handle it. I couldn't stop. His hands press higher, bunching up my shorts and pressing into new parts of my body, never explored by others.

I hesitate above his lips, knowing there'd be no limit he couldn't push, no boundary I wouldn't jump right now. His hand massages me, and I gasp.

And the driver behind us brings me back into the present by laying on their horn.

I jump back, and see an open road in front of me.

My cheeks flush hot as Pierce hisses with laughter.

"Didn't even hear the truck go by," he says with a wink.

"The guy in the car behind us totally saw us." I shake my head, smile plastered on my face, but I'm still too embarrassed to function.

"Mm. He didn't see everything."

A few turns later, he points out the window. "Recognize that?"

We come up on a drawbridge. Two large castle spires stick out of the river, connected by a bright blue bridge and lines. It's massive, and people are crawling all over the lower bridge like ants. I've seen this in every London-based movie.

"Wow," I say. "London Bridge."

A groan escapes his lips, and as I turn he shakes his head

vehemently. "You're one of *those* tourists, aren't you? I thought you looked things up?"

I fold my arms. "What's that supposed to mean?"

"That's Tower Bridge. Which leads to the Tower of London. London Bridge is a piece of crap compared to this."

"Fine," I say, fully aware my ears and face are burning bright red. "I didn't look everything up."

"Hey, I'm just glad I could teach you something." He puts his hand behind my neck and squeezes, relieving some of the tension that's stuck there.

Everything's emotional whiplash with him. I'm sad, he makes me happy. I'm at peace, he makes me frustrated. I'm stressed, he makes me calm. Well, for a couple of seconds, until I'm back where I started, freaking out about the next thing.

We spend the next half hour in more-or-less silence, commenting about the weather or the very British things we're passing. Pub after pub, high street after high street. The city's a beast, but it's more manageable with him by my side.

"Sorry for ranting so much, back there."

"Most I've heard you talk," he says. "I like it when you ramble, if I'm honest."

I nod. Stare straight ahead.

"And I'm sorry you've felt so out of place your whole life. No one deserves to go through that."

How long does it take to fall in love with someone—hours, days, years? It barely seems valid, these feelings that control my body and swim in my blood. The places I've lived, the people

I've known, all seem like temporary shelters now. Love is something entirely different. It's realizing the storm's been raging so long you forget you're drenched, until the sun kisses your cheek, dries your tears, and shows you where your real home is.

TWENTY-TWO

BRIGHTON IS ALIVE. WHERE London's subdued with a quaint charm and bustling seriousness, Brighton is loud. It's loud, it's organic, it's really fucking gay. I stick to Pierce, who leads me down stone streets with coffee shops and boutique stores and through parks teeming with the tiniest of dogs.

We pick out a postcard together.

My hand's in his. And we're in public.

It's the type of vulnerability that makes you feel right, in some weird way. *Look at me now, Kentucky county clerk I still refuse to name.* The wind whips my face, a welcome shift from muggy, rainy London. The taste of salt in the air, the squawk of seagulls in the sky.

"It's been so long since I've been on the beach," I say. Brighton reminds me how similar a place can sound or taste, even though I've never been here before. "My family used to go to the beach when I was younger, but we haven't been in ages."

"I used to come here with my parents too. But they don't even live in London anymore. My gran got sick not too long after I left for the academy, and Mum moved all of them back up to Leeds."

"Sorry about your grandma," I say. "That must be hard, being away from them."

The wind is fierce up here. I welcome it by releasing my hand from his and stretching out my arms, for a brief second. Let the air wrap around my body. Nothing feels better after a long car ride.

We meander down toward the beach, and Pierce gestures out to a bright pier jutting far into the water. Wind carries the cheering sound of a carnival toward me, and I marvel at the bright lights. All around us, the Brighton Marina is alive with activity, even with the sun arcing quickly toward sunset.

We step onto the beach. Instead of the soft sand I was expecting, it looks like the whole beach is made of tan-and-brown pebbles. I make a mental note to google why this beach doesn't have sand, though it must have something to do with the way the water interacts with the coast.

"Thanks for telling me about your parents, and your grandma," I say as the pebbles crunch beneath our feet. "I feel like you don't open up much."

"Ha! What do you want to know about me? I can be an open book."

"What's the town like where your family lives?"

He takes my hand again and smiles. "Quaint. At least in American terms. Actually, it's probably a bit like your

Kentucky, now that I think about it. More grass and trees than you could imagine. It's quiet, peaceful. They're on a train line, so I don't even need a car to get there."

"That's sweet."

There's a peacefulness that comes over him when he talks about home, and a light smile. "It's actually where I grew up. We moved closer to London for Mum's work, but she can work from home now, so it's not as big of a deal. So they're all back there, in that quaint little town outside of Leeds. All but me."

We make our way to the boardwalk, and I look out toward the pier. We don't seem to have any plan for this trip, and for once, not having a plan feels amazing. Pierce and I haven't had much time to talk—like, *really* talk.

As we walk, we bypass the arcade and carnival games. I pull him close to me when a cool breeze picks up.

"Do you want to move back to Leeds someday?"

"Yes, probably. In my dream world, I'd like to work in London, play for the Pops or something and commute in on the train, and live a quiet life in the countryside."

"That sounds nice." I can't stop myself from thinking about how it might look, the two of us following the same path, living together outside the city. It's a long way off, but I can almost grasp it.

He clears his throat. "That all you got?"

I'm comfortable with him. But I don't think I'm comfortable enough to ask him the thing I really want to know about him. Especially when I can't piss him off too much, as I'm miles

and miles from London and that'd be one hell of an awkward
car ride if he just broke it off because I asked too much.

This is dumb.

We lean against the railing near the edge of the pier, and I
take his hand.

"What happened with you and Colin this summer? I need
to know your side of things if I'm ever going to get out of my
head about it."

He sighs. "I knew she'd tell you."

"Sophie did, but she only wanted to protect me, and Colin
was her friend, and he played that awful recital—"

"You think I don't know that? Everyone blamed me for that
disaster. But"—he clears his throat—"Colin and I had issues.
Our relationship was a whirlwind—no, it was a *cyclone*. He was
codependent to a fault, and I don't operate that way."

I release his hand.

"Love, not like that." He lightly takes my hand back. "He
needed more from me than I could give, especially right after
starting at the academy."

"That's vague. What did he need?" What if I need the same
things?

"Babe, I could go on for the rest of the night about his needs.
We were only together maybe three weeks, but he wanted a
husband, like, yesterday. He wanted to go out and be seen
together all the time, and if I stayed in to practice or something, he would flip out."

He walks over to the other side of the pier, and I follow. He
stares out at the water and the shore like some forlorn sailor

from a literary novel. His shoulders are hunched, and I hate making him feel this way. I gently rub his back with my palm.

"Sorry," I say. "Didn't mean to, you know. Start this."

"Do you know what scares me most about being with you?"

I pull back, and he turns to me.

"You're different from Colin," he says. "But the circumstances are the same—no, they're worse. All of your dreams lie in London. You're a hell of an oboist, and I know you'll get a gig soon enough. You emote better than anyone else I've seen, which, as I've been told, is not something I can just learn."

I shrug and back away.

"Please, stop cowering like that every time you get a compliment. If you want to hold your own here, you *must* realize how great you are."

"I'm *fine*." I throw my hands up in the air. "I mean, the last video I made for my portfolio is basically useless. So painful to watch—I missed so many notes."

"I'll tell you something that Baverstock tells me every week." His voice drops. "Music's not about hitting all the right notes. It's about causing a reaction, showing emotion."

"That's a compliment."

"That's not how he means it," he says. "*I* hit all the right notes. I can play higher and finger faster than any trumpet out there, but I'm struggling in this school. Last week, Baverstock called me a marching band dropout. But I'm sure Sophie told you all about that."

"Hey," I say. I grip his shoulders and pull him closer to me. "She didn't tell me this—she's not like that. She wants to protect me from going down the same path as Colin. But that won't be me. And as for you." I kiss him between breaths. "I've felt your emotion. You're an earthquake of emotion, babe, and I know you can find a way to get more of it into your playing."

"I don't think I want to play our piece for the end-of-term recitals," he says.

I pull back. "Oh, okay?"

"No, not like that." He runs his hands through his hair. "I think we should move it forward. Like, do it for one of the Friday recitals. I'm on the schedule in two weeks—I know it's tight, but I feel this whole career slipping out of my hands."

"I can do it," I say. Though my primary incentive for doing it really just went out the window. I've been to a couple of these performances, and certainly no scouts are there. But if it'll help Pierce, I have to do it.

He kisses my cheek. "Thank you, Marty."

After our walk along the pier and the rocky beach, we find ourselves back on the streets of Brighton. Pierce stopped to get iced coffee in a café, one of the three million that line the streets here. And we sit down at dinner, organic and vegan in true Brighton fashion.

I'm still feeling vulnerable after opening up in our earlier conversation, so I continue to lighten the mood with some less divisive get-to-know-you questions.

"What's your favorite trumpet piece?"

"Easy," he says, "Haydn's Trumpet Concerto. It works so well with the rest of the orchestra, and it's technically intense.

It takes major trumpet chops. I always had this idea that I'd show I could play it in some solo performance, and they'd have the whole orchestra play it and give me the solo."

"Wild and crazy fantasies over there."

He kicks me under the table. "Stop your cheekiness right now."

After we're done eating, his phone buzzes on the table, and he steps outside to take the call.

Our waitress stops by the table with the check, and I hand her some cash.

"Oh, was something wrong with your food?" she asks, seeing that I've barely touched it.

I shake my head. "No, it was great. I ate before I came," I say, though in actuality, I had a banana for breakfast and nothing until right now. "Could you bring me a box?"

Wasting food makes me feel uncomfortable. But eating food makes me uncomfortable. I fully plan to "forget" my box here. That way, the waitress will judge my forgetfulness, not my disregard for the hungry. A few minutes later, Pierce comes back in, visibly shaken. He's clenching his fists as he approaches the table. The mood changes. He looks at the table, sighs.

"I should have told you, my friend here—the one we were supposed to stay with?—he's a total flake. He told me we could stay, then just called to say he's actually in Canterbury for the night with his mates. I gave him a fucking earful, but I don't even think he cared. People are the worst."

I place my hand on his, in an attempt to calm him.

Though I'm a bit freaked—I can't miss my FaceTime call

with Megan and Skye. Not again. It's somehow already ten at night here, so I've got two and a half hours to be somewhere with Wi-Fi.

But we can figure it out. It will be fine.

I hope.

"Sorry your friend's the worst. What are our options?"

"It's too late notice to look for an Airbnb. We could get a hotel, but that'd be a couple hundred pounds this time of year. I don't know about you, but I can't swing that."

I pretend to do the math in my head, but I know that would take about a third of my remaining funds, and I still have no source of income on the horizon.

"I don't know. That's a lot of money. You don't know anyone else here?"

"Do you?"

I slap his arm. "Don't get fresh with me."

"Did you just slip into nineties lingo?"

"I don't know," I say. "Sometimes my dad says things so often I think they're phrases people still use today."

"That's wack."

"We don't have time for this," I say, with a hard eye roll. "I hate to suggest this, but any way we can make it back to London by twelve thirty?"

He lets his head drop to the table. His muffled voice breaks through. "It's our only choice, though, innit?"

I give the back of his head a scratch, because it feels right. It feels like what a boyfriend would do right now. Then I pull out my phone and try to find Wi-Fi. After a few unsuccessful attempts—why is your internet unlocked if you're still going to ask for a damn password? answer me that, restaurants—I find one that connects. The signal's weak, but I can tell it works when a couple of emails and texts come in.

I type out an email to Megan and Skye.

Hi guys,

Pierce (yes that guy) and I were going to FaceTime from Brighton (which must be the gayest city in the UK) but our lodging plans fell through, and we need to go back to London. Might be late.

Marty

I take a deep breath and slide my phone in my pocket. The panicking side of me is always there, looming in the shadows. And that side is telling me to worry. That the car will comically break down or we'll get stuck in traffic and I'll never make it. My brain races for backup plans, but there aren't many to be found.

As Pierce walks us toward the car, he places a palm on the small of my back. I look to him, but his gaze remains forward. His confident stride throws me off. It's like he refuses to acknowledge that our plans have changed, or that anything is up in the air. It also comforts me, and his calming presence tells me everything's going to be fine.

I take one last look at the lights of the city and realize this is the first time I've ever gone on a trip with a guy I liked, even as short as it was.

It's the first time I've ever confidently walked through streets while publicly showing off the relationship I was in. Everything about this day was freeing, even learning more about his experience with Colin, and how he never wants to hurt me like that.

I know that if I worry too much about the drive or running late for the call, I could end up ruining this sweet moment. It's all kind of perfect, even with today's many imperfections.

"This is a beautiful city," I say softly.

"Made even more beautiful by your presence." He nudges me with his shoulder, then breaks into laughter. "Ah, sorry, mate, that sounded much smoother in my head."

I laugh too, and that's when I realize that for all the ups and downs this short trip had to offer, I don't think I've ever been happier.

TWENTY-THREE

I START FREAKING OUT once we hit traffic, but then I see that Pierce has got a smile on his face. While I had a good day too, I feel the need to express exactly how important this call is.

"I'm starting to panic," I say. It's been an hour and a half, and we're about halfway there. "The thing you should know about Megan is she's fucking vengeful for a best friend. Like, me and Skye have always been there for her, but she straight up doesn't deal with drama. She ends friendships like it's her job, her calling."

"If she hasn't ended yours yet, she's not going to do it because you miss one stupid call."

"It's two stupid calls!" I run both hands through my hair, which is still windblown from the walk on the pier. "I was gallivanting with you in Cardiff last time and completely forgot to call them. She was pissed. This is how I was supposed to make it up."

"Add 'gallivanting' to the list of words people don't use any-more." He chuckles. "And what is this thing with Fridays? Was this something special for you?"

The traffic eases up, and we fly through a roundabout. I've no idea what the speed limit is, but he's over it.

"We went to this small school, and a few people we knew would throw these bonfires every Friday in the summer. It felt like everyone was invited but us, and we always felt left out. Like, we spent years not getting invited to this thing, but as we got older and people cared less about being cliquey, they started inviting us. But Megan would always make a big show that she couldn't come, that we always had plans. So I guess that's where it stemmed from. Kind of silly, but that's us."

"You didn't mind not going to those parties?" he asks, and I almost laugh.

"They were huge. At least, that's what the pictures made it seem like. Chaotic. Loud. Kind of like those pep rallies we had to attend in school to cheer for whatever football game our team was playing. I wanted to avoid it. I liked hanging out with Megan and Skye anyway. It was so much more chill. More . . ."

"Safe?" he finishes. And in one moment I realize that for all his faults, he really does get me on some level. He knows what triggers my anxiety; he knows my response.

I see him shake his head in the light of other cars. It got dark quickly, but it's peaceful out here. I can't see the stars, but you'd almost confuse this with a country road in Kentucky. That is, if we didn't go through traffic circles every few kilometers and if we weren't on the completely wrong side of the road. Okay, it's a little different.

He reaches into the glove compartment above my lap.

"I was going to give this to you tonight, but I think you should have it now, since you're in a right state."

I take the envelope from his hands, and I pull out a thick piece of paper. I use my phone to see it, and when the light shines on it, my heart rate doubles. It's a ticket. A ticket with my name on it. I scan the details frantically.

"Florence, love. Well, that ticket's for Pisa first, but we'll take the train to Florence, then find our way to Siena."

I melt when he says "love," and I'm a puddle by the time he says "Siena." "Why is my name on this?"

"Usually you need your name on tickets when you try to use them. Or, if you want the actual answer, I was kind enough to have Shane steal your passport so I could get these for you."

"I'm going to Florence? You're *taking* me to Florence?"

"You're catching on. I talked with Dani and Ajay, and convinced them we could use a Tuscany trip next month. I for one definitely need this. A light week of classes, followed by a lovely weekend with . . ." He pauses. "My boyfriend?"

I didn't think he could top the flight. And with one word, he's topped it with a label I've wanted to have attached to me for years. I've wanted a boyfriend ever since I could remember, but I've never allowed myself to feel like this.

But Pierce isn't like anyone else. He's not your run-of-the-mill high school boy. He's not a super-cool, established man.

He's somewhere in between. And that's where I'll meet him, somewhere in the in-between.

"It sounds like you're being presumptive." My gut lifts in my stomach as I talk. I feel weightless. I feel at ease. "But if you're asking, yes. Yes, I'll be your boyfriend."

I take his hand, and he stares straight ahead. The smile never leaves his face. Nor mine.

We make good time for the rest of the trip. I'm late. Later than I thought, but as we come into London, my chest eases, and for the first time I think, *I'm coming home.* About a place that isn't Kentucky.

"Shit," I shout as the realization hits me. "I should have told Shane I was coming back. Is it weird to just barge in? He could have someone over."

"Or I could have someone over tonight." He pauses. "You, I mean. That was an odd way to say it."

I say nothing.

"Do you want to stay with me tonight?"

I smile. "I do. As long as I can use your Wi-Fi to call Megan."

It's a weird feeling, going to someone's apartment for the first time. Wales was fun, but it was neutral territory. So far outside our normal lives that it felt incredibly normal to share a bed—I mean, if I hadn't, I'd have shared with Sophie. So I might as well sleep with someone I can spoon.

We take the elevator to the fourth floor, and walk through the hall to get to his door.

I'm immediately jealous of his flat. It's not huge, but it's all his. It smells of tea and him. The kitchen's spotless, and I don't know if that's because he never cooks or he's just a neat freak. He takes me on a tour of the flat, from living room to bedroom (and nothing in between), and sits on the couch. I take a seat next to him, and he hands me a card with the overly complicated Wi-Fi code on it.

I type it in, and the anxiety levels start to increase. She's going to be pissed. But if I can just get her on the call, I can explain. She'll understand. She'll have to behave if Pierce is on the screen anyway.

The phone connects. I stop breathing. I wait for the hate mail to show up. But nothing does.

I breathe a sigh of relief.

But then I get a call. On the app that gives me free calls over Wi-Fi. I only gave my number to a handful of people—the ones who didn't have iPhones and couldn't FaceTime, basically—but the app doesn't search my contacts for the number, and who memorizes phone numbers? So I answer it.

"Hello?"

I'm greeted with cheers and music and yelling.

"Finally. Um, hey," Skye says. I can barely hear him over the commotion in the background. "You made it back."

"Yeah, Skye, I'm so sorry. Should I FaceTime Megan now or—what's that noise?"

Over it all, I hear his breaths. They're panted, uneven. "I, um. It's not. Well, we're at the bonfire."

"Megan? At a party?"

This is a first. I should be impressed, but I'm unsettled.

"Why are you calling me? Isn't this using your data?"

"It's worth it. I needed to talk to you about this." He sighs; the crackling of the fire takes over my phone.

I stand and pace the floor. I bite my lip. I want him to spit it out, but I can't force him. That won't help.

"Is she pissed at me?"

"More than that. I literally don't know how to say this to you. Fuck."

"Skye." My voice is as solid as I can make it. I know Skye doesn't say "fuck." "What's going on?"

"You're not out to everyone, right? Like, this is still something we don't talk about, right? Because Megan, like, she dragged me to the bonfire. And she keeps chatting with people, and, like, they're like, 'Hey why are you here? You hate this shit.'" He's repeating himself, throwing around the word *like* to delay it as long as he can. I need him to get to the point, or else my grip on the phone might break it. "And she keeps responding that she had plans to video chat with you, but you're too . . ."

He stops.

"Fuck." Fuck. "Say it."

". . . busy with your boyfriend to give her the time of day anymore. She's said it to, like, ten people. I keep trying to stop her, but I literally can't."

So this is bad. This is bad, and I'm sinking to my knees and

I'm on the ground. Sitting. Pierce is coming over, and I think I dropped the phone because Skye's still talking but it's too far away for me to make out what he's saying and I shut down I shut the fuck down because what else do I do here no I am actually asking what the fuck do I . . .

TWENTY-FOUR

"MARTY."

Headache. Pounding headache. It's fuzzy in here.

"Marty."

That's definitely my name. But who's saying it? Are my eyes open? "Ugh," I grunt.

My eyelids peel apart and light floods my pupils. I'm lying back on a bed, head resting against a soft pillow with something cold on my head. Pierce appears in my vision, and when he picks up the dripping rag from my forehead, water hits my face.

"What happened?"

He leans in, cups my face with his hand, and plants a kiss on my dry lips. His hands stay there. His lips stay too. When he pulls away, I see the creases in his expression, the glossiness in his eyes.

"You passed out. Scared the fuck out of me, Mart."

I groan. "People actually do that? I thought fainting was just in the movies. Why did I—"

The call. Skye's voice.

Megan.

The bonfire.

My whole constructed world falling apart.

"Oh."

"Mm-hmm," Pierce mumbles. "I talked to Skye about it once you dropped your phone—he was freaked too, but I let him know you're alive. I can't believe she did that to you. I thought she was your friend. Your *best* friend."

"I don't know." And I really don't. "Megan's view of right and wrong is warped. Once there's bad blood with someone, I've seen her justify about anything."

He laughs drily. "She has her own narrative about what happened. I've never heard someone so delusional."

"How would you know that?" I ask.

"Your mate, Skye, kept saying he tried to stop her. But sounds like he was a bit of a pushover—he was scared of her, like you."

"I'm not—"

He holds a finger to my lips. "She controlled you, she used your anxiety against you, both you and Skye are terrified of her. But I'm not."

A sourness hits my stomach, and I know he's right.

"I didn't want to overstep, but I made Skye give her the phone and informed her that outing someone was an assault, that she was putting you in danger, and that she could be in legal trouble. I said I'd be getting an advocate on the phone on Monday. I think she knew I was pulling all of this out of thin air, but she stopped."

"The damage was already done," I say, bringing him into a hug. "But thank you for fighting for me."

My emotions are one big jumble. I'm angry, defeated, and almost broken, but my home here has softened the blow. It's giving me hope that one day I can return to Kentucky, fully out, without caring what people think. I can *almost* see that Marty.

"Do you think your parents will find out?" he asks.

I give a shallow laugh. "I'm out, Pierce. I actually told my parents first, then Megan. But no one there needed to know, you know? There are only a handful of people I trust there, and even so, you never know if they're a cool, respectful person in the streets, but—I don't know—go to Klan meetings at night?"

"That's still a thing?"

"Unfortunately, yes. Point is, I didn't tell them because I wanted to be able to go back without being the news. I hate knowing that, right now, people are talking about it. Me living in London was one thing people will never understand, but this is another thing. This is how they define people over there. I liked being the guy who stayed in the background, played the hell out of his oboe, then moved abroad to pursue a better life than they could comprehend. Now it's all tainted."

He drops the rag on the floor and crawls into bed with me. Not in a predatory way, not in a sexual way. But in a way that shows me he's there for me, curled up against my side and pressing his lips into my neck. His arm wraps around me, and I let it. I want to stay like this until I feel better. Until the pieces of me are whole again.

I'm out. It's obviously not been easy, but my sexuality is *my* thing. It's my *life*, and I should get to choose what "out" means and who gets to know. I take a look at my phone, and see two or three iMessages have popped up. Already.

None of them are bad. None of them are reminders that I'm going to hell or anything melodramatic. One is supportive, the others ask if it's true. Most start with "I was just talking to Megan," which means Skye was definitely telling the truth.

"Hey," Pierce says. I watch him slowly come into focus. "Who cares what they think? You're thousands of miles away."

"One guy came out a couple years ago, when I was a fresh-man. Most people were great to him. Like, *overly* great." I shake my head. "Telling him how brave he was for being gay—whatever that means—or showing their support by telling him how many queer people they knew. He became a novelty. A caricature of himself. He wasn't the tennis star or the great actor. He was the gay kid."

Pierce laughs, then grabs my hand quickly. "Sorry, that reminds me. When I told people, my mates suddenly started asking me for fashion tips. People are awful. They don't think."

I take a breath, and hold it. My lungs ache, but after a few seconds, the pressure eases.

It's only been a couple of months since I graduated, but I can barely remember what it felt like to walk those halls again. To see the same teachers, the same students. Ducking my head into my locker to breathe when the crowds rushing to class were too loud, too chaotic.

"This was *my* thing to tell or not tell," I say. "And I guess . . . well, I wanted to disappear. And she took that away from me."

My list of friends has always been small, manageable. Until this month, the newest addition to my friends list was Skye, but that was years ago. I imagine Megan, Shane, and Skye's names on a list, followed by Pierce, Sophie, Sang, Dani, and Ajay. But that name at the top, shining bright, just got a big X drawn straight through it.

"Now I'm the gay kid," I whisper.

He plants a soft kiss on my hand. "What kid do you want to be? The oboe guy? The London one? I'll call you whatever you want."

A hint of a smile tugs at my lips. "Just call me Marty."

TWENTY-FIVE

THE NEXT DAY IS a blur. I've made it back to my apartment and given the edited—non-passing-out—version of what happened to Shane, but I haven't gotten the courage to email Megan. I don't even know if it's my place to do this. It's not exactly something you can google and find the proper way to respond when a friend goes off the deep end. But all of our good memories keep coming back to me. Late night Waffle House runs, gas station cappuccinos before school, and that one time we decided we were going to be really good at tennis, before we realized she couldn't control her backhand and I couldn't serve to save my life.

But there are bad memories too. She teased me relentlessly in middle school. Called me a fag (but she called everyone that) and told everyone my head was firmly up the teacher's ass. Word for word, she said that. At twelve. I wonder what made me friends with her in the first place. Was it out of necessity? Did we actually work?

I'm still in bed—I'm always in bed—when I hear voices in the living room. It almost makes me want to go see who Shane invited over. Almost.

I've never been through a breakup, but I'd imagine this is what it feels like. Megan and I kind of worked. She brought me out of my shell. Our demise weighs heavily on my chest, but I'm not friendless. I'm not alone. I can ignore the emails from my acquaintances in Kentucky, and wait for it all to blow over.

I'm hurt, but I'm not broken.

I tap out a quick text to Pierce.

Thanks for everything last night. Glad I can call you my boyfriend officially.

Sophie opens the door and walks into my room. She gives me a look that borders on pity, but there's some fire there that I haven't seen before. Shane seems defeated, and he takes a seat in the chair opposite my bed.

A tapping rhythm sounds from the window by my bed. Rain. I've learned that midsummer in London can be one big puddle. Always raining, heavily enough to make you wet but light enough that it blows around everywhere, rendering umbrellas useless. Sophie's holding a rain jacket in her hands.

"You okay?" I ask.

She shakes her head.

A weird pain settles in my gut, and it's not hunger this time.

I want to make her feel better, and I want to find out what's wrong. Because, what if I'm the reason? I can't lose my two best friends in twelve hours.

"I should be asking *you* that," she finally says.

"Talk to me."

"I don't know how."

"What does that mean?" I ask.

"It means . . . god, Marty. You've fucked up right nice, you know that?"

"Soph," Shane warns.

"I *what*? What are you talking about?"

She paces the room, and I hang my legs off the side of the bed.

"I don't even know which one to start with, mate. Actually, both of them start the same way: I talked to Pierce today."

"Shit." My chest seizes with fear. "Did he tell you I told him about what you said about Colin? It was important. I needed to know—"

"Mart. It's not that. Good on you for calling him out. But he told me what happened with your friend, and that you passed out in his apartment."

Shane clears his throat. "You passed out? You didn't tell me that—I shouldn't be hearing this about my cousin thirdhand."

"It was a bit melodramatic, I guess."

"You think? Marty . . . do you know why you passed out?" Sophie folds her arms and drapes her rain jacket over an arm. She stares straight ahead, out the window. "I need to know if you even get it."

"I mean, I was so stressed after hearing what Megan did, I guess I just lost it, I don't know. That happens, I guess."

"Unless you have a medical condition, that doesn't happen, outside of, like, films and shit. Tell me what you ate that day, because Pierce said you didn't even touch your dinner."

"I had a few bites."

"And the last time you ate before that?"

"What are you getting at? I'm on a fucking diet, Sophie, I'm overweight."

"You are *fine* how you are, but that's not even the point. That's not a diet. When'd you eat before that? Did you eat at all yesterday?"

"I had a couple things," I say. Though I know it was only one banana. And I skipped dinner the night before too. Did I eat on Wednesday? I had a snack, at least. "This isn't why I passed out."

"It's sure as hell a part of it."

"Fuck," Shane says, "I watched this happen too, and I didn't stop it. I was so worried about being too overprotective like everyone apparently thinks I am, so I just watched. This is my fault."

"It's not your fault," I say. "Nothing even happened. You two think I'm anorexic? Do I look anorexic?"

"I'm not here to diagnose you, Marty," Sophie says. "I'm here to point out that if you try to exist off of a tablespoon of food per day, you will pass out, you will hurt yourself, and you will eventually cause damage you can't reverse."

"I know what I'm doing."

"You really don't." She laughs. She freaking laughs in my face.

"I'll stop when I'm at my goal weight," I say.

"What's your goal weight?" Shane asks in a serious tone. "When you magically feel good about your body?"

Sophie chimes in. "When you start to see your rib cage? Please tell us, so we can point out how this is a slippery slope."

"It's working," I say. "I've lost ten pounds this week."

"You *what*?" Shane interjects.

"I don't even know what that means in kilograms," Sophie says as she shakes her head, "but I bet it's more than you should safely lose in a week."

I'm almost out of the overweight BMI. I lose weight every day. I see the numbers going down. This is literally all that matters, and passing out once means nothing. But I don't say this out loud. I'm too angry, and she wouldn't get it.

"Is it because of Pierce?"

"Well, hey, I lost weight and now he's my boyfriend."

I cringe at my own words. That's not how I meant to say it, even if those words are true.

"He's your *what*? He left that out of last night's recap."

I stand up and pace around her. She's infuriating me; she's bullying me like Megan did. She's so wrong.

"Look," I say. "Is there a point to this? I'll make sure I don't pass out next time another best friend turns on me. I seem to be holding it together just fine right now."

"I'm looking out for you, Marty. If you're not going to take care of yourself, someone ought to." She sighs. "And if Pierce is pressuring you to stop eating, or drop weight to be with him, then he can't help you. Boyfriend or not."

I fall back onto the bed. I want to defend Pierce. I want to explain that sure, I might be dieting because of him, but it's not like he's making me do it. Actually, he hasn't said anything to me about my weight, or my eating. Just about his own. Loudly and in front of me, but not *at* me.

"This is my thing," I finally say. "Pierce isn't pressuring me to do anything."

"But you've started checking nutrition labels, just like he does." Shane scratches his head. "You actually *say* some of the same things. Like at dinner a couple nights ago? '*I can't believe this meal has more than half the sodium I'm supposed to consume in a day.*' Like, that's fine if you want to eat healthier, but what you're doing isn't healthy."

"There are people who will look the other way when their friends make bad choices." Sophie glares at Shane. "But I sure as hell am not that person. I don't know how to get through to you. But while I'm on the topic, guess what Pierce announced to the whole class? That you were performing a duet in *two weeks*."

"So?"

"It would take me days to unpack why that's a bad idea. One, Pierce is a flaky fuck with a track record that doesn't speak well of him. But you know that." She hisses a sigh through her teeth. "Two, he's not a good musician. He's a savant in Music History, but you should hear him play—he's so unenthused it's like he's running through the motions. You can't cover up being a boring musician here with a sunny personality and get away with it. Do you know why he wants to do the recital with you?"

"Because he likes me."

"As an oboist!"

Frustration builds within me. I stand up again. "As a boy-friend! As a human being!"

Shane fidgets in his chair, but he doesn't leave.

"I don't think that's true," she says. Her voice is soft, and she looks at her hands. "If you really thought he liked you for you, it wouldn't be like this. You wouldn't be crash dieting like this. You shouldn't feel like you have to hurt yourself to make someone like you."

I say nothing. The rain picks up outside, and Sophie puts on her jacket.

"I've got to go," she says. "This—all of this—is a waste of time. Whether you get taken out in a stretcher, or run away after your inevitable fight with Pierce, or whatever. I can't get close to another person just to have them disappear again. This school is hard enough with Rio going for my blood. I need to make a real friend, and I need to protect myself." She walks away. I almost don't hear her. But I do, and it's a line I'll never forget.

"Good luck with the move back to Kentucky."

TWENTY-SIX

PIERCE STILL HASN'T RESPONDED to my text.

But I need him.

I text him again.

What are you doing?

Then,

Had a fight with Sophie.

I take a walk with Shane, and we find a bench where we can just sit in the rain, even though we're pretty much soaked through at this point.

"Can we talk about anything?" I ask. "Anything that isn't about you-know-who?"

"Well, I'm not sure this is a great time to announce this, but I . . . I got it."

I gasp. "You *what*?"

"You're looking at *Les Mis*'s new fourth horn. I found out just after you left."

"Congrats, Shane," I say. "That's really great."

I should feel more jealous, but I know I haven't put in the effort I should have. The reed I made when I got here is starting to split down the middle, and I haven't even found time to make a new one. The last time I practiced, there was a light buzzing that wouldn't go away.

I've been expanding my portfolio, but I haven't been following through on anything else. I haven't looked for jobs—but it's hard for me to do that when I'm playing in the park with Sang or exploring Europe with my new friends.

But that *is* special and important.

I've never had a large group of friends or a boyfriend, and I never get to play in these pickup ensembles where we just enjoy music together. But maybe I've focused too much on that lately.

"I'd have to quit my bookshop job," Shane continues, "but that's fine with me. I can always try and get you an interview there if you want—it's a great job, and it's super flexible."

"It doesn't seem like it. I mean, you never get to hang out with the group anymore; you missed the last group jam session because of it. Seems like it gets in the way a lot."

A pause. Then he takes a breath.

"So, that's the other thing. I've kind of been seeing

someone. And we've been having so much fun we didn't want to jinx it by telling people. But I think we're going to start telling people soon. So I want you to be the first to know."

I cover my mouth with my hands. "Oh god, it's Sang, isn't it?"

"Ding-ding-ding." He runs his hand through his hair, causing a halo of mist to surround his head. "We seem to be an item."

Shane accentuates his point by eventually leaving to go meet up with him, and I ask him to pass along a hug to Sang.

I get the feeling I should kick it into gear. That I need to make a change, soon, if I want things to work out my way. If I don't want to get my ass kicked back to Kentucky, quickly. But my mind's caught up with Megan, with Sophie, with Shane, and with Pierce—especially our forthcoming recital. I worry about his playing—I've never actually heard him play on his own. All I know is he admits he struggles. Sophie said he struggled. And he's still playing third trumpet.

But is bringing someone up so wrong? And maybe with my help, we can blow everyone away.

Both of us.

"Boyfriend." I try out the word again on my tongue, but it doesn't feel real. "Boyfriend."

My stomach growls. And I can't deny Sophie has a point. I press into my gut to quiet the sound. It's starting to be embarrassing—people give me that look when it happens in public. It used to be a funny smile, but they've since darkened into real concern. Does everyone know what I'm doing to myself? Do I even know?

My phone vibrates as I head back to the apartment. It's Pierce. The tension releases, until I read it.

On a train to Leeds to visit Mum for a family do. Sorry about Sophie.

And,

Let's run through the recital piece when I get back.

Before I can truly react, my finger holds down the power button until the screen goes black. Fire lives and breathes within me. My steps echo against the brick walls of the bridge. I've turned away from the park, away from the flat. I keep walking, and I wish I brought headphones or something to drown out the city. I need to facilitate an escape.

An escape from my escape.

Everything feels like it's falling apart, and the universe is definitely giving me a sign. Shane told Sang the universe is wrong, but what does he know? Pierce is gone when I need him, and is already showing how greedy he is about the recital.

Or maybe I'm reading too far into it, thanks to Sophie.

I keep walking, for ten minutes. Twenty. Longer. I follow the same road north, until I see tourists starting to gather up ahead.

Suddenly I'm on the Beatles cover. Abbey Road. *The* Abbey Road with the iconic crosswalks and the tourists lined up to take their walking picture. I lean against the brick wall surrounding a nearby residence from the chaos, and I'm in perfect view of the crosswalk.

And I study them.

Here's the thing about Abbey Road. It's a real road. With cars that get really pissed by the pedestrians blocking the way. I snap a picture—not that I want to remember this moment, but I want to remember this place. The anger of the drivers and the obliviousness of the tourists.

I sit on a bench across from Abbey Road Studios and watch the never-ending flow of people and cars, joy and frustration. A woman starts playing "Hey Jude" on the guitar nearby, though no one is paying much attention to her.

But I am. Her vocals lull me into a sort of trance, until my lips perk up into an attempt at a smile. Anytime I'm too low, music can pull me back, and it reminds me why I'm here in the first place.

Moping isn't helping. Worrying isn't helping.

I have to pull myself out of the darkness.

TWENTY-SEVEN

"SOPHIE WAS TRYING TO make a point, I believe." Shane leans against the wall of his bedroom. "She wants you to bounce back. To be a stronger advocate for yourself, you know?"

"I don't think I can. I don't know what this is, this haze that's fallen over me."

"You could eat." He tosses me a bag of crisps. "I didn't want to admit it at first, and I don't know how to talk to you about it. But I do worry about you sometimes. Your eyes glaze over and you hold your stomach. Plus, you sleep all the time. How many naps does one guy need?"

I pull both ends of the bag. It opens.

The tang of barbecue crisps hits my nose. I stare at them. Turning the bag over, I read the calorie information. I don't know if I should.

He rolls his eyes. "Eat. You're not doing yourself any favors."

I want to end this . . . crash dieting. But I can already feel

Pierce slipping away. He's barely been in contact this week, and I wonder if maybe it was all too much for him. If *I* was too much for him.

But we've got our trip to Florence soon, then our recital after that, and if I can drop another ten or so pounds, I'll be closer to my goal.

Though I still don't know what my goal is.

"I'll have a few," I say. And I put two in my mouth.

Two becomes four, which becomes half the bag. He watches me eat like I'm some sideshow act. I quickly fold the bag and put it to the side. No more of that, for now.

The weird thing about having a roommate is that for your entire roommateship, you've got one open-ended conversation going. He's there when you wake and when you sleep, and all the hours in between. He's there practicing for his new job while you're watching a movie. And your trains of thought can travel on, day by day, an ebb and flow that never seems to end.

It's been a full week since Sophie first brought it up, and he's finally talking about it. He'll bring this up again, but for now, I turn away. To my computer. To the phone in my hand.

My fingers type the numbers I know by heart. The *only* number I know by heart that isn't my home landline.

And it belongs to someone who fucking wrecked me.

Skye's texted intermittently over the last few days, but he's got no answers.

It would be so easy to cut her out of my life, but I can't. I can't recede into my turtle shell and wait for this to blow over, because I know it never will. I need a resolution—some kind of resolution to keep me going here.

"Hi." I clear my throat to lower my voice, which echoes back to me. "Take me off Bluetooth."

"Yes, sir. I can't believe you're actually calling me. Is this a confrontation?"

"I thought it was about time," I say. "I don't know where to start."

"How about starting at the point in time you got too good for us."

Is Skye there too?

"Megan, do you want to know the truth? I think that was ages ago. Years. Before we were even friends." I choke back a tear. "I've always felt like a bad fit for the life I was given."

"Because you were *gay*?"

"Yeah. In a state where half the people there would prefer I just die than be myself, it's either you make yourself feel superior or you let them make you feel inferior. There's no in between."

"Well, great news. I'm giving you fucking wings, Mart. You're on your own. I'm done holding your hand, and it's clear you *think* you can function just fine without me. So I kicked you out of the nest."

"And waited for me to splat all over the pavement."

She laughs. "And you did splat, didn't you? God, I hate knowing you so well, I really do. I was just telling Skye—"

"Keep me out of this," he says. "This is your thing. You crossed lines."

"Skye, please. I told you what I was going to do; you still came to the bonfire with me."

"I didn't think you'd actually do it!"

"Skye!" I say. "She told you I was gay, even when I didn't want her to. What makes you think she'd be bluffing about outing me to everyone else?"

My hands grip the throw pillow by my side. Shane's quickly gathering things to leave the room. Living in the same apartment may be one open conversation, but he's ending it now, and I don't blame him.

Skye's silent. Megan's silent. I'm silent.

The door clicks as Shane enters his bedroom, and I grit my teeth.

"Megan," I say. To make the conversation more serious. "I didn't know where I wanted this to go, but I do now. I'm sorry I was running thirty minutes late on a call and you took that as me blowing you off for my boyfriend, which you said menacingly, but for your information, he is officially my boyfriend. But I'm sorry about a lot of things. I'm sorry I never stood up to you, and gave you this perverse superiority, where you think you can control what happens in my life. You were always pissed I told my parents first, and you next, so I'm sorry for that. Because really, you should have been the last one I told. Because every single memory about me coming out is tied to you. How you claimed you always knew. How you started quizzing whether or not every guy in my vision was hot. How you felt you needed to push me further and further out of the closet, like that was the thing holding me back."

I stop, and give her one last chance to interject.

"There was one thing holding me back from being myself, and you know who that was?"

She scoffs. "I can guess."

"You." I let the word sing out. "I think we're done here."

"I think we were done a long time ago."

TWENTY-EIGHT

THE ONLY THING I regret, days after my fight with Megan, is this:

I let her have the last word.

She's a debater at heart, and she knows how to flip the subject over and attack the jugular. She's not one you battle in words (or with fists either; she's got the strength of an MMA fighter), but I held my own.

I said what I needed to, which I've never done before.

Beyond that, I'm looking at the positives: I leave for Florence in two days, and today's the first day I get to see Pierce since I passed out, since he got stuck in Leeds longer than he planned and we never got to have that practice session. I'm still losing weight, but I'm eating more, if for no other reason than to not pass out. I still feel funny sometimes, but when I do, I take a nap. And naps fix all things.

Right now, I'm just getting back to the flat after an especially distracting practice session. But when I stop to check mail on my way up, I see a package. I take it in my hands, and glance at the label from the bottom up.

It's from America. Kentucky.

The address isn't my mom's.

My hands start shaking, to the point where the contents of the box start shaking too.

I take large steps to the apartment. The thudding of the contents of the box matches my heartbeat. I fling open the door and set the box and my oboe case down on the coffee table. Then I back away from it.

Shane jumps up. "What are you doing?"

"She really got the last word."

"What?"

I snap out of it. "Sorry. Megan." I gesture to the couch, where I made the call that ended our friendship. "She sent me something."

He bounces on the front of his bare feet, looking between me and the box.

"Are you going to—"

"I don't know!"

"Avoiding it won't stop—"

"I know!"

"Then open it!"

I sigh. "Fine."

Shane darts into the kitchen and brings back a butter knife. I ignore the bits of curry and lamb on the serrated bits. (I can only identify this because it was our dinner last night.) I cut into the tiger print duct tape, and the anticipation builds in my chest with every pull of the knife.

I open the flaps, one by one, delaying the process as long as I can.

It's a scrapbook. A red bound folder with a picture in the center. The picture is one I haven't seen in years. It's of our middle school homecoming dance. It's the first picture of all three of us.

"Wait, is that you?" Shane asks. "And her?"

I laugh. "Megan and *Skye* went to this dance together, which was the extent of their dating life. I wasn't friends with either of them yet. I'm that guy in the background with his mouth hanging open and looking surprised at the flash."

"How photogenic you are. Why did she send this? Is she sorry?"

"It takes over a week for mail to come here." I pick up the scrapbook and run my hand across the fabric. "She sent it before our fight."

I open it up.

The first page is a letter:

Happy Valentine's Day, BITCH.

Okay, that was harsh.

Okay, it's July. But it takes a few months for packages to go overseas. Or was that the Mayflower? You answer that—you're the H.S. graduate, not me.

Truth is I didn't really know what to make of my utter need to scrapbook. Here are some memories of us from my iPhone.

I could have done this online and saved a lot of time. But my
mom likes to scrapbook a lot and she bought me all of these
things from some Etsy store, so here you go.
    With all the love in my heart . . . BITCH.
               Megan

If I had magic powers right now, I'd use them to stop the laughing. Each chuckle feels like betrayal, but I can't help it. The letter's so her. This scrapbook is so *not* her. I sit on the couch, and Shane takes that as a cue to leave the room. I take it page by page.

I stare at an immaculately matted picture of her car, with cursive stenciling above that reads, "Where it all started." We'd hated each other for years, mostly because she wouldn't stop talking over the top of every single person in History. She was a know-it-all who didn't know shit, but she wouldn't let anyone get a comment in. I snapped at her once, ages ago, and she held the grudge for years. I'm talking hard eye rolls when I walked into the room, glares when I passed in the hall. All for nothing, really.

It was all fine, until I needed her.

Shane comes back with a plate of mini samosas he made for us in the oven, and points to the spot next to me. "Can I join?"

I nod.

"Nice car." He takes a seat.

"It's hers. I usually took the bus to school, but I was finishing up designs for the yearbook one day, and had to stay super late. I'm within walking distance to school, but it would've been a long walk, and I was in a fucking leg cast—long story. When I left, there was only one car in the parking lot, hers. No one else in my family was answering, and I didn't have many friends who could drive yet, so I was stuck. I asked her for a ride, and somewhere in that six-minute drive, a friendship was born."

I turn the page, and suck in a breath. The burning starts in my eyes, and I know the tears are coming and they won't stop once they do and—

"Um, do you need a tissue?"

—I feel myself breaking apart. Sadness tears at my muscles, and I feel simultaneously hollow and overloaded. That picture. Her dad pulling me close, smiles plastered on our faces.

"We—" I start to sob, but I pull back and force the words out. "We had just won a game of cornhole. It's some lawn game you play in America. I don't know if you—well, anyway, we won. Beat Megan and her mom, and took this picture. And he died. Just a few days later."

"And you were close?"

"No, it wasn't even that. But having your best friend's dad die? It's a mess. You're sad, you're grieving, and that doesn't compare to what they're feeling. You're sad, they're devastated, broken, losing faith, and scared. But they have to get it together in an instant. She gave the eulogy."

A tear makes its way down my cheek.

"God, it's hard when friendships end," I say. Shane puts his arm around me, and I hold my breath to keep from losing it. "Let's keep ours going for a bit longer, if you don't mind?"

"Are you going to make up with her?" Shane asks. He nods reassuringly, like that's the obvious choice for a lifelong friend. And it kind of is. But . . .

"A little perspective helps," I say. "But this fixes nothing. You should have heard her trying to justify outing me like that. I can't believe I kept her in my life for so long."

"True. It's good you made it out of there," Shane says with a scoff. "That whole town is full of idiots."

"Last week, I would've agreed with you, but I don't think that's true." I shake my head. "Since she did that, I've gotten a ton of supportive messages from people back home. Skye keeps checking in on me too."

"Huh," he says. "So there's more to Avery than meets the eye?"

"I didn't give any of them a chance to actually know me, so I guess I'll never know. When I found Megan, I thought she was all I needed. That is, until I got here." Shane smiles, and I continue. "With Pierce, and Sophie, and everyone else, I was able to be myself *right away*. A group like this was something I never knew I needed. I've got my own family here."

Once I get my emotions back in check, I dip into the bathroom and reflexively take out my scale. It's midday, and I've already checked my weight once, but I like to see how it changes through the day. Pierce asked me out to lunch today, so the number might go up later. I slip off my shoes and jeans and step on.

My weight's about the same. I don't know what I expected, and I can't explain why I feel compelled to do this so often, but there's definitely been progress. I pull out the front of my shirt and see the extra room where my stomach used to be. It's still there, but a little smaller.

I put my pants back on. They're a snug fit—I had to get them from Primark yesterday, as my old ones looked huge—but I like them. My shoulders pull back on their own, and I feel confident.

Until I hear someone knock on the front door.

Shane heads out for one of his final bookshop shifts as Pierce comes into the apartment. He gives me a quick hug without much of a glance at my new jeans or acknowledging the fact we haven't seen each other in days. He sits on the couch and offers a wave.

"Hi," I say. It feels awkward, but I don't know why. There's tension in the air, but I can't place why his shoulders are slumped, why his gaze is stuck to the floor.

"Hiya," he says. "Sorry, I'm not sure I'm up for lunch. But I still wanted to stop by."

I sit next to him, and put my hand on his back. "Everything okay?"

"This school is hard, sometimes. I keep getting so frustrated. No one listens to me. It's like they don't think I'm trying or that I'm letting my cockiness get in the way. I'm a reasonable person. I set goals for myself. I meet those goals. I—fuck, I don't know."

"Pierce," I say, scratching the back of his neck.

He swats my hand away. "I'm not looking for pity. I just need to practice more or something, I don't know."

"I'm not pitying you. You're my boyfriend; this is what we do—listen and support each other, right?"

The silence lasts for far too long. And eventually, he shakes his head. "I guess. Never been the boyfriend type."

I don't have a response, so I stay quiet.

He sighs. "I talked with Dr. Baverstock yesterday, about the recital piece."

"Oh?" I ask. "What did he say?"

"That he was excited to hear *you* play. Apparently he's heard your practice sessions lately. I had to sit there, and smile, and listen, while he praised you for everything he critiques me for. I was gutted."

"I'm sorry," I offer weakly.

"It's not your fault. Anyway, I should get out of here. There's probably a practice room open. This isn't helping. I'm sorry, sometimes everything is just . . . so hard."

I know what he means.

He stands, and the tension sprawls out through my chest and shoulders. I stand, and try to follow, but he's out the door. I didn't even get to tell him about the scrapbook, or the earlier friendship-ending phone call. We could have stayed together, helped each other, but he didn't want that. A part of me knows he's right about one thing, and it worries me: he still might not be the boyfriend type.

Our time outside Parliament comes back to me, and I remember the rush of emotions I couldn't stop—whatever version of Pierce that was. He stuck with me, and he listened, and he adapted. And as much as I want to close off and sulk, I think it's my time to do the same.

I bolt out the door, oboe in hand, and spot him a few paces

away, running his hands through his short hair. He's pacing, back and forth, trapped by his emotions. I know that feeling, or something like it if it's not the same.

"Pierce," I shout. He looks up and I smile.

It takes a lot out of me to smile. Yes, I may be a good liar in some instances, but in most I'm crap. Especially when it comes to my mood and how I feel about someone.

When I catch up to him, I put an arm around him. Heavily enough to show support, but lightly enough so he doesn't think I'm trapping him.

"Spending the rest of the day in the practice room might not be the best thing right now. Let's grab a quick lunch, then go to Rio's jam session. You still get to practice, but it'll be for something fun. Might get you out of that headspace. I know I could use it."

There's this hesitation in his expression, but eventually, acceptance creeps into his gaze.

"Okay. You're right. Let me grab my trumpet and we can go."

We wind through the park hand in hand—our instrument cases taking up our other hands—and an unusually cool breeze cuts through us. It's a literal breath of fresh air. Time is resetting itself, and *I* had the power to change things.

The sound of clarinets hits my ears, not unlike the last time we did this. But this one doesn't sound like a fight. Sophie's not showing off. She's running through some scales and warm-ups with Rio. Their fingers fly faster and faster, until they both run out of breath. I stop, pulling Pierce back a bit as anxiety creeps into my shoulders.

It's Sophie's smile. I don't want to ruin it, but I know my presence will.

"What's going on with them?" Pierce whispers. "No, you don't think they're . . ."

He drifts off, and I get his meaning. Rio's smile beams back at Sophie, and to be honest, I've *never* seen a happy smile from her. A confident smile? A semi-spiteful one? Sure. But a purely happy one?

"Looks like they found a way to resolve all that principal clarinet drama," Pierce says as Rio closes the distance between her and Sophie with a light kiss.

"Dani and Ajay are here." Pierce starts off in the other direction, and I follow.

But before I do, Sophie's gaze locks with mine for a moment, and I see a wealth of emotions bubble into her expression before she looks away: there's a gravity to her expression. I wonder whether it's disappointment, or anger, or maybe something more?

I don't press it. I follow Pierce and pick up my music from Dani. He gives me a peck on the lips before leaving to join his trumpet companions, and I notice the perk in his step as he goes.

"Sharing with me again?" Dani says. "I was able to pull a shitload of Queen this time, plus some *Star Wars* medley because Ajay has been asking for one all summer. Get ready for some trills."

I laugh. "Let's crush it."

TWENTY-NINE

IT'S SEVEN IN THE morning. And not only am I awake, but I've also endured a forty-minute tube ride with Pierce sleeping on my shoulder, all our bags surrounding me. Now we're at this grab-and-go café at the airport, mere hours before I fulfill my lifelong dream of going to Italy.

To pay me back for being his pillow and making sure we didn't miss our stop, Pierce volunteered to grab breakfast for us and bring it back to the table.

The smell of espresso and bacon comforts me, wraps me up and tells me I'm just fine. But I miss Megan. I miss my parents.

Fuck, I even miss Kentucky.

The coffee's no good in this country. I didn't even know how much I wanted a good cup of coffee until I realized I could never get one again. The food's fine, but the produce sucks. I'd like to buy fruit without it having to be shrink-wrapped.

The cheese is great, though. Bacon's different here—thicker, and a bit chewy—but it's good too. Maybe I should curate a pros and cons list.

I feel trapped in this airport, in the very spot where I could go anywhere else in the world. Even though I'm leaving for Pisa in an hour.

This is when I decide to look through my emails, and I find two from my parents, which I've never opened. I sigh. It takes a great deal of convincing not to open emails that have the potential to hurt me, but I force myself to read the one from my dad. (Since I still haven't talked to Mom since the incident, I don't even want to know what that one says.)

Marty,

Mom and I have been talking a lot—actually, a lot more than we used to about you and your relationship with religion. I'm disappointed that you haven't been more honest with us, but I understand why you might feel unwelcome. Mom still doesn't, but I think she's trying to understand.

We had our big Fourth of July party, like we always do. I attached a few pictures of the family. For once, all my brothers and sisters came! It was great to have them all in the room. But it was also a little weird when they kept asking questions about you and we just didn't know the answer.

I'm not sure what else to say. I am going to try and get

Mom to start talking with you. But I think she's just
scared. I hope we can all catch up soon.

Love,
Dad

The pit in my stomach grows, and I feel the tears welling in
my eyes. I haven't talked to them in weeks. We have a typical,
huge family, and I can't imagine how they feel not knowing the
answers to everyone's questions.

I go to open Mom's email, but I see the subject line and
freeze: *Bonfire.*

I have no idea what she's going to say, but I know it won't be
good. One of her biggest fears was of other people "finding
out" about me, so she must know that everyone knows. I hate
that I spend so much of my time trying to make my sexuality as
little of a deal as possible, while everyone else in my life seems
to be making it into a huge thing.

I respond to Dad, and I tell him I haven't read Mom's email
because I'm scared to. And I don't want her judgment. I don't
want our church's judgment. I just want to be understood.

I don't know if this will help you understand anything
about me, but I'm not sure anything else will. The lying
and the pain didn't start last year, but *something*
definitely did. And I don't think either of you understand
exactly what happened.

So? I'm attaching an assignment I had to do for English

last year. Ten journal entries from my week in London last year. It's not the one I ended up turning in—you'll see why—and I'm sorry for cursing in it, but if you want to start to understand me, here's a good place to do that.

Marty

That pain balls up inside me and puts pressure all throughout my body. It's hard to breathe and not burst into tears. I hate feeling sorry for myself, and I hate the building anxiety that I just made a mistake.

A palm rests on my back. I look up and see Pierce, and smile. The breath that leaves my lungs takes as much of the sorrow as it can hold, and when I stand and wrap my arms around him, I almost feel whole again. I pull away and look into his eyes, and wonder why mine tear up.

"You all right, love?"

I sit. He joins me.

"I just really needed a bacon bap right now." I shake my head. "I don't know; that was a dumb joke. So much has happened in the last week. My parents are being confusing, Sophie won't talk to me, I had a massive breakup with my friend back home. I looked it up—this apparently happens all the time to people once they move away to college, but I never thought it'd happen to me. I don't know."

He takes my hand and offers me a smile.

"Plus, I am a little jealous of Shane."

"You and me both." He sighs, and I feel so much frustration

in his labored breath. "I can't believe I'm busting my ass at this school and I have nothing to show for it."

"That's not true," I say.

"No, it's really been a right disaster from the start. I thought I could coast through—typical trumpet mentality, I know. My first recital was the same week as Colin's. Actually, I went on *after* him. I played 'Flight of the Bumblebee.' Technical masterpiece. Nailed it. Everyone thought I could be the new Sang."

I'm impassive. I'm worried. I have no idea which expression shows more on my face.

"But then I did a different piece for my placement audition, 'La Virgen de la Macarena.' It's a boxing match—fast punches and slow footwork all wrapped into this killer piece. I loved it. The quick parts flew through my fingers, and I could tell the panel was rapt, but the rest . . ."

He rolls his eyes. "I don't know. I thought it was good—vibrato was there, tone was on point—but Baverstock didn't think so. Since then, I've just been another middle-of-the-pack player. I can't get off third trumpet to save my life, so how am I going to land a real audition, let alone get a part?"

We sit in silence for a bit, as I consider the new dynamic. Pierce is hurting, that's for sure. But it doesn't help his case in Sophie's accusation—that he's using me to look better at the academy. It's a weird feeling. It gnaws at my insides like a dog trying to get at the squeaker in a chew toy. It's desperate to make me upset or make me paranoid.

I've still never heard him perform, really. I guess I will once we start practicing together. Except our recital's in one week.

I've got my part down, but even if he's the best player in the world, it doesn't mean we'll be great together.

We eat our breakfast and drink our shitty coffee, and I lead Pierce to the gate. We board quickly. Everything goes smoothly. As it does at Heathrow.

"I can't believe Dani and Ajay went out of Stansted Airport," I say. "I've heard it's impossible to get to."

"Yeah, they got up at four to catch a bus out there. They'll be half-asleep by the time we meet them in Florence."

We're ushered into the plane, and stress creeps up on me again. Dread is always hanging around lately, in my mind. I should be happy, content. Not paranoid and messed up. But maybe that's what having a boyfriend does to you.

Some positives:

- I'm getting a stamp in my passport that says "Italy" on it.
- I'm going to my dream country with my boyfriend.
- I'm still able to call him my boyfriend.

We take our seats. I release a deep breath, hoping some nervous energy goes out along with it. The plane takes off smoothly.

I see his hands grip the armrests, hard. His knuckles are white. Like all the warmth has left his body. I try to ignore the uneasy feeling in my gut. I put in my earphones, lean back in the airplane seat, and we fly off into stormy skies.

DIARY ENTRY 4

I'VE NEVER SEEN ANYTHING like this. Well, outside of Instagram. It's all bright colors and music and cheering and dancing. I read once about how unique glitter is, because it can be both a celebration and an effective protest: it's cheap and easy to use, it sticks to everything and is impossible to ignore, and it's gorgeous—bright, gleaming, unrelenting.

London Pride is all of those things. A celebration and a protest all in one, generously sprinkled with glitter. We're waiting for Shane and Aunt Leah to join us for lunch before the big audition, so while Mom and Dad went in to grab a table, I came outside to write in my trusty journal that will never see the light of day, and to see if I could get a glimpse of the parade.

I hear it more than I see it, but everyone rushing around me is part of it too—pride flags of all varieties line the street, whether they're on clothing, painted on faces, or flying in the air. One girl even has the bi flag painted into her hair. Now *that* takes dedication.

Mom just sent my dad out here to come get me. They want me to wait inside with them. I mean, I knew they were uncomfortable just walking around this area, but I hoped it was just because of how many people were in the crowds. But seeing their faces, and knowing them, I worry that it's something more. That pride scares them. That it's not the crowds in general; it's worse. They're scared of the people themselves.

THIRTY

I'M TOLD WE MADE good time. But that flight was anything but a good time. Incredibly turbulent. I don't get motion sick, but I am almost proud of myself for not hurling up my bacon bap and coffee. Though that could *still* happen at any second.

My stomach grumbles.

We land at eleven thirty in the morning, local time, but the skies say late evening. The sun has no chance against these dark clouds, and god, the rain.

London's rain is ever present, a mist that pings off your face and finds its way into your lungs. But this is worse. Running from the airport to the bus depot involves being exposed for about thirty feet.

So why am I drenched?

"I hate this," Pierce says.

He slams his bag down, which garners concerned glares from strangers.

I get it, these strangers on the bus get it, everyone gets that you're mad. Now, let's calm down.

"It's okay, we'll dry off eventually."

He groans. "I'm in a puddle. I am a puddle. I am made of puddle. This is shite."

I gesture around. "You're making a bit of a scene."

"Who cares? I doubt these wankers speak English."

"Well, actually, most—"

"Yeah, yeah, you looked it up. Get off Google, Marty."

My head shakes on its own. I sigh, then wonder if this is what being in a relationship is all about. Put me down as not a fan. Not a fan at all.

The bus takes us quickly into Pisa's main square, and I get my first glimpse of Italy. Cobblestone sidewalks lead to old off-white buildings. Hundreds of little boxes in this area, little windows with green shutters on top, and a kitschy gift shop under a red, green, or striped awning. The clay roofing gives the buildings a bit of charm, but otherwise . . .

It's a little fake.

The bus stops, and we file out into the rain and quickly run to the nearest awning with fifty thousand other tourists. We're in Italy, but we're in what's probably the most touristy spot in the whole country. The Piazza del Duomo, with the Torre di Pisa.

I let all of these thoughts run through my head because I'm one-hundred-percent not here for this. I'm not ready to talk to that bad mood bastard, and he doesn't look to be ready to apologize anytime soon. Plus, I'd hate to bother him with more of my issues.

We don't even stop to take pictures of the leaning tower. It's there; it's definitely an architectural marvel. (By "marvel" I mean "mistake.") The grays of the sky mute the loudness of the white tower. When you see it in photos, it looks oddly grandiose. Bright green grass under this white marble megalith.

But a memory makes me pause. The guidebook from my childhood had this image on it. I would stare at the tower for so long, imagining I was one of the hundreds of tourists gazing at the tower. When you're stuck in a place like Kentucky, these dreams always feel like dreams. Unrealistic. And I'm finally here, and I'm bickering with my fucking boyfriend instead of enjoying this.

I look up and realize Pierce hasn't stopped. He's leaving me behind. I charge forward, through the crowds and the rain, and with massive effort, I catch up to him. He doesn't say anything. He knows I stopped, I know it, and he didn't wait for me.

Eventually, we make it to a nondescript depot, and I breathe a sigh of relief as we board the docked train. Until I realize all the coupled seats are taken. Pierce throws his bag above a seat and takes it, so I quietly place mine above the seat across the aisle.

Within minutes, we're on the way. Conversations buzz all around us, but we don't add to the noise. For better or for worse, we've stopped talking. And I hate this feeling.

"So how's Music History going?" I grasp for anything to talk about. "Sophie said you were doing really well in that class."

He just shrugs, then grunts. "Fine."

The pressure builds, and I take deep breaths to calm down. But it's no use.

The view from the train is not of the Tuscan hillside. It looks like anywhere else, with dead grasses and garbage all around. The towns we pass seem run down, and the length of the trip is full of graffiti.

I wonder how this trip could get any worse.

About two hours and one cramped nap later, we're in Florence. The rain has ebbed, the sun peeks through the sky, and I find myself determined to make things better. Pierce and I walk side by side through the exit, and find ourselves in a very real city of love.

Unlike Pisa, Florence lives up to the hype. Old brick buildings flank the alleys we walk through, each with quaint shutters and working clotheslines crisscrossed every which way. Signs of neon and wood and metal hang off the side of the brick, announcing trattorias, bars, gelato, and everything in between. The tension pours off me like water.

I slip my hand into his. And every second we touch, I feel stronger, more connected. He has to feel this city like I do. He can't stand there, numb to the smells of the pastry shops, flower stands, and restaurants.

He lets go.

My chest falls, but he pushes forward. We take street after street, and he checks his phone.

"Where are we going?"

"To find Dani and Ajay."

"Oh."

It's as colorful as our conversations get.

THIRTY-ONE

"MARTY! PIERCE!" DANI WRAPS us into a strong hug, though it seems impossible, since she can't be taller than five feet four. "*Benvenuto!*"

"*Buonasera,*" I say. "Or is it not late enough in the day to say that?"

She shrugs. I give Ajay a hug.

And then it starts to get awkward.

Pierce's issues are beyond me, and beyond our bickering. And I wish I knew what they were, or how I'm a part of them, or if I could fix them. I want him to let me in, but I don't know how to show him.

It's especially worrisome because he's closed off to his friends too.

But we charge forward, and I walk in line with Pierce the whole time. Ajay leads the way through cobblestone alleys and plazas. Our shoes hitting the stones matches that of my thudding heart. Dread creeps through me, and I can't make it stop.

I take a cleansing breath, and clear my throat.

"We don't have time to see much," I shout to Ajay. "Where are we going?"

"Gallery of the Academy of Florence," he says. The smile shows through his voice. "I looked it up. Zero percent chance we'll get lost."

"David," Pierce says. "That's where that statue is."

Dani cackles. "Pierce, you are the only person I know who could make a masterpiece seem dull and depressing. Perk up, honeybuns."

That makes him smile, briefly.

About thirty minutes and two wrong turns later—turns out Ajay researched the gallery but not how to get there—I walk into the gallery, and I'm surprised to see there's more than just David in this museum. In one room, giant oil paintings of portraits and landscapes surround us. In the next, sculptures of a hundred nameless heads and faces watch us pass by.

But when I turn back, I see him. David. And I see *all* of him. He's a spectacle, and a representation of the human form that would make any guy feel fat. Sculpted—literally—abs, defined arms. I walk around to the back to find more defined regions.

I see the awe in Pierce as he stares up at David. And that makes me relax, even for just a minute. There's hope in this situation.

We meander and work our way up the Arno River until the Ponte Vecchio appears in the distance, causing nostalgic chills to flood my body. The guidebook on Florence had a few pages on this bridge slash market, and just like the rest of the Florence section, I wore through the pages.

The shops on the Ponte Vecchio are unlike anything I've ever seen. They're all old-looking jewelry shops, and the shine of gold and silver catches my eye as we walk through the bridge. Dani stops to look into the window of a shop, and I get out my phone to take a few photos of the bridge.

"Did you know these all used to be butcher shops in the 1500s?" I ask.

"I did not, but I was hoping we'd get a lesson from you," Dani says with a laugh. "Wasn't sure if his bad mood would ruin our whole tourist experience."

"So you noticed."

She rolls her eyes. "Yeah, it's clear. Anyway, butchers. Neat."

"Apparently the grand duke would cross this bridge a lot and didn't appreciate the, um, smells," I continue. "So he put a stop to that."

"I don't think I blame him."

The rest of our sightseeing plans quickly devolved into eating and drinking at the Italian (obviously) restaurant by our Airbnb. We ordered based on the words we could figure out and ended up with a feast complete with a five-euro jug of their finest house wine. I took a small glass and nursed it the whole evening.

But back in our room, we're out of distractions. There's nowhere else to go, and I feel stuck with him in this bed. It hasn't been a great day. But a part of me, a *huge* part of me, wants to be able to curl into him at the end of the day. Or to hold him close to my body and pretend we didn't just go through a ton of annoying shit.

He comes back from the bathroom and strips quickly to his briefs. He's got the same smoldering glare that's been on his face all day, but it takes on a new manifestation when he looks at me. His chest and abs are covered with coarse hair. The last time I saw him, he must have trimmed. Because now, everything seems wild.

And I can definitely see his package, bulging out of his tight briefs. He wants me to see him. See all of him. And I'm not sure why. We've been anything but consistent lately, and the allure of being in Italy can't override that. But I want to be close to him.

He crawls into bed slowly.

It's weird, seeing someone confidently crawl on hands and knees, in front of another person. It's a nightmare for me, with my still-flabby stomach. There literally couldn't be a less flattering position.

So I stay with my back on the bed. Sucking in my gut, for some reason. Not like he's going to see—

He kisses me.

His body's over mine, his . . . everything pressing into mine. I feel him through my shorts like I feel his tongue pressing into my mouth. We've never kissed like this. The passion's too much—I pull him into me, and hold him close, but he fights away. He points to my shirt.

I hesitate.

It's the moment I've been waiting for, but I'm not ready. My BMI is in the normal range but too close to overweight and the flab's still there and I—

He kisses me again, and reaches down to the base of my shirt. Why's the fucking light on? He pulls the shirt slowly, tugging it to slide up my fat back, and in a moment it's up over my stomach.

I'm exposed. Well, sort of.

He presses his hairy belly into mine, just lightly, and his body heat radiates through me.

He's pulling my shirt over my head. I can't breathe.

This doesn't make up for anything.

His lips are down to my neck now, and I've never felt anything like it. Feelings pulse—*literally pulse*—through me. From my neck, down my shoulders, teasing my back, and disappearing into the sheets. I pull his face off me. He looks at me.

Then he looks down. At my chest, my chubby self, the growing lump in my shorts.

"Wow," he says. "You look good."

This is it.

My goal. The moment I've been working toward. And it's supposed to make me feel better.

Because, the crash diets worked. The passing out, the naps, the depressing smile, it was all supposed to be worth it in this moment. My confidence should be roaring, urging me to press my body into his without any qualms.

My shoulders should be pinned back.

My smile should be huge.

My back should be straight.

But it's not.

He's down at the foot of the bed, and his hands are on my shorts, pulling them down. I gasp—it's too fast. We're in a fucking fight, this can't be my first time, and his hands are on me, all over me, but I can't do this. I can't, even if it's what I thought I wanted for months.

I'm exposed, as exposed as possible. He's so close to me I could hit him on the chin if I flexed the right way, but it's not . . . it's not right.

I grab his hands. "This isn't how I—I want this to happen."

"But I'm your boyfriend," he says.

"That's the thing," I reply, pulling up my shorts, draping an arm casually over my stomach. "That's the first time you've used that term since we got back from Brighton. When I use it, you almost physically react. This whole time, you wouldn't even look into my eyes. Are you sorry? Can we talk about it?"

He rolls over to his side. "That's what this is. This is how adults make up."

"Don't patronize me," I snap.

"You can't blue-ball me like this. I was about to break through my briefs."

I turn away from him. My shoulders tense up, as I realize how weird I feel.

"We don't have to talk through everything," he says. "There are other ways to work through our problems."

I shake my head. "Maybe." And maybe he's right. What

would I know? But I'm freaked. This is my first time, and it's all I can do not to think of my exposed side right now. Love handles galore. "I don't want my first time doing, well, any of this to be with someone who pressures me and calls it a form of apology."

"Jesus, Marty. You've got some issues, you know that?"

It's clear that I have a *lot* of issues right now. I know that. But I also know none of them are going to be fixed by hooking up with him right now.

"It's not worth it," he says. He stands, abruptly, pulls on his jeans, and storms out. "I'm sleeping on the couch."

So I hold my pillow tightly, listening to the shouts from the busy street outside, and beg for sleep to come.

THIRTY-TWO

WHEN WE STEP ON the bus from Florence to Siena, there are only two pairs of side-by-side seats together. Ajay grabs one, and Pierce forces himself in the second.

I look back to Dani. "I guess we'll take the other one."

We put our stuffed backpacks up above our seats, and sit. I'm still on edge from last night—a lack of sleep and two double shots of espresso from an Italian espresso bar will do that for you.

Pierce hasn't said much, and I wonder if I should go apologize.

"Issues?" Dani says. When I turn, I see she was looking at me eye Pierce and Ajay's seats. She's smiling.

"I guess you could say that," I say. "It's becoming clear I have no idea what happens in relationships."

She pauses. It's a thoughtful pause. Or it's a worrisome pause.

"Pierce doesn't either. Fuck, me and Ajay are going on three months, and I still have no idea what's going on."

It makes me laugh. I savor that moment, because it's been far too long since I've smiled.

The bus takes off toward Siena, and the view changes drastically once we leave Florence. Winding hills and ancient villas with clay-tiled roofs flank us, the greenery doubles, and it all feels calmer. People go about their days here, their normal lives, not knowing how freaking amazing it is to live in a place like this.

"Can you imagine being, like, a farmer here?" I say. "You come out, check on your crops, and take this stunning view for granted every day."

"I get that. Malta is a little bit of Italy, a weirder kind of Italy. It's like a few of the rejects came to the island and started building houses on top of each other. You have the beautiful, resort-level buildings and areas devolving into slums, but the views are amazing."

"Do you miss it there?"

"Yes and no. I don't think I can get a job back home, so I hope to get one here. And Malta's so overpopulated it's probably for the best."

I smile. "I'd like to go to Malta. Do you speak Italian there?"

"Most people in the city speak English; everyone else speaks Maltese. It's a mix of Italian and Arabic. It's cute."

I pick the hints of Arabic from her voice, the lilt in her speech, the *shhhh* hiding in every consonant.

"How's your composing going?" I ask. "Still working on a few pieces?"

"Haven't had much time, but I think I've got one piece I'm happy with." She pauses. "That reminds me—let's busk in the town center in Siena. Pierce doesn't want to, and Ajay didn't bring his electric piano."

"I can't imagine why he didn't bring a piano on the plane." I laugh. "But, um, sure."

After feeling a little left out back when Dani played on the streets of Cardiff, I decided to bring my oboe. The thought of playing in front of so many people again, in a new city, is terrifying. But I'm ready to push myself out of my comfort zone. Not because anyone's making me, but because I *want to*.

"We can just alternate our memorized pieces. Whatever you've been working on for auditions should be fine. I'm going to have Ajay record mine, so he can do yours too if you're still working on a portfolio."

"Why doesn't Pierce want to?"

"We used to do it a lot earlier in the summer." She shakes her head. "But I don't know, Marty. He's the master of self-sabotage."

THIRTY-THREE

SIENA HAS THE BEAUTY of Florence, the hills of Kentucky, and the square footage of a two-bedroom apartment. Okay, that's an exaggeration, but it's small. Within an hour, we've done a citywide *tour de gelato*, and I've already got my postcard. There's not much else to do here but explore and walk around, so we do those things.

We walk along the Fortezza Medicea, a fort dating back to the 1500s. It's old, not Cardiff Castle old, but it'll do. The structure is a large rectangle of clay brick, elevated up a zillion stairs.

"Bored," Ajay says.

"I'm with you," Pierce says.

I walk out, toward the center of the plaza. "You can't really feel the history here, compared to the rest of the town, but it's a beautiful space. And look at all of these people jogging."

"You want to be running right now?" Ajay says.

I laugh. "Not even a little bit. But good to know I have the option."

Pierce continues his sulking through another espresso shop. I pray his mood turns, quickly, because the next stop is one that's been on my bucket list since I first got the guidebook to Tuscany. The Siena Duomo.

I'm used to winding paths, from London parks to Kentucky roads; everything winds out with no real origin. Siena's different. The feeling's the same, but we zigzag through harsh brick turns, narrow alleys. It's all angular and disorienting—in a good way. Too often London has felt like *home* home with its open spaces and cloudy skies.

We maneuver through the angles, corner by corner, and it all comes into view. Wood doors framed with ornate stone carvings, trailing up traditional peaks found in cathedrals. In the top, near the center of the building, there's a large pane of stained glass that sparkles with multicolored light. I'm frozen here. It feels like a back alley on one side, and it looks like the holiest place in Catholicland on the other.

It's not technically my religion, but it's close enough. And it really feels like I am about to have one literal come-to-Jesus moment. But I'm ready for it.

I break off from the group and find myself walking the stairs.

"Did you want to go in?" Ajay asks. "I think I will."

"It's seven euro—if that doesn't stop you, then I'm in."

He nods. "The Catholic side of my family would kill me if

I didn't go inside one *duomo* while we're in Italy. The Hindu side? They probably wouldn't mind if I skipped it."

With a glance back to Pierce, I file into the building. It's like we're on two separate trips. But maybe Dani can make him a bit perkier before we continue.

Ajay takes the lead, and we quickly get our tickets and file through the line.

I haven't been in a church like this since my parents took me to St. Patrick's in NYC, and even so—this is way bigger than St. Patrick's. The green-and-white marble columns hold up the building. There's so much to focus on, the dark wooden pews or the massive gold-plated organ, but the columns catch my eye.

It's so quiet in here.

I hold a euro between my fingers and hesitate by the votives. St. Patrick's comes back to me. I've always been raised Christian, and my mom's always been all in on it. The mega-churches are her happy place, the more opulent, the better. She'd go every day if she could. My dad's family is a mix of religious and not, but my mom's clearly pulled him allllll the way to the dark side. It's hard to tell how much that means to him.

For Mom, Christianity replaced the family she had been separated from. And I guess religion has that way of connecting you with people. And right now, I feel oddly connected to them.

I think I remember how this works.

I drop a coin in the donations box; Ajay follows suit. I take a wick, light it, and transfer it to a candle. After dropping the wick, I bring my hands to my forehead, chest, then left and right shoulders.

"Do you really believe all this?" I ask him as we slowly walk down aisles, into more rooms with ornate altars.

"You know what I like about you?" Ajay laughs. "This is, maybe, the second time we've ever talked, one-on-one, and you're asking me the hard-hitting questions."

I shrug. "No better place to ask this question."

"I do, I think. There's so much I don't know, and I admit that, but I've not come across anything that made me stop believing in *something*. Oh, and I like the pope. That a good enough answer?"

"Works for me. It's hard to be in this place and not believe in something."

He looks up at a gold-plated cross, set over an altar. "I get that."

Outside again, we move quickly to the piazza. I try to get Pierce's attention by coming close to him. He shies away every time. He's cold, even though the sun is hot this July day. I'm defeated. I hold my oboe case tight in my hands, and I'm looking forward to playing pieces with Dani, but there's a knot in my chest that won't go away.

It should be Pierce out here with me, but maybe there's a new friendship in Dani and Ajay that I can make, so when Pierce and I are better, we'll all be closer. Maybe.

The Siena town center is positioned around a tall clock tower, with the facade that looks like a castle. It's bright red, in stark contrast to the darkening sky. People sit around it, all over the varied levels of seating in the open space, and loud laugher comes from the patios of restaurants around the perimeter. It's a summer day in Italy. And my boyfriend's being a wanker.

Dani's already got her flute out, and she's warming up. She overturns a knit cap for passersby and starts running through scales and arpeggios. Her fingers flit over the keys almost magically.

I put a new reed in my mouth to wet it. The tone won't be great, but it'll be good enough for this. I think I've learned to just play. Perform. Live it.

"This is going to be such a great shot," Ajay says.

Dani's quickly in performance mode. She takes a deep breath, raises the flute to her lips with the grace of a queen, and launches into the music. I've no doubt why she's here. I'm rapt—I've never heard a flutist this good. It intimidates me, it makes me want to be better, it challenges me. I want to cheer when she finishes, but the clink of change in her hat does that for me.

"Count it," I say. "I'm going to double that."

I stick my tongue out as I fit the reed into my oboe. Ajay keeps recording. Pierce is watching. He seems embarrassed, and I wonder if it's because Dani's performance was on point, or something else. Is it me?

But when I play, those insecurities melt. I play my go-to audition piece, a staple of mine. Something I could play all night, all day, warmed up or not. My lips, fingers know what to do, and I pour all my energy into the piece.

I open my eyes to see the camera, and I smile. People are coming up to drop money in the hat—not much, but a few euros. Probably nowhere near what Dani got, but this is her element. She knows how to capture an audience like this in a way I can only hope to learn over time.

Pierce comes up, drops a euro in the hat, and turns to leave. No wink, no smile.

I don't let it trip me up. I finish my piece with enthusiasm and emotion and everything I have. I killed it.

Ajay applauds, causing others in the crowd to do so as well. Most of them still ignore me, which does not offend me in the least. Since Ajay's got footage of both of us, he leaves too, and I'm alone with Dani.

She plays another piece—aggressive, quick, but still melodic and powerful. Effortless. Her cheeks turn red, and I feel the vulnerability creep through her fingers. I've never heard the piece, but it's contemporary and new, like nothing I've ever heard before. But I've felt this passion before. The pull of the melodic hook, the lightness in my body.

It's her piece. It's so distinctly Dani, light and airy, fast and articulate, sweet and serene. It captures mood like film scores should.

I want to counter with "Gabriel's Oboe," but she's heard it. And I want to shock her. There's a piece I worked on last year, and memorized, but I've never performed it. I run through the fingerings as she finishes up.

She plays the final cadence, and I go. My trills are sharp, the bright runs up the scale are impeccable, the phrases connecting them are off, but only enough to make Dani chuckle. I play the piece faster than I've ever done, closer to the tempo it was written (by someone who must really hate oboes). And when I'm done, I'm panting, and fall back to take a seat on the ground.

She laughs and joins me.

"You wrote that piece!" I say. "I could tell."

"Because it was awful?"

"Because it was *you*. God, Dani, I'm so impressed."

She lifts up the hat, and pokes through the change.

"We've got, like, twenty-five euro here," she says. "We should make this a daily habit."

"Yeah." I nod. "That was fun."

She looks at me, hard. "No, really. We can get a busking license or something—we could really make this work."

I stare off in the distance, things clicking in my mind. If this was my main source of income, I would love my job. And it would be a great way to extend my time here. But I'd never make rent on that alone.

"Is it like that when you and Pierce play together?" she asks. "I mean, I've talked to him about it a little, but he's so defensive about his playing."

"We still haven't practiced together."

She sighs, and chills—the bad kind—claw up my body.

She breaks eye contact first. "I was worried that was the case. He told us you'd been working together on that piece for weeks."

"What? When? Why?"

She turns away, just slightly. I see the rise and fall of her chest. "He said it to shut us up, and make us stop asking questions. This is so typical." She trails off. "Fuck, Marty. I need to tell you something."

My body constricts. Anxiety's burn spreads through my shoulders. The tone's serious, and she's avoiding my gaze. I feel myself zone out, starting to disassociate with the situation, but I snap back. Take a breath. I can't disconnect. I force myself to be present, to listen to what she says and deal with it. I clench my fists, tense my core.

I'm here, and I'm ready.

"Pierce is one of my close friends, and he's a good trumpet player, whether or not he believes it. But I think he's only doing this"—she gestures to me—"to bring up his status at school."

"The recital, you mean?" I ask. "That's what Sophie thought, but I—"

"Yeah, that. But also, your *relationship*."

DIARY ENTRY 5

IT SEEMS LIKE THE only times I've been calm this trip have been when I'm writing in this diary. So thanks, Mr. Wei, for assigning this, I guess. As the world crashes down around me (it's my diary, I can be as dramatic as I want), it's good to know I have something to turn to.

I'm having a hard time processing everything that just happened, that's happening, so maybe I should make a list about everything that's causing me anxiety. I love lists.

- I am late to the audition, but they were able to slot me in for another time since I'm in the waiting area, but I have no idea how much longer I'm going to be waiting.
- The fight between Mom and my aunt started right after Aunt Leah got to the restaurant. Immediately, Mom started being nitpicky about her being late, but then the

real issue came out. She thinks Aunt Leah chose a restaurant close to the pride parade on purpose.

- Pride parades, according to my mom, are evil? Like, straight from the devil, a celebration of temptation, that sort of thing. She made it clear that she's "okay with me" but . . . apparently she isn't okay with *them*. That's not a wildly shitty viewpoint at all. Cool.

- Mom said she's not letting me come live with them next year. How could she trust her sister after being tricked like this? How could she let her son live in a place like this, with so many obvious temptations? Melodrama aside (I'll spend the rest of my life processing those two rhetorical questions, no big deal), that means I'm at this audition for no fucking reason.

It turned out Aunt Leah did do this on purpose. She wanted me and Shane to be able to see pride, and it came out that she didn't think my parents would let me experience it any other way, so she set up a meeting spot where pride was unavoidable.

But her doing this didn't bring out the fun, carefree side of my mom like she thought it would. It brought out the devil.

Aaaaand shit. I forgot to soak my reed, so I need to do that right now and hope I don't get called. Fuck this trip.

THIRTY-FOUR

MY NECK'S TENSE TO the point of near spasm. I almost drop my oboe. It's the warning I've heard from Sophie, the fears I've had lately, but it's different coming from Dani. I can't rationalize it away when his best friend tells me I'm being used.

"I mean . . . does he like me at all?"

"I like you a lot," Dani says. "And I think Pierce likes you too. But he's not a relationship kind of guy. After Colin, he promised us he wouldn't do that. He put everyone through a lot of pain, because we were all becoming friends with Colin too. He was in my section, and I saw him crushed on a daily basis." She pulls the headjoint out of her flute, grabs her case off the ground. "I told Pierce I wouldn't let him do that again."

"I'm not like Colin," I say. "I wouldn't just disappear."

But I don't know if that's true.

"Well, either way, when he said you wanted to do a duet with him, we were really uncomfortable with it. He's a fine player, but he's desperate to get in Baverstock's good graces. I've never seen him so desperate."

Our kiss outside the Southey hangs in my thoughts. It pushes everything else out. It crowds out all the bad, and it has been doing so for a long time. I still feel the butterflies, the rise in my chest and the ease in my shoulders. How could something so perfect fall so fast?

"He was so nice to me," I say.

"He's also been a dick to you." She shakes her head. "Thin walls in the Airbnb."

"You don't under—" I stop. I've said it before. I've thought it countless times.

Context is important. If people only see the good, or they only see the bad, they can't understand any of the complexities of any relationship. And ours has its complexities. But she understands how I'm hurting. I see it in her gentle expression and hear it in her hushed voice. I can't cling to the only good memories we have anymore.

My cheeks feel flushed. "I've got to talk to him."

"He's going to be so pissed at me," she says with a sigh.

"I've had some shitty experiences with this in the past, so I want to know: Are you my friend? My real friend? With no attachments?"

"Of course." She laughs. "Like I told you—I like you, Marty. And I don't want you to be even more hurt in the long run. And I don't want your music career to suffer."

I clench my fists when I realize I believe her. I'm wounded from Megan, eviscerated by Pierce. But I can't let that keep other friends at bay. I can't fear being close to anyone. I want to keep her as a friend.

"Okay." I give her a hug, and her thick hair bunches in my face. I whisper through it. "I won't tell him you said anything, then. I'll keep this focused on me and him."

I pack up my oboe and hold it close to my side. My feet lead me down the jagged alleyways, to my destination. I see the espresso bar through the window, and through the window I watch Ajay and Pierce chat. Well, I watch Ajay chat and Pierce nod. His posture's wrecked, like he's trapped in a fishing net that's pulling him under the table.

I walk in and then order an espresso from the bar. I hate this. I hate this. But I have to do this.

I take a seat with Ajay and Pierce.

"Dani wanted to show you something," I say to Ajay. "She's at the tacky souvenir shop next door."

"Right, okay." He hesitates, then stands.

His footsteps echo through the bar, and there's a part of me that wishes he would turn around, or Pierce would follow, or the espresso machine would explode, so I didn't have to have this talk.

The feelings are back. The constricted chest and lightheadedness, and there are only a handful of people in here, but it might as well be Trafalgar Square. The breaths don't come easy anymore. Ajay is out the door, so I turn.

I look at Pierce, who looks down. The act brings back the fire from before, the clenched fists and tense shoulders. I flip so fast between panic and rage it's like I give myself whiplash.

I don't know how to feel. I've never googled how to have a serious conversation with your asshole boyfriend, but I know what it'd say.

The chair legs groan as I make room for me at the table. Across from Pierce, not beside him. He looks to me, and I take my shot.

"What are we doing?" I ask. "Look at you! Hunched shoulders, eyes glued to the ground. You don't even like being around me."

He looks down in response.

"I don't know what changed," I say, "but all you care about is minimizing your time with me, or forcing me to do stuff I don't want to. And making me feel bad for it."

"That's not fair," he says. His voice sounds off. Too low and scratchy to belong to him. "I haven't been feeling it lately."

"Lately? Pierce." I sigh. "You never felt it. Why are you acting like you did?"

"I'm going through a bad time right now," he says. "And if you can't stick with me through it, you might as well not even be my boyfriend."

I clench my fists again. I feel my pulse skyrocketing, but I grit my teeth.

"You've never stuck through anything with me, Pierce, and it's clear you never will. This isn't an even relationship; it's not a relationship at all. You can't talk your way out of it. You can't fuck your way out of it." My fist pounds the table. "Tell me now, did you ever actually want to be my boyfriend?"

He hesitates, but his gaze drops again. Silence.

I think I have my answer.

A rush of emotion flows into me. I want it to be anger, I thought it would be anger, and I beg for denial or rage or anything.

But that's not what's coming.

I tear up, and the breaths come hard. And god, the pit in my chest. It's like someone's squeezing my lungs and I'm begging for them to pop. For it to just be over with. I hold my stomach—my dumb stomach that is slimmer, but at the expense of so much.

"Why would you toy with me like that? It's not fair. You're not that desperate; you're not that callous." I blow air through my mouth carefully, like I'm blowing on soup, but I'm really trying not to pass out from over-oxygenation. I clench my abs. I have to be strong, while he's still weak and sulking. For a little longer. I can do this.

"I can't believe it," I finally say.

"Look, I didn't mean to . . ." He shakes his head. "What I'm trying to say is, I'm sorry."

He reaches out to take my hand, and I hate myself for wanting his touch. He hesitates, and I feel the tips of his fingers brush over mine. It makes me hurt that much more. I pull away. I find my strength.

"You may have started this," I say, my voice wavering, "whatever your intentions were. But now, I'm ending it."

I leave the café, and loneliness hits me like a truck. I walk in the opposite direction of the others; I need to be alone. I need to go home.

Flying to London was scary. I left everything behind, everything I knew, everything that was safe and secure. And for the last six weeks, I thought I was replacing it with better things. More secure things. But that's not how it works.

There's only one thing that can offer security: me. If I make my own decisions, if I follow my own path and still let others in along the way, I'll be protected from this.

Heartbreak happens. I looked it up.

I tried to imagine what it felt like, even though I'd read it in dozens of books and articles. But it's nothing like that. There's no way to describe it in words, except maybe if you repeated the word "fuck" for four or five pages.

That's what heartbreak is, an endless string of "fucks" shouted from your heart, making it hard to hear, hard to see, impossible to breathe. It's melodramatic, sure, but what isn't about this moment? I'm literally sitting in a gutter.

My eyes must be bright red, because I can't stop rubbing them.

Tears are coming out so fast I can't even dry them on my shirt.

I know I'm not far enough away from the others, but I can't go on.

I can't go on.

People are staring. People are definitely staring. But if they knew what was going on, how much I've lost, how hard I've hit the bottom, maybe they'd let me carry on. Or maybe they'd judge me. I don't know. It's hard to experience anxiety when I'm crying. It's hard to worry or fret or whatever it is that takes up my whole day. I'm all out of fucks, and I want to be left alone. This gutter is my home now, and no amount of concerned Italian chatter is going to change that.

Some time passes. I think of Sophie and how I need to apologize to her for her pointing out the awful things I was doing to my body. I think of Megan and the scrapbook that I haven't even acknowledged. I think of Shane and how I haven't been supporting his potential big break nearly enough. I can't help but think of the opportunities I missed—I could have shown the world, or at least London, my talent.

But I let Pierce eclipse all that.

The thoughts lead me back to myself. I need to make things right again. I need to make a change.

THIRTY-FIVE

I DIVIDE MY THOUGHTS into two parts: old Marty and new. When I think of something that old Marty would do, I do the opposite. Even if it makes me uncomfortable, I do it. At least, that's my plan.

My panting's stopped, and I'm sort of held together now. That's good. There's a lot of good in this situation. I'm in a beautiful country. I've shed my attachments. I'm free to do as I want, as long as my newfound confidence doesn't get the best of me.

I put my palms to the gravelly road and prop myself up. I stand, dust myself off, and raise my arms to stretch. The bad feelings threaten to pull me back as a haze falls over me. That's what this sadness is, a haze that makes me move slowly, interrupts my train of thought, and makes me all-around uncomfortable.

But I press on, because old Marty wouldn't.

Siena's not hard to figure out. The center is the piazza, and out from there in a semicircle will get you to where you need to go. I need to go to a bus station, and I can find it if I go outside the city.

But that's not what happens. In minutes, I'm lost. Siena's small, but made of hills—I scale a hill and look out between buildings, but see nothing except another street. Siena is taller than a corn maze, more complex than those extreme sudoku puzzles. I walk by a large brick wall three different times, wishing and begging for the bus station to appear, but nothing does. All at once, I realize I'm not panicking. I know I could just ask someone, but I'm determined. My breaths aren't shallow; my palms are only wet from the residual tears.

I'm almost too crushed to worry about being lost. The realization makes me sad.

Suddenly, I turn a corner and the brick maze releases its hold on me. I'm free.

To reward myself, I stop by a small market for a Fanta and some crispy M&Ms. I try to keep my thoughts light. I even half smile when I finally make it to the station, and think about getting home early in the day. Old Marty would go straight to bed. New Marty is going to do whatever he can to stop sulking. He won't be that person.

I won't be that person.

Not now.

I get back into Florence about seven hours early for my flight, but I go straight to the airport. Florence is beautiful, but I'm on a mission right now, and I'm going home.

Home! It's still weird to think about. But it *is* my home, damn it. And it's time I stopped acting like an intruder and started acting like someone who belongs. I can do this.

At the ticket counter, I try in vain to exchange my ticket, and I'm stuck buying a new one. It drains a lot of my funds.

I connect to the airport's Wi-Fi and shoot out a message to Dani.

> Sorry to bolt like that. I'm in Florence now, flying out soon. But you've probably figured that out by now. Wanted to catch you before you got on the bus in an hour or so, thinking you left me behind. Thanks for talking to me.
>
> P.S. I'm in. Let's try for that busking license.

I hope that's enough as I hit send. They still have time to get the message, so they don't freak out too much. Pierce will have an empty seat next to him on the flight where he can store all his bad attitude, all his assiness. I feel okay.

For a while.

I board the plane, and once we take off, I stare out the window as all of Italy grows smaller beneath me. I'm starting to get used to this—this flying thing.

Before we even hit cruising altitude, I start to cry.

There was a part of me that knew Pierce could've been my first love, and thought he actually was. Will he be the *one that got away*, like you see in movies and books? The guy who sticks with me, always in the back of my mind, for the rest of my life? I might have loved him, the times he was sweet to me. The way he picked me up at the airport and welcomed me to London immediately.

Fuck, some part of me loved him when he took me to Big Ben.

I pull my knees to my chest and lean against the window, and I let it out. As quietly as I can, but I don't care about the people around me. I don't care about anyone else. Old Marty would've cared. Would have been strong to save face and not embarrass himself. New Marty cries in public. New Marty makes an ass of himself and doesn't care, because they don't know about the hole that was just punched into his barely beating heart.

I close my eyes, and I don't open them until I'm in London.

I land, and shoot a text to Sophie right away.

It's over. You were right. Sorry.

A breath escapes me, and I feel the tears start to come. But I'm not letting it happen again. Later, maybe. Now, I'm getting off this plane a new person. After we deplane, I sit on a bench and take my oboe case out of my bag. I drop my reed into the small cup of water I kept from the flight.

I walk through Heathrow, slowly, taking in how alive it feels here. People always in a rush, dashing back and forth.

I maneuver through the airport until I get to the tube. It's here I know what piece I'll play. I put my oboe together, leaving my case open—might as well start making money to pay for that flight now. Then I play. I start off with "Gabriel's Oboe," and it makes me think of Sang. Which makes me think of Shane.

So I play.

And I go through my entire collection. I'm there, off to the side, for forty minutes. I thank the busking gods that no one asked for my license.

I feel freer after the performance. More confident. If I can do that in Heathrow Airport, I can do it anywhere. I look into the oboe case, surprised to see that New Marty just made bank.

"Huh. This is not how I expected to find you."

I look up as Shane drops a couple of coins into my case. The look of confusion fully takes over my expression, which causes him to laugh.

"Hey, mate," he says. "Dani texted me. I hopped on a train as fast as I could."

"You didn't need to do that," I say. "I'm fine. Really. Sort of."

He pulls me into a firm hug. "It's okay not to be, you know."

Tears pool in my eyes, and I blink them away. I feel shaky and so drained. When we pull apart, Shane takes my backpack from me and guides me toward the platform.

"And actually, I *did* need to do this. I promised my mom I'd take care of you this summer, and I don't know if I've really done that."

I stop walking and grunt a disapproval. "You *tried*, though. Way more than I tried to take care of myself."

"I wasn't even here when you landed, Marty. I keep thinking that if I just—"

"No, Shane. Really." I put my hand firmly on his shoulder. "I don't think there's anything you could have done. I was so stubborn about this, about everything."

He sighs in relief. "It's nice to hear you say that. You've been so different lately. I mean, that's a good thing too! I was shut in that bookshop while you did some really brave and incredible things." His smile is so bright my face starts to mirror it. He laughs. "I know I'm not really responsible, but I probably would have done a few things differently if I could do it again."

"Uh, yeah, me too," I say with a laugh.

"Anyway, I thought it was time I finally picked you up from the airport." He nods toward the tube entrance.

"You're only six weeks late," I say, causing him to give me a light shove.

"Don't push your luck," he scoffs. "Now tell me about your trip. Everything."

I talk more on the ride back than I've ever done before— with Shane, with Pierce, with Megan, with anyone. The walls within me have broken, and I give in. It's hard to get the words out at times—about my crash dieting, and everything I tried to change for a stupid boy—but once they're out there, I don't feel so alone anymore.

Ever the practical one, Shane helps me make a plan for the

rest of my time here. Tomorrow's the day I will get serious about my portfolio and put up my videos on YouTube. Tomorrow's the day I start over again, as a single guy, but as someone with a lot of close friends. Old Marty wouldn't be ready for this.

But fuck it, I am.

DIARY ENTRY 6

DEAR FUCKING DIARY: IT'S over.

I'm sitting in the lobby waiting for my parents to come back from their coffee run. The audition was supposed to take a lot longer, so they probably think they have a ton of time. But things didn't exactly go to plan.

I can't blame everything that happened during the parade for why I flopped, but I can't say it helped. I've been in a daze this whole time, lower than I've ever felt. They could tell too. The teens in the office looked at me with a confused pity on their faces as I left the audition. I don't blame them . . . I'm confused too.

My reed hadn't soaked enough, and I knew it'd be an issue. But we were late enough as it was, and my parents had already made it clear that they weren't sure London would be a great place for me, so I didn't really get the point of following through with the audition.

But I still sucked it up. I played the piece. And I left.

I missed so many notes. Runs I know I had under my fingers mushed into a squeaky blur. My fingers felt tingly and numb as I played, and with every wrong note, I could only focus on how I was blowing this opportunity. But I made it through the piece.

"Do you want to run through that last part again?" Dr. Baverstock offered kindly. "No need to be nervous—we know you can play, and we enjoyed your video audition."

"I don't want to play it again," I replied.

What I didn't say was that my parents had just pulled the rug out from under me—in more ways than one—and that they weren't even planning on letting me come to London anymore.

I put my oboe back in its case and grabbed my sheet music.

"I'm just wasting your time, sorry."

I couldn't even look him in the eye as I left.

THIRTY-SIX

THE ANXIETY'S FADED. SORT of. Okay, it never truly fades, but maybe I'm learning how to work with it. At various points of the day, I still feel sad about myself. My shoulders ache and my mind alternates messages of hate. I almost lost it all. I definitely lost him. And that's supposed to be a good thing, but it rarely feels like it.

At a small two-top in the back, I see her. I run and wrap her in a hug.

"Sophie," I say. "I missed you."

"It's been, like, a week, Mart. Let's calm down."

I sit down and order a traditional English breakfast—eggs, beans, bacon, sausage. Sophie and I catch up while we wait for the food.

"What's new with you?" I ask. "What did I miss?"

"Biggest thing is, well, I gave principal clarinet to Rio," she says, shaking her head. "I realized it meant so much more to her. But Baverstock wanted to do an audition for the solo. I'll find out soon about that, but the audition went well."

"It's good he opened it up to auditions, and didn't give it straight to Rio."

She laughs. "I think Rio wasn't too happy about that. She's an odd person, very intense about everything, but I think we're starting to be real friends. Better than what we were when we first got here."

"*Just* friends?" I ask coyly.

"We're, um, taking it slow."

"By kissing in the—"

She kicks me under the table, so I stop. But the smile never leaves my face.

Our plates come, and I dig in. I'm starving, and for once, I'm not going to ignore it. I'm going to eat this sodium waste-land like a real Brit, and my kidneys can just be happy I'm not washing it down with beer.

"Are you mad at me for everything I said?" Sophie asks.

I shake my head, slowly. "This will sound so cliché, but I think I needed to hear it. It set everything in motion that led me to realizing Pierce was not right for me. It's hard, because the good times with him were *so good*. But I was a mess. I still am a mess. It's going to be nice to pull back and focus on myself for a bit."

"Sorry it didn't work out. You deserve better, anyway."

She flashes a genuine smile, and I feel it reflected on my face.

"You're a good friend," I say. "I've been burned before, and I know you have too. But I trust you."

She rolls her eyes. "I've come to the conclusion that people are, in general, nicer than not in the real world. But I was shit to you. I got so scared you'd be another Colin situation, and I hate it when people look for advice, then blatantly don't take it." She pauses. "But I walked out on you, even though I knew you were flailing and not eating and needed someone. What I'm saying is, even though you're a git, I'm sorry I abandoned you like that."

I chuckle, and when I stop, I take time to look at her. A real friend. The girl who fought for me, freaked out about losing me, and . . .

Apologized to me.

I suck in a deep breath and think about Megan. How toxic she is for me, and how I still don't want to be around her. There are two Megans: the one who made me the scrapbook and the one who outed me to my whole school. Dealing with the second isn't worth it, just to stay friends with the first.

Sophie clears her throat. "So yeah, tell me all about Italy."

And I do, between bites of food.

I walk into the apartment, and immediately lock eyes with Aunt Leah. She's not supposed to be back for another month, so even though she gives me a sweet smile, a chill runs through my body.

"Marty!" She pats the seat next to her on the couch, and as

I come in I see Shane sitting at the kitchen table, a hesitant look on his face. I feel everything start to unravel as I take a seat, but I hold it together. Or at least, I try to.

Because I'll never know if I can until I try.

"You're back early," I say.

"Yes, I am. I want you to know, first, that I'm not angry with you." She looks up to Shane. "Maybe a little with you, but I understand why you did what you did."

She sighs, and I think about interjecting or playing dumb, but really, what's the point? I sent my parents all my old diary entries; they detail pretty clearly how much of a flop I was in that audition. The pieces must have come together.

"Your mum called me," she said. "And she was not happy."

"I'm sorry." I say it quickly, but she just raises a hand before I can elaborate.

"Apologies can come later. I need to talk for a bit." She sighs again, blowing out a chest full of air and looking to the ceiling. "You know, our family was never religious? It seems odd, looking back, because all our friends were super Catholics, but that was just never something we were a part of."

"I guess I never really thought of that," I say. "Our mega-church kind of took over our whole lives, so it was hard to imagine anything came before."

"I'm not sure what drew her to it. Maybe she was trying to find her own family, which is probably something you can relate to. But anyway, I got pregnant at around the same time your mum did, which you could probably figure out since you and Shane were born a month apart. It was unplanned, it was a scary situation for me, but I was so glad I had a pregnancy buddy. I was already doing this without any 'dad' in the picture, so I *really* hoped it would bring me closer to your mum. I needed her.

"This was, unfortunately, a few months after she joined that big fundraising machine she calls a church, and I had started to see changes. She always distanced herself from me, from her life here, and I can only guess why. But it escalated when she knew I'd gotten pregnant. Out of wedlock. The *horror*." She rolls her eyes.

"She turned her back on you for that?" Shane asks. "That sounds nothing like the aunt I knew, the one who'd send me birthday cards every year. They were the tacky Jesus-y inspirational ones, sure, but she still wrote so much in them. I remember because they seemed even more out of touch than the ones Nan would send."

"She loved *you*, of course. And she's obviously not all bad— she's a normal person, just easily influenced by anyone with a cross hanging around their neck. Point is, I can't imagine your experience being raised in that environment as a gay teen, but I do know what it's like to be young and have someone turn their back on you in the name of religion. I know the shame that comes with that. So, after Shane came out—and told me you had too—I vowed to do what I could to help you."

"I know," I say. "And I . . . took advantage of that."

I run a hand through my hair and try not to let the guilt gnaw at me, but it still creeps into my stomach and builds like a full-body cramp.

"So, like I said, your mum called. And it took us a while to sort out the truth. She said you sent them a diary you kept from your time here last year. I could tell it really affected her, because she wasn't yelling at me like she normally would, and we sorted through all your lies without her once calling it a sin. Which we all know is big for her. But she was genuinely worried about you and couldn't get ahold of you." She opens her laptop, and taps a few keys. FaceTime pops up. "So I told her I'd go back immediately and we could all talk it out."

I nod. "Okay, I'm ready."

The call connects, and my parents are in the view. Mom and Dad sit at the barstools at the counter in our kitchen back home, and Aunt Leah adjusts the view so both of us are in it.

"Hi, Marty," Mom says. "First of all, we love you. I hope you know that. Secondly, we have a lot to talk about here. But maybe you should catch us up on your time in London."

"And . . . Wales. And Italy." Dad laughs. "You never should have showed me how to use that Find Your Friends app."

My cheeks flush hotly, but I hold myself out of my shell for just long enough to explain myself. From the beginning. The full story. New Marty's got one last job to do.

"Marty," Aunt Leah says once the call ends, "I know it's hard. But you've got to give them a chance to—"

"How can I? My family is supposed to be my rock, the one thing that keeps me going no matter what. They're not going to just become understanding and start waving pride flags overnight, and I shouldn't be forced to wait while they figure it out."

"You're right," Shane says. "But you can have more than one family. You can *choose* your family."

Aunt Leah laughs. "And remember that adults like me and your mum—we don't have our shite together. We can try to be a rock all we want, but we've got plenty of cracks. It's rough to grow up and learn your parents aren't quite as put together as you think they are. So be mad, be resentful, but most of all . . . be honest. Things may change, or maybe they won't, but you won't know until you try."

"I can choose my family," I echo. "I mean, you're my family. And so is Sophie, and Dani, and that whole group."

Shane comes over to give me a hug. My aunt makes it a group hug. "And we're not going anywhere," he says.

THIRTY-SEVEN

I BARELY PICKED AT my dinner last night, which was the latest reminder that there's a lot still lingering inside me. But I asked Shane to help me be accountable for it in the future. After the call with my parents, and the lie unraveling, it's clear: a guy can't change overnight.

I've dropped the New Marty persona. I'm trying to learn and get better every day. I'm doing things that make me happy and make me closer to my new family.

Today's a big day. Dani used our videos and got us an audition for a busking license. And after that, it's London Pride. Take two. I've got a sack of glitter, and we're all going to be decked out in the brightest colors we can find. We're doing it right this time . . . as long as we can get through this audition in one piece.

Before I get out of bed to start this hectic day, I decide to bite the bullet and pull up Mom's email. The one I got in the airport, right before I sent them last year's diary. I'm still try-ing to figure out if I want them in my life, and if so, to what extent I want them to be here. Aunt Leah's given me an exten-sion on my stay here, but I don't know how long that'll last.

I don't know anything. But I open the email.

Marty,

I am furious right now. I know your friend Megan has been acting strangely lately, but I heard what she did to you, telling everyone at Avery High about your sexuality without your permission. It's disgraceful, and I am so sorry you're going through this.

I want you to know that I found this out at church. It was everything I had feared. My "friends" all finding out that my son was gay, then coming to me offering scriptures and fake support . . . and one even mentioned a special program I could send you to that was sponsored by this very church.

Now, I know I haven't been the most accepting, and I know that won't change overnight. But when these ladies came to me, honestly offering a thinly veiled conversion program as support, a piece of me broke straight in two.

I was too appalled to speak, but your father stepped in with some choice words for them. We left right then, and by the time you get back, we will hopefully be a part of a different church. A more accepting one.

This doesn't exonerate me. I know this. I've prayed a

lot about this, and I don't know what I can do. But your
dad thinks this is a good start. I'll try calling you soon,
though I know you hate when I call out of the blue.

I love you,
Mom

The email sits with me all morning. I wish my feelings
about this weren't so complicated, but I've learned that pretty
much everything is complicated, especially when you're gay. So
I might as well do the best I can and try to cope.

Shane, Sang, and I sit on a train, off toward Trafalgar
Square, which is full of a few hundred billion people on a normal day, so I can only imagine what it's like during pride. But
they're holding busking license auditions in a private room
in the National Gallery.

I look over to Shane, who's got his arm casually around his
new boyfriend, and I try to make sense of the jumble of thoughts
knocking around in my brain. All of them are probably far-
fetched, but since I'm off to my first and only audition of the
summer—and Shane's just a few weeks away from starting
work in his *Les Mis* run—now seems like the right time.

"Okay. Now that you got your dream gig, I have a favor to
ask. Would you put in a good word for me at the bookshop
before you go? I'm looking for part-time jobs, and I've applied
to a few American-style restaurants that might appreciate having
someone with real American diner experience under his belt.
Actually applying this time, not just dicking around and falling

in love with a jerk. Between that, and if this busking thing works out with me and Dani, I think I could make it work."

"Does this mean you could really stay? Like, for good?"

"Yeah," I say. "Should we start looking for a flat? I kind of like having you as a roommate."

"I don't know." Shane sighs. "I kind of liked living alone this summer, while you were out touring. Maybe I'll get my own place."

Sang snickers. "I definitely appreciated the, uh, private time we had there."

Shane winks, and I just roll my eyes. "Be serious! You had me freaked."

"Yes, let's do it," he says with a smile.

A silence passes over us, and I look around the train to see bright colors all around. Queer people of all ages flood the car, some quiet, some excitedly cheering, some already drunk. Okay, a lot of them are drunk.

But everyone is *so* happy.

"Seriously, Shane." I keep eye contact, which is a challenge. But I have to keep it. "I'm sorry about being MIA this summer. And for not taking your advice about Pierce. And for . . . scaring you."

"You don't have to apologize. Boys make us do stupid shit. But thanks."

This is where we'd probably have a touching bro moment, but it gets cut short by us getting to our stop. We finally make it out of the station with the other thousand queers, and head to our meeting spot: Trafalgar Square, the fourth plinth.

Sophie and Rio lean against it, hand in hand, waiting for our arrival.

"We come bearing face paint!" Sophie announces as a hello.

Rio laughs. "And stickers!"

I give each of them a hug and take the paint from Rio. "I've got a shit ton of glitter. But, uh, let's get through this audition first. Has anyone seen Dani yet?"

While we wait, we settle into conversation. How Sophie interacts with everyone is different than it was earlier in the summer. She's more relaxed, less guarded. Sure, I could be her *one* friend that she wanted. But she doesn't need *one* friend. Like me—like all of us—she needs a family, and she's got one.

Rio lifts up to give her a kiss on the cheek.

Dani taps me on the shoulder.

"Ready?" she asks.

I turn, but my gaze slips past Dani, right through Ajay, and on him. Pierce. I knew I'd have to be around him again, with my growing friendship with Dani, but I didn't know it'd be this soon. Too soon. He has bed head; he hasn't shaved. He looks like he's running at ten percent, and his gaze misses mine and scans the ground.

Dani comes up to me and pulls me into a cheek kiss, whispering, "Do you want him to go? We were hanging out today, and he asked to come. I said that he could, only if you approved. Do you?"

My eyes haven't moved. With each passing breath, I feel more tense, and I feel the awkwardness levels rise within me. Do I approve? How could I? It's a public space, so I can't stop him from being here. Plus, how could I turn him away and not be an ass?

And I remember, vaguely, what Sophie told me about Pierce when I first met her. They were cliquey and standoffish, and clearly didn't make Sophie feel comfortable or invited.

It's that memory that makes me tell Dani, "Yeah. He should stay."

He's here because, for some reason, he wanted to be. And if he wants to celebrate pride with me, as a friend, with his other friends, I can't stop that. Rather—I could stop that, or I could run away, but I won't do either.

Because I'm a hell of a lot better than he is.

"Pierce," I say. I take slow steps toward him, and I feel the eyes of the others burn into my skin. "How are you?"

"Feeling pretty rubbish right now, if I'm honest."

I run a hand through my hair. "I mean, you don't have to. We're all friends here."

He laughs, then says, "I wasn't great to you."

"I know. And I've recovered. So, things are good." I bend down to make eye contact, and he gives me a light smile. Vulnerable. And I know it's the only chance I'll get to ask this question.

"How—" I clear my throat. "How much of this was real?"

"I liked you. But I used you."

"Let's take a quick walk," I say before leading him farther away from the group.

With each breath I strengthen. I stand straight, pull my shoulders back, relax the tension in my face, and put on a neutral expression. I have the control in this situation, and I should relish it . . . but the dynamic makes me feel uneasy.

"Shane showed me your audition video once, before you even got here. You were *so good*. You asked me early on whether I liked you as a person or as an oboist, and the answer is still both." He sighs. "But the harder Dr. Baverstock pushed me, the more I focused on Marty the Oboist."

"I know," I say. "It wasn't a great feeling."

"I wasn't ready for a relationship, especially after what happened with Colin. But I really saw *something* between us. I had this vision of us as this power couple that pulled off wild duets."

Despite myself, I chuckle. All this time, he thought of me as a duet partner, not a boyfriend. And I don't think he even knew it.

"I wish you'd have liked Marty the Person more," I say.

"I certainly could have treated you better. I'm sorry, truly."

It doesn't excuse much. From the beginning, he wanted Marty the Oboist to make him look good, to up his street cred in this school. Maybe he doesn't even know how much he used me, how far he tried to push me that night.

"I feel like an idiot." The confession weighs me down. "I wasted this whole summer because I was trying to please you or be with you. Pierce, if there was ever a part of you that really liked me, you'll find a way to make me trust you enough to be friends with you."

"Right," he says. This time, his gaze doesn't fall. He keeps eye contact. "You deserved better. You really are—"

I throw up my hand to cut him off.

"I'm going to join my friends, crush this audition, and have the most epic pride the world has ever seen."

"I suppose I'll just . . ."

He turns to leave. Each step he takes resonates within me. The tension inside me is intense, but I know what I need to do, to start to get over this.

I do the strongest thing I can think of.

"You should join us."

When we return to the group, Dani rushes to meet us.

"Everything okay, boys?"

There's a nervous edge to her voice, which I try to calm with a smile. Pierce still trails me, and I speak without looking back to him. "No, but we're working on it."

The crowd has doubled in size, in density, since we started our little heart-to-heart. High-energy music pumps through a giant speaker as two drag queens have a lip-sync dance-off. Cheers come from all around, making my spirits lift instantly. Sophie takes my hand, and we look out on a sea of rainbow, full of pure energy.

"I'm so sorry to do this to you," she says, before throwing a handful of glitter up in the air and letting it cover us completely.

Rio comes up behind me and gently slaps a rainbow sticker on my face. I turn to her and shake some of the glitter out of my hair before looking back at the rest of our group. Ajay's donned the bi flag as a cape. Shane and Pierce start painting pride flags on each other's faces.

Dani appears next to me, dripping in glitter. I turn to her, and she shrugs.

"Let's hope the judges like a little sparkle," I say.

"If they're going to schedule an audition during London Pride, they should expect nothing else." She picks up her flute case, now covered in Rio's stickers. "You ready?"

"Let's do this!" I shout.

We make everyone promise not to have too much fun while we're gone, and then we head out to the audition, our friends cheering for us the whole way.

Diary Entry 10

I'M STILL NOT TURNING in this diary, but I wanted to finish the project anyway. The assignment was ten journal entries about an experience you had over the summer, which sounds easy enough. Actually . . . I stand by my earlier point that it's a little juvenile. Regardless, I'm finishing this project with the real story, for me.

When Megan has to take this class, she'll flat-out refuse to do it. When Skye has to take the class, he'll spend the day before school starts writing up these diary entries about a real event that happened over the summer. But I'll try something new: I'll write the diary entries, but about a fake experience.

I'm not a liar, but I need to do this.

So I'll redo the London trip through my journal entries. They'll be through a rosy lens where everything is all right. Where we stumble upon a pride parade, and my parents show me who they are—but "who they are" turns out to be accepting, loving, and understanding.

Maybe I'll refurbish the story. Mom didn't pick up that discarded rainbow flag to throw it in the garbage; maybe she started waving it around. Dad will find us the best spot to stand so we can see the floats, so the colors can be absorbed into my soul and I know I'm welcome *somewhere*.

Maybe in this version I didn't bomb my audition, which means I'll be on my way to London in eleven months. On my way to London, one of the only cities where I've found true acceptance—from pride, sure, but also from Shane and Aunt Leah.

Because otherwise, I'd have to turn in *this* diary. One that shows a guy who doesn't have a future. In music *or* in the real world. But that's not going to happen, because I think I have a plan. And until I can leave this place, and find my own family, make my own life . . . I'll just lie. Smile. Keep my head down. And get out of here.

I may be gay. I may be flailing.

But I won't suffocate.

Thirty-Eight

AFTER AVOIDING IT FOR literal months, I decided to fix the one thing still sticking out from everything that happened this summer. The email I sent Megan was short, yet took hours to write. I could feel things resolving around me. I could see the light at the end of the tunnel.

Megan,

You know me better than any person on this planet. Sometimes that's good, like how you'd choose the perfect playlist to match my mood whenever you picked me up for school. Sometimes that isn't as good. You know how to get a rise out of me, you know how to make me uncomfortable.

You *like* making me uncomfortable.

I'm trying to be someone else. A better version of
myself. Someone who's more present, happier. The
person you always wanted me to be.

But that couldn't be my story. I ended the email with a few
lines that took seconds to draft and hours to make right.

But I have to do it for me. Not for you.
    Oh, and I really love the scrapbook. It's something that
I'll look back on many times in the next few years and
remember how much fun we had together.

Marty

Had.

That word tripped me up. Because we're in the past tense
now. You don't have to be friends with everyone, and you don't
have to hold on to friends who aren't great for you. According
to the internet. Even ignoring the fact she's the reason I still get
"IS IT TRUE?!?!!" messages, though it's been a couple of
months, she isn't a good person to have in my life right now.

I'm seeing Skye tomorrow. I didn't want everything to end
with him, but I know it won't be the same. We'll talk about all
the things we used to, and we might talk about Megan. I'm
preparing for it, at least.

Airports are more manageable now. But that's because there
are fewer unknowns this time. I'll land in Kentucky at the

awkward hour of four in the afternoon, so by the time I get settled at home, it'll be bedtime in London. And when I wake up, it'll be time to face life in Kentucky as an openly gay man.

Even if it's just for a week, until I'm back on a flight to my new home in London, I'm ready for it.

My new life: a shitty two-bedroom apartment with Shane, a part-time job, busking in the underground with Dani, fitting auditions in where I can. It still seems impossible. I just turned eighteen, but I'm not nearly old enough for this. Or mature enough. But I'm doing it. New Marty is committing to his new life.

Megan is in the past, but Pierce is back in the present. We can manage it. I don't think I judge him for doing what he did, and I don't care if he judges me. There was once a day when I wanted him to have all my firsts, but there are many I still hold on to. I'm just waiting for the right one to share them with.

I hold the phone up to my ear.

"Hi, Dad. We're boarding the plane now."

"Marty! Can't believe you're coming back so soon." He laughs. "Nah, it's been ages, really."

"It feels like it's been years. I'm excited to come back, even though—well, you know."

"Don't worry about that. Your mom and I won't let anyone be weird around you."

They've been better, but it will take some time to put things behind us. There's so much we need to talk about, but we have time. And for once, it's like we're all on the same page. I'm even a little excited to see their new church. (Though I may have booked my travel specifically so I'd miss Sunday service—oops!)

I board the plane, take my seat, and put in my earphones. When the cabin doors shut, the anxiety creeps back in. It's the normal kind, I think. If there is such a thing. It's a beast of a flight—ten hours, over an ocean.

And this time, I have a two-way ticket.

A week in Kentucky will do me good, but I'm going to miss Sophie, Shane, Dani, maybe even Pierce. And I have the rest of my life, theoretically, to hang out with them.

With trembling hands, I take a book out of my bag and clutch it to my chest. It's a journal, one I picked up shortly after everything went down this summer. I've been writing my experiences in it, and it's been helping. Aunt Leah introduced me to all these great meditation and breathing apps. Nothing's perfect, and it might never be, but it helps.

I write the date in the top-right corner, and start to fill out a page of fears, of joy, of everything in between. Airplanes have a way of bringing all the emotions out of you.

On my last transatlantic flight, my dream was to escape. Get as far away from there as I could. But despite the hitch in my breath and the tension snaking down my shoulders, I'm ready to go back.

A wave of excitement washes over me as the plane accelerates down the runway. My heart rate kicks up, and my breaths become shallow as the front wheel lifts off the ground.

London shrinks beneath me, and it finally hits me. I never

wanted to escape from Avery. I never wanted to disappear, or fade into the background. I wanted to go someplace I could conquer my fears and become my own person.

And I freaking did it.

AUTHOR'S NOTE

Dear Reader,

When I was a senior in high school, my friends won superlatives like Future Leader of the World or Class Clown. Me? I won Most Musical. This was fitting, because, from choir to marching band and everywhere in between, music defined my teen years. That continued well into college, where I studied music and joined every ensemble I could find. *As Far as You'll Take Me* is, in every way, a love letter to music and the sense of family you get when you fall into the right ensemble—in music, or in life.

Unsurprisingly, it's also my love letter to London. Not long ago, I went to graduate school in the UK and saw firsthand just how overwhelming and wonderful an international move can be. My husband and I traveled some while we were there—to Florence, Cardiff, and a few other cities that might seem familiar after finishing this book. I wanted to give voice to that rural American teen who dreams of traveling the world and also capture the joy, wonder, and, yes, anxiety that travel brings. Giving these experiences to Marty was one of my favorite parts of writing this book.

Marty's story may be fiction, but it's underscored by the real lived experiences of queer teens, including my own. In *The Gravity of Us*, I showed an aspirational world where two boys could fall in love without any blatant homophobia or issues with identity holding them back. In this book, things don't go quite as smoothly. But between the family Marty was born into and the family he finds along the way, he knows he'll be okay.

Like Marty, I struggled with anxiety and disordered eating while trying to find my place in the world. As a queer teen, I was always looking for love and acceptance, and when I couldn't find it, I thought it was easier to change myself than to change the world around me. I always discuss mental health in my books, in part to destigmatize conversations about it, but also to show queer teens who share these experiences that they're not alone, and that the fight to survive and thrive is so worth it.

If you're struggling with disordered eating, call or text the National Eating Disorders Association's helpline at (800) 931-2237. If you're a young LGBTQ person in crisis, don't hesitate to call TrevorLifeline at (866) 488-7386. These resources, and many more, are just a call away whenever you need them.

As always, it's an honor to be able to write the books I'd have needed most as a teen. Thank you for reading.

Until next time,
Phil

ACKNOWLEDGMENTS

THERE ARE SO MANY people who helped bring this story to life, from my friends who taught me what "found family" really meant when I needed it the most, to my publishing team and industry friends who gave me the courage to tell this incredibly personal story to readers across the world. Some special thank-yous are in order:

To my agent, Brent Taylor, who is the most fabulous, joyful, kind, and wise (not to mention the hardest-working) person in this entire industry, and to my editor, Mary Kate Castellani, for having such a clear vision for each of my projects, and for always finding a way to bring out the joy in every scene I write.

To my publishing team in the US, including Claire Stetzer, Lily Yengle, Phoebe Dyer, and Ksenia Winnicki, for everything you do to help get my books in the hands of more readers. To Diane Aronson, Erica Barmash, Jeff Curry, Beth Eller, Alona

Fryman, Melissa Kavonic, Cindy Loh, Donna Mark, Jasmine Miranda, Daniel O'Connor, Valentina Rice, Teresa Sarmiento, Chris Venkatesh, and Katharine Wiencke for putting in a ton of work behind the scenes to make this book a success. Extra-special thanks to illustrator Jeff Östberg and designer Danielle Ceccolini for their work creating this beautiful cover.

To my international team—Hannah Sandford, Ian Lamb, Mattea Barnes, and Tobias Madden, to name a few—for getting my books in the hands of readers all over the world, and to Patrick Leger for illustrating the UK cover.

To Anna Priemaza and Chelsea Sedoti, who read the earliest draft of this book back in 2015 and were among the first to fall in love with Marty. It's been a long journey, but I'm so glad you were there along the way to give me confidence in this story. And a sincere thanks to all my writing friends for their overwhelming support of me and this book.

To the Pride of Dayton Marching Band and my UD music family for accepting me for exactly who I was when I needed it the most, especially Kiersten M., Greg M., Lauren P., Laura M., Adam N., Sarah N., Brian D., Danielle D., Courtney B., Peter H., Brooke L., Jen B., Christine W., Hollie R., Andrew R., Bill R., Hannah B., Alex B., Mandi A., Megan M., and Lauren H. And to the rest of my found family—from Dayton, to DC, to London, and finally NYC—for helping me build my many homes away from home.

To the Stampers and Lambs, the families I was born into, for showing up for me constantly and surrounding me with love my whole life. To Mom and Dad for your overwhelming support and love, and for your constant commitment to spoiling your only child over the last thirty-two years. To the Steins for welcoming me into their family over the last decade. I love you all so much!

And finally, to Jonathan. Thank you for always being there for me in a way no one else ever could. You're my biggest cheerleader, my happily ever after, and none of this would be possible without you. Thank you for showing me a true love story.

Four best friends
One unforgettable summer

Don't miss

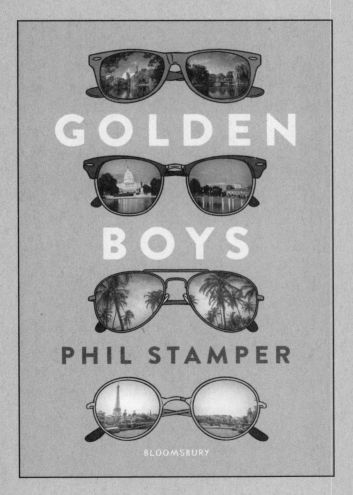

Turn the page to read a sneak peek . . .

GABRIEL

BEING THE BIG SPOON is such a chore. Don't get me wrong, it's nice having Sal curl into me. The warmth coming off his body is calming. My heartbeat thrums through my chest, but I feel my heart rate slow.

Breathing is a bit awkward, though. First, his lightly tousled blond hair keeps getting in my mouth. Second, it's like I can see my hot breath curl around his neck—is it uncomfortable for him? How fresh *is* my breath, exactly? And how does Sal not worry about all this when our roles are flipped.

Mentally, my body's suspended in this kind of light, peaceful state. Physically, I'm *sweating*. We've kicked off the blankets, but not even the constantly running air-conditioning his mom insists on can combat this heat wave. My left arm is fully asleep, and I'm not sure where to put my other one. Right now, it's draped awkwardly around him, rising and falling slowly with his breath.

Every time I shift my body, my skin peels lightly away from his. Normally, this is when I'd call it quits and roll over, but if this is the last time . . .

I can't think about it. So I think about him.

He seems comfortable and safe in my arms, in his bed, in his house. His confidence claims ownership over everything in his sphere, and sometimes I feel like I'm pulled into that, even if we're not actually, officially a thing.

Something in the way he softly presses his hips into mine and arches his neck back reminds me he's in control of this situation, even as the little spoon.

I place my lips on his neck, then give it a playful bite. He laughs and jerks his head away from mine.

Sometimes it feels good to remind him that, of all the things that are his, I am not one of them.

"What's up?" Sal asks, rolling over to meet my gaze. Our foreheads touch, and a smile pulls at my lips. My breaths grow longer, smoother. "You're stiff today."

I arch a brow, which prompts him to say, "Ugh, not like that. I mean it, though. Are you worried?" he asks. "About this summer?"

"I'm worried about a lot of things," I admit. But it doesn't exactly take a mind reader to figure out what worry is at the top of my list. "Don't get me wrong, I'm excited to volunteer with them. And it'll look great on my transcript. And I'll help save the trees, which is cool."

Sal pulls me in for a kiss. "Are you worried you'll miss me too much?"

"Right," I say with a laugh. As much as I do love this thing we've had going on for years, I don't love *him* like that. "We could probably use the time apart anyway. Give me a chance to find a boy who doesn't consider C-SPAN recaps to be pillow talk."

"Ah. I see. You want the good stuff." He pulls closer to me, and the chills fly up my back and settle uneasily into my shoulders. "Don't make me use my secret weapon."

"Oh my god, don't!" I shout, slapping him away while holding in a laugh. But he leans into me. His voice drops to a whisper, and his breath on my ear sends shivers down my whole body. I pull up the blanket, despite the heat. "*Où se trouve la station de métro la plus proche?*"

My heart plummets into my stomach, and I hate myself for being so basic. I mean, he's saying nonsense he picked up from French III, I know this. *But.* He says it so directly, so boldly, that I almost see myself falling for him in a real way.

"*God*, why didn't I end up taking French?" I say. "What the hell are you even saying?"

"Oh, you know, romantic stuff." He clears his throat. "*Je voudrais acheter un billet.*"

Despite myself, I shudder. "Sounds pretty romantic," I say dryly.

"Ms. Brashear always said I had the best accent of the whole junior class. Reese hated that, but maybe he'll pick up the accent after living there this summer. A few of us might get to go on a trip to Paris next year for French IV, so I've got to keep practicing. Wouldn't that be freaking awesome?"

"Wow. The Village of Gracemont, Ohio. Taking over Paris." I pause. "I kind of feel sorry for them."

He laughs, and I do too. But when the laughter stops, an unsettling silence replaces it. Without thinking much of it, I roll away and stare at Sal's room. It's so tidy you'd think he doesn't have any stuff. But there's hints of his personality throughout the space. A ring light and a selection of makeup in one corner. A tie rack filled with bright bow ties, most with price tags still attached. A large desk with a spinning chair and laptop, adorned with academic medals, trophies, and one term paper. He's got his good grades pinned to a corkboard like he's his own proud parent.

"I'm excited to go to DC this summer," Sal says. "But I'm almost more excited for you to go to Boston. For Reese's design school in Paris. Heck, even for Heath to get to Daytona."

"Heck?"

"An upstanding young gentleman never curses."

Simultaneously, we roll our eyes. He's quoting his mom right now—she was bad before, but she pivoted to full helicopter mode the moment he got the call about his summer internship with Senator Wright.

He reaches around and pulls me into him, and a rush of calmness floods my body. He never wants to be big spoon, so I savor every moment. "I mean it, about all of us. We've been inseparable for years, but . . . there's only so much we can do here, you know? Mom's always pushed me to do this kind of stuff. She was always making time to take me away from here, to show me what life is like outside Gracemont. She even opened this particular door for me, by helping me get this internship. I know I can pick up where she's left off and turn this into my life." A darkness fills the silence. "We need to get out of here."

"That's so easy for you to say," I push back. "You're comfortable in big cities, you fit in everywhere. Nothing scares you." I don't mention that he also has the money to do these things, while my parents are eating into their savings to send me to Boston. "But it's hard for me to even think about. I want your confidence, you know?"

"You still *did it*, Gabe. You have to be confident and brave to make these plans—to apply, to tell your parents, to actually commit to this bonkers save-the-trees passion. You saw the opportunity, and you said yes. That's brave. Don't let your anxiety overshadow everything you've already done."

I sigh, long and slow, as he holds me tighter. "I keep thinking of all the people I need to impress, all the crowds I have to deal with. I'm going to hate Boston, I know it. Seriously, what the 'heck' did I get myself into?"

He laughs, then mumbles something about how I'm going to do great. He's so casual with how he holds me right now. His sticky body is pressed to mine, and he's not even doing anything, but his intensity still radiates. It's addictive . . . his energy, his confidence, his drive.

He's always striving for more: better grades, more accolades for his desk, but he's somehow as content with me as I am with him. I can't help but think we both deserve better than content, though. So, maybe this summer apart will be good for us.

He holds me close, and I breathe him in. I ignore the part of me that never wants him to let go.

SAL

I DON'T KNOW WHY, but something hits me when Gabriel and I step onto the porch. Something other than the heat wave, that is. A wave of longing, maybe? Remorse? *Fear?* But I smile and push through it. Those feelings will just hold me back, so I can't let myself think too hard on it.

We're already running much later than we planned. Reese wanted us at his goodbye party early to help set up, and if Gabe doesn't leave now, we don't have a chance of getting ready, picking up supplies, and making it to Reese's on time. But something's stopping him from going.

"So," he says. "With how Reese's family is, his goodbye party's bound to go on all night. You've got family stuff Wednesday; I've got family stuff Thursday."

"On Friday, the four of us will be together all night," I say, catching on to what he's saying.

"And we leave Saturday."

"We leave Saturday," I echo.

He shifts uncomfortably, and the longing settles in my chest again. "Which means, this is it for us, in a way?" he says.

"It'll never be *it* for us." I wink. "But yeah, we won't have alone time for a while."

Our friendship is unconventional, to say the least. We've always been able to talk through it, though. Even if Gabriel's anxiety sometimes gets in the way and makes it hard for him to express his thoughts. But today is different. It's never felt clipped like this. He's never seemed so guarded.

I reach out to him, and he pulls back at the last second.

"I . . . don't know why I'm thinking so much about it," he says. "Three months is a long time, I guess. And we finally have our first chance to date other people."

"And you've suddenly realized you love me."

Our eyes meet, but he busts out laughing first.

I know I love him. It's not *that* kind of love. But it's not nothing. There's something there, and it's just that everything around us moves so quickly. I'm freaking busy, Mom's always breathing down my neck, and everything is hard.

But this isn't. In fact, sinking into his lips is easy.

"I'll miss this, though." I admit it with a gentle smile on my face. "And if we never get to hook up again because we're off falling in *real* love with our cosmopolitan boyfriends, then good for us. Right?"

The silence after I ask is full of emotion. We knew there was an expiration date on this, but I didn't think I'd be staring it in the face so soon.

"Right." His voice is quiet, but it doesn't reveal much of anything. "And if this is it for us, just know I've appreciated it, Sal. Even if you are just *awful* in bed."

I scoff and pretend to turn away, but he grabs my arm and spins me toward him.

"Joking," he says. "I really will miss us."

With Gabe, I always have to be the strong one. The confident one. And I *like* that dynamic. I like feeling in control, taking the lead, but right now I don't feel so confident.

He turns to go, but he stops when I let out a whimper.

"Did you say something?"

I bite my lip. "No. It's nothing."

It's not nothing, of course. I'm stressed about moving to DC, about our friendship, about the other guys. About my mom's three hundredth lecture on "college strategy" last night. I'm *scared*. I want to say that, and I need him to hear it. But I can't cling to this dynamic we have. This *whatever*ship that we've been in, off and on, for years. I need to move forward, and he does too, and this summer is the perfect time to do it.

He must sense my hesitation, because he comes back onto the porch and wraps me in a hug. We break apart, just briefly, and I bring my mouth to his. We have a million unspoken rules to our hookups; the most obvious one is that we never do it in public. But here he is, biting my lip and pressing his tongue into mine. We kiss, and we kiss, and we kiss.

But I'm still scared.

• Golden Boys •

GABRIEL + HEATH + REESE + SAL

Earth to Sal

Earth to Gabriel

What exactly is the point of a group chat if no one responds to me R

 I respond!!

Don't text and drive R

 We're at a stop sign and you're in the passenger seat??

Shut up and drive. R

Guys, whenever you're done doing whatever it is you're...doing

S, can you still pick up ice? And G, you're bringing your dad's cookies right?

Don't be late 😠

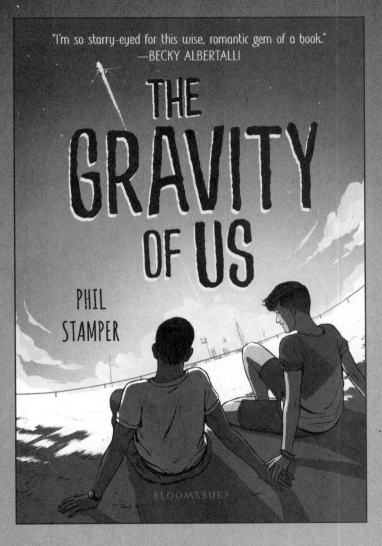

"I'm so starry-eyed for this wise, romantic gem of a book."
—BECKY ALBERTALLI

THE
GRAVITY
OF US

PHIL
STAMPER

BLOOMSBURY

PHIL STAMPER is the bestselling author of *The Gravity of Us* and *As Far As You'll Take Me*. His stories are packed with queer joy, and his characters are often too ambitious for their own good. Born and raised in a rural village near Dayton, Ohio, he now lives in New York with his husband and their dog.

WWW.PHILSTAMPER.COM

@STAMPEPK